Discarded

L.A. CADIEUX

Evernight Teen

www.evernightteen.com

Copyright© 2014 L.A. Cadieux

ISBN: 978-1-77130-895-3

Cover Artist: Sour Cherry Designs

Editor: JC Chute

L.A. CADIEUX

DEDICATION

It's not what the world holds for you. It's what you bring to it.

— L. M. Montgomery, Anne of Green Gables

This is for anyone who has been a part of this journey.

You can achieve your dreams.
And with perseverance, you will.

No matter the miles that separate us and in no particular order, you're appreciated for:

Sharing time with my characters.
Believing in me.
Inspiring.
Never letting can't be an option.
Being beacons of light.
Believing in Teddy.
Representing my work.
Being a friend.
Publishing my novel.
Building a website.
Being an early reader.
Encouraging.

Being a difference maker.

Mom & Dad, Crystal & Trent, Laurie, Ryan, Shea & Sheldon, Charlee, Marisa, Samantha, Brittany, Ryland, Anne, Stacey, Jane, Mrs. Strauss, and to all my teachers and professors along the way.

A million times over, thank you.

ONE LIFE

A Teddy Owens Story

L.A. Cadieux

Copyright © 2014

Never say can't.

Where you tend a rose, my lad,
A thistle cannot grow.

—Frances Hodgens Burnett, *The Secret Garden*

Chapter One

Three Sisters Mountain Manor

9:40 P.M. CDT, Sunday, August 29th

"Admit it, you're a mess." My words were thick with accusation as I showed her the bottle. The lines separating a mother from her daughter began to blur, the tighter my fist clenched around exhibit #1: the medication bottle. "I found this in the trash."

Angelique placed the soda she'd been sipping onto the kitchen counter. "Stop worrying about me. Honey, I'm *fine*. It was an accident—those merely fell into the garbage earlier," she said. A bead of condensation rolled down the side of the aluminum can, seeping into a chip in the counter.

"Do you take me for an idiot? The trash isn't exactly accessible." I pointed to the cupboard beneath the kitchen sink. As I leaned forward my wet hair hung over my face. I'd gone and dyed my locks red a few weeks earlier. Fortunately, the color had faded after two washes.

"It's completely plausible it fell under the sink," she argued. Angelique turned to search the deserted street outside our tattered screen door—her actions were a clear indication of what I'd suspected all along.

"Please, look at me for one minute, and don't start with one of your conspiracy theories—seriously—I can't take another. This *full* bottle was in the washroom trash. I found it after taking a shower." A knowing expression dawned on her face…she'd been caught in another lie. "You haven't been taking your prescription. Why?" I shoved a hand into the pocket of my cut-off shorts and pulled out the telephone wiretap.

Angelique's eyes narrowed in on it. "Teddy, give me the bug," she demanded, placing a thin hand on my shoulder.

I tore out of her grasp. "In case you missed the memo, this isn't normal. It's not okay to spy on me. Angelique, I'm not your naïve little girl anymore." I held up the listening device. "Your sickness is worse than ever. Your paranoia is out of control—you need help. I'm tired of trying to fix it."

"I'm fine," Angelique shrilled. Her hair was matted to her forehead, saturated with the humidity. "You have to trust me. I have my reasons."

"I want to trust you." I noted how her cheeks and eyes had sunken in. God, she wasn't eating again. Her anxiety had worsened significantly since my sixteenth birthday. Lately, she'd watched me like I was going to burst into a man-eating tarantula at any moment. "You make it hard."

"You can't possibly understand." She reached over to tug at my arm, resulting in a tussle over the bug. "Give me that already—it's not yours," she ordered.

As I ducked out of the way, she jerked my arm. "Let me go!" I tried to snatch my arm away.

"Please, can you try to keep your voice down?" She released me, only to glance outside in search of her imaginary tormentors.

"Why can't you try to be a normal mother?" I asked, red-faced.

"It was never in the cards for you, honey." She pushed a limp strand of brunette hair out of her face.

"You don't listen, not even to the doctors," I said sadly. "Try to keep care of yourself." Taking aim, I flung the bottle against the refrigerator and watched with disdain as it burst open, sending pills spewing across the floor. Many of them disappeared into a filthy crack in the linoleum floor under the counter. "I'm not your babysitter!" Angelique stood rigidly, staring down at the pills. Considering her current state of mental health, and knowing my mother, she was probably asking herself if they could possibly be poisoned.

I opened my mouth, then closed it, and then opened it again. "Forget this—I'm done." I threw my fists up into the air.

"Teddy," Angelique shouted as I ran from the house. "Get back here this instant," she ordered. "It's dangerous—"

I slammed the squeaking screen door behind me, cutting her off.

If I wasn't so livid I'd have taken notice of the police car sitting at the end of our street, but it was too late: the cops were stepping out of the car. An officer waved me over. Angelique was going to lose it on them, and it was my fault.

Making my way toward the cops, I started to panic. *What should I say?*

"Hello there," the first officer said. "Is everything okay?"

"Yeah, nothing to report." I stared down at my sneakers, not wanting to meet their cynical gazes.

"What's your name?" the second asked.

"Teddy Owens, sir."

"How old are you?" He leaned against his cruiser, tilting his head to the side to consider me.

"Sixteen—at the beginning of August." I cringed as the screen door on our house banged shut. The officers wore amused expressions as Angelique stomped toward us. They wouldn't be smiling if they knew what she was capable of.

"It's going to be one of *those* nights," the first officer said under his breath.

It was one of the last times I'd play the role of an innocent spectator.

~Two Weeks Later~
1:15 A.M. MDT, Sunday, September 12th

After the authorities had placed Angelique on an involuntary hold she was shipped off to the psych ward—

spewing nonsense the whole way about an alliance of human mutations. I spent two miserable weeks in temporary custody with an old couple that drank too much tea. Luckily, or maybe unluckily, my social worker Tulia Rivera managed to work a miracle and track down Angelique's only living family member: a long-lost brother, Delmont Owens.

Tulia had been dead set on keeping me out of the foster care system—I'd been resigned to ending up there, mainly because I didn't know who my dad was. As it turned out, fourteen years ago my uncle had emigrated from England to Canada, to work as an investor of some sort. Even though I was more than cynical of my uncle's story, to Tulia, the most important part was he had no criminal record—and on top of being willing, he was financially secure enough to care for me. To convince me of my good fortune, Tulia showed me a photo, and even I had to admit we did resemble each other, a lot: both with an Angelina Jolie pouty lip, almond-shaped emerald green eyes, and naturally blonde hair. Soon after, my uncle pulled a few strings with friends in high places and I was shipped off by the state to live at *Three Sisters Mountain Manor.*

"I hate insomnia." I hadn't slept well in days. Not since I'd been taken away from home. I pushed my comforter away and peered down at the cat near the foot of the four-post bed. The cat's coat was shining darker than the espresso stain of the bed frame as she stretched out her paws, baring her pointed claws. I tapped my fingers against the intricate detail in the headboard. With a frustrated sigh I threw off the rest of the comforter. "This is hopeless." I stepped out of the bed and curled my toes on the cold floor as I walked over to the window. My gaze narrowed in on a light piercing the darkness like a knight's sword. "Maybe fresh air is the key to defeating a sleep issue?" I turned from the window.

With calculating yellow eyes, Koko didn't dare blink as I slipped on a jacket. "What are you worried about?" I pulled on my sneakers. "There aren't any man-eating moose out tonight—are there?"

A motion detector blinked as I tiptoed down the hallway of the manor. Koko followed in hot pursuit, dodging flecks of mud falling off my shoes. I waved apologetically at a security camera as I passed. This manor was as strongly guarded as *The Louvre*. I couldn't help but wonder if my uncle struggled with paranoia as Angelique did. Why else would anyone need all these cameras? It was like I'd moved from Corpus to a whole other world, hidden deep in the Rocky Mountains.

The manor's grand foyer, as the housekeeper had called it, was cloaked in darkness. Mr. Green, the butler, was certainly fast asleep in his apartment at this hour. Pretending to be a Charlie's Angel, I stealthily snuck down the staircase and headed toward the kitchen. If I remembered correctly, the cook mentioned there was a door there, which opened onto a patio area.

A moment later, as I reached for my target—the doorknob—I closed my palm around it and turned carefully, fully expecting it to disintegrate into my palm with a sudden movement. Unfortunately, as I feared when the door clicked open the security system made a loud beeping noise. One of several cameras whirred as it moved to stare down at me with a creepy mechanical eye.

"Leave me alone," I muttered under my breath. I reached over for a telephone book on an entryway table and headed out the door. "They still make these?" I whispered to Koko. With a shove, I lodged the book between the door and frame.

It took less than a minute before Koko and I had entered a wooded area. We followed a paved pathway, enjoying the crisp air tickling my nose. It would have been a perfect night to escape, if we weren't surrounded by soldier-like trees, their branches stretched out like arms trying to capture—I totally know how Snow White felt. And to be honest, I had nowhere to go.

The crisp smell of bark and pinecones was my new reality. Their scent was thick in the air as a sliver of the moon shone down, casting an indigo shadow over my uncle's remote estate. I shivered as the breeze drifted through my hair. The leaves of the trees fluttered like a stadium full of clapping hands.

"Koko? Do you hear that flapping noise?"

A high-pitched screech echoed through the night.

I stooped to pick her up, covering my head with an arm. There was a beastly bird stalking us, I could hear its heavy wings beating the air black and blue above us. I'd been battling an uneasy feeling all evening—this certainly wasn't helping me to erase my anxiety. Out here, amongst nature and all its glory, the estate seemed darker and scarier than it had in the warmth of the Rocky Mountain sunlight.

"What is this Canmore place like?" I had asked Tulia.

"Couldn't tell yah, Teddy," she said, flipping through the contents of a manila envelope.

"Aren't there polar bears in Alberta?" I asked, flinching as I imagined a sparse land of man-hungry animals with pointed teeth. *"Heck, I'm afraid of anything with sharp canines."* Goodbye, rattlesnakes. Hello, carnivores.

"Maybe you'll like it there—you're lucky it is the beginning of a new school year." Tulia smiled, bending

her head over her papers. *"Think about it,"* she'd said off-hand. *"No more sharks and alligators to worry about."*

"I'll take an alligator over a grizzly bear," I'd grumbled. *"And the ocean over a hulking mound of rock."*

Back at the manor, I was relieved to hear the heavy flaps of the eagle's departure.

"Looks like you won't be bird food tonight," I assured Koko, hugging her as we continued on past a bend, after which a pristine cabin appeared like an apparition. On the west side of the carefully trimmed front yard was a swaying hammock—the kind one would buy from a street vendor. With Koko hugging my chest, I approached and carefully put a hand out to sit down. The hammock ropes creaked with my weight as I leaned back to stare up at the twinkling stars, pushing back and forth with a foot.

"What are you doing?" a young man's voice asked. Startled, Koko scrambled off my chest. "Dude, it's the middle of the night. Shouldn't you be sleeping?"

Seriously, I want to hide under the hammock. I know whom this voice belongs to.

"Why does it matter?" I asked slowly recovering from my surprise. "Dude," I added sarcastically.

"It doesn't—but it's two o'clock in the morning," he said, stepping out from the shadow of an evergreen. The light filtering over the hammocks from a nearby yard light provided me with my first glimpse of his boyish face. I was pleasantly surprised to see he had dark brown hair and a mass of curls on his head, which totally looked better on a guy than I'd have guessed. His hair was messed up like he'd just rolled out of bed. Oh wait, he probably *had* just rolled out of bed. Even his blue jeans were rumpled like he'd snatched them off his bedroom floor.

"Let me guess." He placed a callused hand to his chin. "You were...out for a late-night stroll." He stepped closer with a mock-serious expression. "And then you somehow lost your way," he smirked. "You came here...because?"

"I couldn't sleep and thought fresh air would help." I blushed. "Am I in trouble for trespassing?"

"Nah," he grinned. "You're not in trouble."

Up close I noted he was a couple inches taller than I was and definitely my type—it was totally the mop of curls laying in wisps across his forehead. I was pleased to see he also had a kind smile. *Oh, save me now*, and he had dimples in both cheeks. I *loved* dimples.

"You must be Theodora Owens," he said, his voice distracting me from staring at his dimpled smile. "I'm Kane Piers: the estate gardener's grandson." He stuck a broad hand out toward me.

"Hey." I shook his hand. "It's nice to meet you." Shaking myself out of a stupor after being blindsided by the dimples, I somehow managed to say, "Call me Teddy, Teddy Owens. I despise the name Theodora."

"Cool," he smiled, "Teddy." We held hands about ten seconds too long. It was Kane who pulled his hand away first. "Nice," he grinned. I caught a mischievous glint in his eyes as he noticed my lavender pyjamas. Seriously, I probably looked like some halfwit trespassing lunatic sitting in her jammies. *Perfect.* Kane tried to hide another smirk behind his arm. "Glad to finally meet you."

"What's funny?" I asked, blushing again.

"Nothing." Kane steadied the hammock and squeezed in to sit next to me. We fell awkwardly into each other as the hammock bent in the middle. He placed an arm protectively around my waist to steady us, pausing for a second to smell my hair, sending tingles up my spine. He frowned.

"I'm sorry for waking you up."

He shifted, taking back his arm, and bent his head to the side to consider me. "I'll forgive you, but only this one time." He filled his lungs with a deep breath. "But don't get me wrong."

"Wrong?" I asked, looking down at my foot.

"Teddy, you really shouldn't be sneaking around the estate by yourself at night." His brow furrowed. "What if you were mistaken for an intruder?"

What? Do they shoot intruders upon first sight around here?

"I'm not—and I wasn't," I stressed. "But thanks for the advice. I'll try not to walk around on your property in the future."

He placed an arm over his forehead and leaned back, copying me, but looked way more comfortable than me. It was like he was one with nature…Kane belonged here in the mountains. I did not.

"By the way," Kane patted my knee, "don't worry about the pyjamas."

I hugged my arms to my chest. "I was kind of hoping you wouldn't notice."

Kane kept one of his legs dangling. "I like it." He shrugged. *Good!* "We're pretty casual around here." He plucked at his forest green windbreaker.

I nodded, pleased. "Good to know." Maybe I would fit in around the manor after all.

Koko was sitting by the cabin listening to our conversation, closely. "Koko, here girl," I urged, reaching a hand out toward her. She didn't move, merely cast me a *please don't patronize me* look. "Have you ever noticed that Koko acts...weird?"

"You think Koko is...weird?" Kane asked, jostling the hammock. "What did she do?"

"I can't put my finger on what's different about her," I admitted.

Kane's jaw went slack as he stared over at Koko, then back at me, like he wasn't sure what to say. "She only wants to make sure you're okay."

"How do *you* know what Koko is thinking?" I asked with my eyebrows knit together.

Kane touched his forehead and wiggled his own brow. "I read minds."

An awkward silence followed.

I was waiting for the punch line, but it became apparent there was none. "Are you trying to be funny...or serious?" I asked after a moment.

Kane laughed and burrowed his head into his hand. "You're funny." He raised his head, and even his eyes were smiling. "No—of course I can't read minds. I'm not a telepath."

"You never know," I said leaning toward Kane, drawn to him. "There are people in this world who do some strange things."

"True." He nodded, but I couldn't help note he had pulled away from me slightly. Maybe he wasn't interested the way I was? "Can you do anything out of the ordinary, Teddy?" Kane asked, jostling the hammock as he sat up shoving both hands into his jacket pockets. I couldn't help having the distinct impression he didn't trust them out in the open—what had I said?

I snorted...and it was definitely not attractive. "I'm simply Teddy Owens from Corpus. No mind reading. No future telling—and to be honest not much of

17

anything special. All I really have is a wealthy uncle, and I still haven't met him yet."

Kane's mouth fell open. "Teddy," he choked out. "It's impossible for you to be, ordinary."

"You don't even know anything about me."

"You're an Owens—I don't think Owenses know how to do ordinary." His words were said with such conviction even *I* almost believed him.

I sighed, burrowing my chin in my chest. "You'd know better than me. The only Owens, other than myself, I've ever actually met certainly does redefine the word."

"You're talking about your mom, aren't you—it's been a tough go, hey?" His words were full of compassion.

I placed a hand to my cheek, turning my neck slowly to face him. "Let me guess, you know about my mother's issues?" *Of course he did. Everyone working at the manor was probably talking about Delmont's poor niece and her crazy mother.*

"Yeah, I know," he said.

I lowered my gaze to stare at the ground as we creaked back and forth. "Great," I muttered mostly to myself.

Kane sat up and lowered his other leg, grasping the hammock with his hands. "Well." He was staring at me out of the corner of his eye. "I should head back to bed—school tomorrow."

"Hey, Kane?" I said trying to stall his leaving. "Before you go...can you promise me one thing?"

"What's that?" he asked. Both his feet were firmly planted on the ground as he prepared to stand.

"Don't tell anyone my name—seriously. I hate it."

"Sure, Teddy," Kane said. He stood up, leaving me alone on the hammock. It was instantly uncomfortable without his warmth. Kane leaned a shoulder on the tree trunk, frowning down at me. "Did your mom ever tell you anything about taking oaths?" he asked curiously.

"Sure—she told me never to make a promise I couldn't keep." I rubbed my hands together to fight off the cold.

Kane smiled. I was relieved to see it. "Good," he said. "Would you be willing to make a forever promise? You know, the kind you can't take back?"

"It depends on the promise." I lowered both my legs to the ground.

"Dude, what if it would save lives if you *didn't* make the promise?" Kane asked.

"Easy, then I wouldn't promise anything."

"But what if either way you'd save lives—and either way people would die?"

I pulled my shoulders to my ears. "Honestly, it sounds like an impossible situation. I don't think there's a right answer."

"Promises make this world go around, Teddy," Kane said hauntingly.

"Why do I get the distinct feeling this isn't about our promise *not* to talk about my name?" I stood up, wanting to feel him close to me again.

Stepping away from the tree, Kane lowered his arms. "Oh I haven't forgotten about our promise. Dude, but we totally have to make it binding—for fun." He held out an open palm toward me.

I stared at his palm, uncertain. "Do you want me to shake on it?"

Kane twitched his pinkie finger. "We need to make an earth-shattering, life altering...pinkie oath."

"Life altering and earth shattering?" I tried to keep a straight face. "Wow, that's serious stuff."

"Yep—are you willing to make that kind of an oath?" Kane asked cocking his head to one side. "Pretend it is unbreakable. The forever kind of promise."

"Are you serious?" I met his gaze and my cheeks probably could have lit a fire.

"Yeah," he said, taking a long deep breath. *This pinkie oath business was sure important to him.*

"If those are the terms…" I held up my pinkie, trying to keep a straight face. "It's a promise."

"*Teddy* Owens." Kane stooped to wrap his pinkie around mine, smiling shyly. "I swear from this moment on to never bring up *the name which shall not be spoken.*" The polite laughter in his eyes shadowed over for a moment. "Do you accept this pinkie swear oath?"

Charmed, I grinned ear to ear. His hand closed around mine, his fingers wrapping around mine. I loved how safe he made me feel. It was like we could take on the world together.

"I do—Sir Kane." Was it possible to fall in love at first sight? I didn't think so, until now.

"Maybe I'm Sir Lancelot," Kane said, as he let go of my hand. He stepped away, his cheeks flushing brighter than mine. "Either way—we're in for a truck load of trouble."

"Why would we be in trouble?" I asked. He'd pulled away fast as a rodeo bull out of the chute.

Kane stared up at the stars twinkling up above. I marveled at the way his face shone in the mixture of moonlight and porch light. The hollows of his eyes and cheekbones had shadowed over, creating an air of mystery about him. "Teddy, consider me your friend. As your friend, I should let you know—if you're like any of the Owenses I've known—trouble is never far behind."

L.A. CADIEUX

Chapter Two

Timbuktu?

2:20 A.M. MST, Sunday, September 12th

"Teddy, we should head back now," Kane said, rubbing the back of his neck and taking another step away from me.

"I was planning to head back about now anyway," I said slowly, not wanting to spook him again.

"Can you promise me something," he asked, still wearing a troubled expression. What was the problem? We'd been having such a nice moment.

"What?" I asked. It would have been polite, if earlier he had mentioned there would be strings attached to our 'forever' pinkie swear.

"I want you to promise not to wander around at night. It's dangerous." The serious edge to his request sent a shiver up my spine.

I rubbed my arms. "Do you want to pinkie swear again?" I asked, trying to lighten the mood.

"No, but don't go poking your nose into things you don't understand." Kane glanced back toward the cabin. There were no lights on inside. "I had to learn this the hard way," he said.

Was there something so terrible on this estate I should be as worried? "Be honest—did you come out here to lecture me?" I wondered. "What happened to make you so nervous?"

"I don't like to talk about my life story." He paused and stared down at his hands. "Anyway," he said,

"I heard your Uncle Delmont is helping you out, because of your mom troubles?"

Hiding my embarrassment was like hiding an elephant behind a teapot. "Well, to be honest, I don't like to talk about her."

"Don't worry about what anyone else thinks," he said.

"I don't want people asking me about her," I admitted.

Kane stared at me intensely for a moment. He sighed. I wasn't sure if it was a sigh of frustration or of acceptance.

"Teddy, your innocence is sweet. I like it. However, considering everything, it could be dangerous..." his words trailed off.

What was there to consider? It wasn't like I was a porcelain doll—heck—just living day to day was dangerous for everyone. I merely didn't want to explain Angelique's sickness to anyone. I still didn't get it.

"I have an idea." I looked up to search the night sky for the luckiest star. "Kane, see that star." I pointed. "Right there—the brightest one." He looked up trying to find the star I was pointing at.

"Do you see it?"

"I think I see the brightest star." Kane narrowed in on a star. "Um, Teddy, what if it's a planet...or a satellite?"

"Doesn't matter. Now, make a promise on your star—it's like making a wish, but if you go back on your star promise it'll be bad karma. I call it a wish-promise."

"What should I wish-promise?" he asked.

"Wish-promise...you won't ask any questions about Angelique. I don't want everyone in town knowing about my trouble back in Texas."

"I wish-promise on the brightest star," Kane said without hesitation. "I won't ask about her, but..." I hated the word "*but*" and when it was followed by a silence it could only mean trouble. "Wish-promise me you'll stay out of trouble."

"That's a broad promise to make," I said weakly. "I *can* promise to *try* and stay out of trouble," I added quietly, "but only if you tell me what the big secret is around here."

Kane wrenched his gaze away from the sky.

"Dude, there is no secret—what are you talking about?"

"Fine, don't tell me," I huffed. "I should head back. If Ms. Lillian discovers I'm missing she'll be looking for me like a pit bull."

"Ms. Lillian is more like a golden retriever than a pit bull." Kane buried his hands deep into his pockets. "Believe me—I know a few pit bull types."

"Good to know." I shuffled my feet as I remembered the creepy eagle. "If it's alright, can you walk me back to the manor?" *And, if it's okay, can we go back to being romantic?*

Kane placed a hand on the small of my back as he guided me back down the path. "I'd always intended to walk with you back," he whispered near my ear.

Okay, this was nice, but there was no reason to be feeling giddy about him touching me.

"Hey," he asked. "What is your first period class on Tuesday?" Kane somehow knew I'd been ordered to stay home until Tuesday. Ms. Lillian said it was to allow for time to adjust. I'd rather go to school.

"Math with—," I paused as I tried to remember, "—I think her name is Mrs. Jordan."

Kane placed a warm hand on my shoulder. "Dude, I have her first period too, but it's not really my cup of tea."

"Really?" I laughed. "Are you an anti-academic jock?"

The curls on his forehead fluttered in the wind. "No, and I totally don't dig the whole dumb jock mentality."

I smiled. "Good—and I agree it's a silly stereotype."

A few minutes later Kane and I stood on the patio outside the kitchen—the door was still propped open with a telephone book. We both shifted back and forth on our feet as Koko slipped back inside…leaving us alone.

"Kane, before you go," I rushed to say as he started to turn away. I grabbed his arm. "Thank you."

Kane stared down at my hand. I felt uncertain. Maybe I'd imagined us connecting earlier. I dropped it to my side.

"Sorry," I apologized, looking away.

"It's fine," he said, and then tenderly reached over to touch my cheek with the back of his warm hand. I looked up at him, surprised. He also looked a bit taken aback, as though his arm had moved without his permission.

With his other hand Kane reached over to fiddle with the zipper on my jacket. I tried my best to ignore the excited swelling in my chest. He took both my hands in his—was he going to kiss me? He didn't. Instead he let go of my hands, and then took a step back, putting a sensible distance between us.

"Sorry," he mumbled.

"It's fine. I'll see you at school," I whispered weakly.

"Yeah, see you Monday," he said, having done a three hundred sixty-degree turn in about three seconds flat. I kicked the phonebook out of the way a little too aggressively. The door slammed shut.

~Two Days Earlier~
2:00 P.M. MST, Friday, September 10th
  Where was this manor, in Timbuktu? I wondered after Ms. Lillian had picked me up from the airport. We'd been driving at least an hour and half, leaving the city behind us.

Earlier in the morning, after a sleepy drive to Houston, Tulia had dropped me off at the airport. "Teddy," she'd said, "Angelique has been transferred to a dissociative personality center in Los Angeles. A specialist there took an interest in her case—and in the other personality she calls Lynette."

"She needs all the help she can get," I'd said, slumping in my seat.

I played with a frayed end of my hair, rubbing the split strands between two fingers. Was it possible to wear hair dye off with friction?

I admit, for a pathetic moment I had searched for a polar bear or man-eating moose out the airplane window when the plane landed at Calgary International. It was a positive sign when I didn't see any wild animals. The Canadian customs agent was a tired looking Asian lady. She read my passport and then looked me up and down.

"Miss Owens." She closed the passport. "Why are you coming into Canada?"

"I'm visitin' my uncle, Delmont Owens."

Her dark eyes narrowed. "And where does your uncle live?"

"Canmore, Alberta."

"How long do you plan on staying?"

"A week." *If I had somewhere else to go, it was the truth.* She handed back the passport.

A couple hours later and Ms. Lillian had driven down a long, but picturesque mountain highway lined with spruce trees and then turned onto a roughly paved and winding side road—hence, Timbuktu. Finally, she slowed as we approached a substantial black iron gate. The walls on either side of the gate were stone and at least fourteen feet high. A couple of gigantic security guards in navy blue uniforms were standing near the gate. One man was taller than the other and looked like Andre the Giant, the other was half the height—still large by my standards—and had lighter hair. In a fancy calligraphic scroll on the side of the rock wall were the words '*Three Sisters Mountain Manor*'.

"Three Sisters is the name of that mountain," Ms. Lillian explained, gesturing toward the jagged triple peaks overhead. She slowed the vehicle to a crawl and powered down her window.

"Hello, Barney. Fred." She waved a manicured hand as we waited for the gates to fully open.

"Please tell me their names aren't really Fred and Barney?" I asked as we accelerated past.

"We like to tease them," Ms. Lillian said as she stared back in her rear view mirror, examining her short grey, perfectly styled hair. She smiled. "Fred and Barney are their nicknames."

"It's funny."

I played off my sudden interest in their names by powering down my window and pulling on my hood. There were billowing bushes on either side of the road. Would it snow by Christmas? I had convinced myself

Santa Claus couldn't land on a roof that was not covered with snow. Obviously, Santa had never visited me.

We took a bend in the road and my gaze was torn away from the tranquil landscaping of evergreens and crab apple trees when epic *Three Sisters Mountain Manor* erupted into view. The manor was an English Baroque style mansion and what I thought *Pemberley Hall* would have looked like in Jane Austen's *Pride and Prejudice*. It felt out of place in the land of ski lodges and log cabins.

"Impressive."

I didn't know what else to say. All I knew was that Uncle Delmont and I would not have much in common at all.

The venerable manor had a grand, circle-shaped driveway. Across three stories of the manor's stone walls were tall windows. The windows reminded me of castles from fairytales. A huge cherry wood door was the focal point of the entrance where four columns supported a covered porch.

The white-haired butler, who looked like he had a surfboard clasped to his back, smiled at me as we drove up. He held the door open for us and his eyes crinkled like a grandfather's would with a friendly smile.

"Hello, *Miss* Owens. I'm Mr. Green, pleased to meet you."

"Hi," I said shortly.

A marble staircase with dark stained mahogany railings graced us with its regal presence, beckoning us to continue onto the second level. In the center of the foyer there was a massive ceramic vase. Ms. Lillian gestured for me to follow her up the staircase.

"Your new room is on the second floor."

The front door clicked shut behind me. Mr. Green did not follow us up the stairs. Down the hall a vaulted ceiling was showcased by floor-to-ceiling windows. The ceiling was held up by impressive, distressed wooden beams and columns. Ms. Lillian stopped in front of a door framed by two wooden beams. She gestured for me to enter and stepped aside.

"Dear, I do hope you like your room."

I took my first step into the room. I swallowed.

Everything was...immaculate. The bedroom was charmingly decorated in a way most teenage girls desired: all white, fuchsia, expensive and frilly. Curled up in a ball in the center of the four-post bed near a soaring window was a little black cat. The cat's head poked up out of the plush fabric to greet me with curious amber eyes.

Pretending this extravagance was nothing new for me, I said through a frog in my throat, "Who is this little guy?"

"Her name is Koko," Ms. Lillian informed me.

I sat carefully on the bed and scratched behind *her* ears.

"Hey there, Koko," I said.

"Here you go now." Mr. Green entered and placed my backpack on the bed. "I'll be downstairs if you need anything else, Miss Owens," he said, bowing slightly.

"Thanks, but please call me Teddy."

"As you wish, Miss Teddy," he replied with a stiff bow and retreated through the open door.

Dropping off the bed, I walked closer to the window. Behind a large greenhouse one could see the front porch of a simple two-story log cabin.

"Here is your en-suite bathroom." Ms. Lillian's voice caused me to turn around again. She was pointing to a closed door.

"And your closet."

I glanced over at the door.

"I'll have to check it out," I said.

The housekeeper smoothed her crisply ironed shirt and flattened her palms against the expensive fabric of her pintuck skirt—she was dressed like a Dillard's sales lady.

"I'm sure you need a few moments. My girl, I'll return in a half an hour to show you to the kitchen."

"Thanks, I'd actually like a few moments to myself...before any more tours."

"I'll leave you to it." Ms. Lillian gently pulled the door closed behind her.

I turned back to the window to stare outside and my gaze narrowed. Inside the greenhouse two people moved slowly through the rows of hydrangeas with a long watering hose in hand. One was an older man with short grey hair and a younger man with curly dark brown hair, wearing a black sweater, which appeared to hug his athletic build. I couldn't see his face because it was blocked by plants. I leaned forward and squinted while trying to gaze past the greenery. I felt like a voyeur. He must have felt my gaze because he looked up and our eyes locked for a half a second.

"OMG!" I ducked onto the floor and buried my head in my knees. "Koko—he saw me totally checking him out!" I groaned in horror.

When I did have a chance meeting with Kane Piers two days later, the idea of living on my uncle's mountain estate suddenly didn't seem so lonely after all.

11:00 A.M. MST/MDT, Monday, September 13th

I awoke to golden rays spilling through my bedroom window, the towering snow-capped Three Sister Mountains a heavenly backdrop. I stayed in bed adjusting to the light and replayed the run-in with Kane during the night over—and over—again. After all the serious contemplation, all I concluded was there was definitely something suspicious going on around this estate. At 11:40 a.m. I decided to make it my business to find out what was going on. I jumped in the shower, then dressed casually in my typical jeans and t-shirt and headed downstairs for lunch.

Ms. Lillian was already at the mahogany kitchen table reading the *New York Times* on her laptop, sipping her soup from a steaming bowl. I sat down next to her wondering why she didn't read the local news. The cook, Mrs. Abasi, was quick to bring me over soup. She was petite, barely as tall as I, sitting in a chair.

"Teddy," Ms. Lillian said looking up. "I'm going into town. Would you like to come along?" she asked.

"If it's alright...I'd like to stay here at the manor," I said. "I don't feel much like going anywhere."

Ms. Lillian looked downcast. "What are your plans, my girl?"

I looked sheepish. "I *was* hoping you could trim my hair, that's if you're not busy—it doesn't need to be anything fancy." I pointed to my grown out roots. "Don't know if you noticed, but I need it fairly badly."

"I'd love to," Ms. Lillian said and lowered her spoon. "I'll leave for town this afternoon. I'm yours for the next couple hours, if you'd like."

"I'd like it," I replied, smiling for the first time since I'd arrived. After lunch we headed upstairs to start my makeover. I should not have been surprised there was a hair salon in the manor. The room was even complete with a salon chair and a brightly lit mirror—the kind with lights all around the edge.

I sat down in the chair and stared at my make-up free reflection in the mirror. "Ms. Lillian, here's to hoping you're a miracle worker." I met her gaze in the mirror.

"This will be easy as pie." She smiled. "I have the perfect model. I've been cutting my nephew's hair for years," Ms. Lillian said, taking out a pair of scissors from a case.

Please don't make me look like a little boy, I silently wished.

"What would you like me to do?" she wondered. "Just a cut, or more red, maybe brown—blonde?"

"Do you have the dye for hair colors?"

"Oh yes, most colors."

"Then lime green, yes. Red, no—and not purple," I instructed with a grin.

"Alright..."

I held the side of my hand up to my jaw and considered my reflection. "I'm totally joking about the lime green. I want my natural color back."

"Whatever you'd like, dear."

It scared me a little Ms. Lillian would have accepted any whim.

"Do you feel brave enough to trim it to the jaw line?" I ran my fingers through my tresses, which currently fell just below my shoulders.

"That's more than a trim," she noted, running her fingers through the back of my raggedy strands. Ms. Lillian studied my frayed roots. "Girl," she clicked her tongue against the top of her mouth. "You have natural blonde hair, the color of grass in the Serengeti, like your uncle."

"Yeah…or maybe my dad was blond." I shrugged.

The hands running through my hair paused.

"That's possible," she said with an edge. Ms. Lillian ran her hands down the length of my hair to just below my shoulder blades. "Are you sure about losing this length?"

"Cut it off—it's all split ends."

I was enamored with the way Ms. Lillian stripped the red color out of my hair, and then dyed my hair the same shade of blonde as my roots. The woman had done this before. She was talented as any professional hairdresser. After washing the dye out and combing out my hair, she unsheathed her scissors. She gathered my hair into a ponytail at the nap of my neck.

"Ready?" she asked nervously.

"Ready."

All it took was a couple snips and then *voila* — I had short hair.

"Gross!" I squealed as Ms. Lillian held out the ponytail.

"It's the same hair you were walking around with a moment ago," Ms. Lillian grinned, before she continued to snip my hair into a layered style. To keep my new look a surprise, she'd kept my chair turned away from the mirror. Unplugging the blow dryer, she frowned and tapped the end of the round brush to her chin.

"What's wrong?" I asked.

Without a word Ms. Lillian picked up a small makeup brush. "Just a couple more minutes, dear." Sure enough a few minutes later she'd lightly dusted my eyes with green and bronze, and even applied a thin layer of lip-gloss and mascara.

"There." She put her hands on her hips with a look of triumph. "My girl, you were perfect before but this look is like the cherry on top of the delicious ice cream sundae—a sundae smothered in caramel sauce."

"Now you're just making me hungry."

"Close your eyes—don't open until I say," she instructed.

Ms. Lillian swivelled the chair around.

"Can I open them now?" I asked nervously.

"Open them." She clapped her hands together.

Blinking a couple times, I opened my eyes and reached up to touch my hair. I felt healthy ends. In the mirror a stranger's huge almond-shaped eyes were opened wide with surprise.

"Ms. Lillian—this is miraculous'!" I jumped up.

Ms. Lillian accepted a hug. "My girl, a cut and a little makeup can't make you beautiful." She put her palm to my chin. "You have an infectious sweetness and intelligence—no one can manufacture personality."

Sweet and intelligent? I usually thought of myself as stubborn, and nothing came easy for me—including academic success.

I let go of her and continued to stare into the mirror.

"It's just...nothing like I expected."

Smiling, Ms. Lillian grabbed a broom and swept the hair off the floor into a dustpan.

"Go now. Enjoy your new hair," she directed with a slight tilt of her head.

****

When I opened my bedroom door the next morning I found Ms. Lillian dressed to the nines with a makeup case in hand. She was far too happy for the hour.

"You ready for your first day at CCHS, dear?" She sashayed in wearing her crème pantsuit and black Jimmy Choos. Did the woman ever rumple?

I rubbed my eyes and stepped aside.

"No, not even close. See—bed hair."

"First question," she asked. "How tall are you?"

"5-foot-10," I replied with a groan.

"I'm going to help you get ready," she said, revelling in the possibilities. *Save me now*.

After a few minutes my newly appointed stylist had picked out a pair of dark washed skinny jeans, brown riding style boots, a crème color cashmere sweater, and blouse for underneath.

"Ms. Lillian, this is going to be embarrassing for me." I stared at my reflection in the floor mirror with uncertainty.

"You look fabulous." She handed me mousse for my hair.

"I think it's too much," I tried to argue, not really sure what to do with mousse.

Ms. Lillian snatched away the mousse preparing to style my hair for me. "Nonsense."

"Look, this whole look is more New York Fashion Week—not Teddy Owens goes to school."

"My girl, let's have fun with your look today."

"This is only for today," I said.

"Cross my heart—just today if you prefer." Ms. Lillian looked pleased. "You'll be lovely either way, dear."

She tossed me a trench coat style jacket from the hanger. "White?" I asked shaking my head. "Black, okay. Brown—sure. White, no."

"Yes, white."

"I'll get it dirty," I complained.

"Then you pick another jacket tomorrow," she suggested.

Okay, now she was having too much fun.

"See," Ms. Lillian grinned as she tied the jacket's belt, "The fit is perfect." I felt like an apple, fallen from a tree of sustenance—far too exposed and vulnerable for my liking. Downstairs, the aroma of cinnamon raisin bagels met us in the parlour. I found my backpack stuffed full with school supplies on a chair. Mr. Green busily trotted around Ms. Lillian and me as we ate.

"The school will provide a combination for your locker," Ms. Lillian informed me while tapping her chin thoughtfully. I could picture her putting a mental check mark next to those tasks she had completed.

"Thanks." I sipped my juice. "I'm sure you included everything."

The minute I finished the last bite of my bagel, Mr. Green swiftly took my plate away.

Ms. Lillian handed her empty cup to Mr. Green on his way past.

"My girl, it's time to head out." She stood up and picked up her Prada purse from the floor, then rummaged through it to locate her keys.

"Oh yes, I failed to mention Kane Piers will be waiting for us outside." Mr. Green pulled out my chair for me, balancing the teacup. "Teddy dear, you do remember I mentioned Kane, don't you?" Ms. Lillian guided me toward the door.

She opened the entryway closet and pulled on a black blazer. *How come she gets to wear black?*

I sighed. Mr. Green rushed over to open the door for us.

"Kane? Yeah...I remember you mentioning him," I said. Wonderful, this could be an awkward drive into town. "Didn't you mention he has his driver's license?" I reminded her hopefully.

"He'll drive with us today," she told me as she stepped outside.

I hesitated. "Why?"

"Because, dear, there is no use driving *two* vehicles into town."

Fantastic.

Mr. Green waved and then closed the door behind us. We were met with a gust of chilly September air. I followed Ms. Lillian across the length of the covered porch.

"Ms. Lillian, what happened to Kane's parents?" I wondered. "Why doesn't he live with them?"

Ms. Lillian's car keys jingled in her hand as we headed for the garage.

"Maybe if you ask him, he'll tell you." She patted my shoulder.

"I'll ask..." My voice trailed off as we entered the garage through a side door. Inside we found Kane and his grandfather in the middle of a conversation. Kane lifted his gaze to stare at me—his eyes widened in surprise. Self-consciously I fiddled with my waist tie.

"Mr. Piers. Kane. Good morning," Ms. Lillian beamed as she greeted them. Mr. Piers stepped forward with his hand drawn out politely.

"This must be the much talked about Miss Owens, from Texas," he said. "Hello." I shook Mr. Piers' hand.

"Mr. Piers, please call me Teddy," I said.

"Glad to meet you, Teddy." Mr. Piers reached over to squeeze the back of Kane's arm. "Kane, son, don't be rude. Introduce yourself properly," he scolded.

Kane looked handsome in khaki pants and a brown suede jacket, but then, Kane would look hot dressed in a paper grocery bag.

"Hey." Kane cast me a sheepish smile and shoved his hand into his jacket pocket.

"Teddy, this is Kane Piers," Ms. Lillian said for him. "Kane, this is Teddy Owens. Remember—we talked about her coming to live at the manor."

"Nice to meet you," Kane and I said in unison.

He reached out with his free hand and there was a twinkling laughter in his eyes.

I let go of his hand first.

"It's time to head out." Ms. Lillian hit the unlock button on her keys and the X5 beeped. "My girl, I don't want to drop you off late on your first day of school." She headed for the driver's side.

"We wouldn't want that," I said under my breath.

Kane headed for the rear passenger side seat and opened the door.

"I can sit in the back seat," I said, playing the seat-martyr.

"Nah. Take the shotgun position." Kane jerked his thumb toward the front seat. "I prefer the backseat."

"Nobody likes the backseat," I said.

"Well, I do."

As I got into the front, he closed the door and I buckled my seatbelt. A moment later, Kane leaned toward me from the back seat. "You clean up well," he whispered, and then chuckled to himself as he settled back in his seat. I was glad he could not see my face because I was probably tomato red.

"It's just hair," I said. I pressed my back into the seat and clung to my backpack. "It won't be like this tomorrow."

The road into Canmore was busier than when we'd driven in from Calgary. The small community bustled with activity as a main stop for tourists travelling to visit the Rocky Mountains. Ms. Lillian made sure to mention about 12,000 people lived there.

"Teddy?" Kane tapped my shoulder from the backseat. I turned my head and caught a glimpse of his dimples, and my stomach twisted. "If you want—sit behind me in Mrs. Jordan's class," he suggested. "No one sits in that desk right now."

"I might be taking you up on that offer." I faced forward again.

"Good." Kane sounded pleased.

Ms. Lillian glanced into the back seat at Kane. I could have sworn she'd cast him a warning glance, and then reached for the volume dial to turn up her crooning country music. Up ahead I could see a row of school buses lined up in front of Canmore Composite High School—also known as CCHS. The school resembled an oversized ski lodge, but it was also obviously a school. Near the football field the school shared a parking lot with the town's recreation center.

Ms. Lillian parked along the sidewalk, near the largest congregation of teenagers she could find. Naturally, they all turned to stare at us. I felt like a goldfish stuck in a fish tank. A huge guy with black hair approached the vehicle, waving. The guy was a few inches taller than Kane—darned near a giant with a t-shirt barely concealing his rippled muscles.

"Connor!" Kane shouted. In a flash he'd jumped out of the SUV. "What's up, bud?" They exchanged goofy grins.

I opened the door a crack and placed one foot tentatively out of the car.

"Piers—yo—I *have* to tell you about this chick, Meg," Connor told Kane. "I met her this weekend—man—this girl was ho—" Connor stopped talking when he caught sight of me.

I couldn't help but notice he had ebony eyes. Everything about him screamed *mean*.

"I heard there was a new girl," he leered at me. "Bud, are you going to introduce?" he asked Kane, sizing me up like a rancher would a cow at an auction.

"Connor—dude—I swear, you have girl radar." Kane motioned for me to get out of the vehicle. "Just give her a second—she's shy," he suggested to Connor when I didn't budge.

Ms. Lillian smiled apologetically and placed a supportive hand on my arm. "Teddy, I have an appointment. I'm sorry to drop you off like this and leave."

"I'm fine." I pushed open the car door the rest of the way, then stepped out.

"Teddy?" Ms. Lillian called before I closed the door. I turned and she handed me something flat and shiny.

"Call if you have any trouble. My number is programmed into the phone," she explained. "Hit one for speed dial."

"This is mine?" I stared down at the metallic cell phone in my palm.

"Kane has one too," she added. I knew Ms. Lillian was trying to say: *Don't worry. You're not getting any weird special treatment or anything.*

"Nice." I stuffed the cell into my jacket pocket. "Have a good appointment." I closed the door and in a few moments the SUV disappeared behind another school bus pulling up.

I couldn't help but notice two girls staring at me curiously. The dark-haired one was the kind of girl boys loved to dream about at night, with her silky brunette curls, porcelain skin, and pretty round eyes. She resembled a baby doll. Her gaze did not waver, but merely shifted after a moment to land possessively on Kane. The curvier blonde with wavy hair next to her was the typical sidekick. She was pretty, but not enough to be competition. The Baby Doll leaned over to whisper in her friend's ear and their pointed stares turned hard as they glared at me.

Well, that was fast. It took all of two minutes flat before I was no better than the grime caught in the drain of a kitchen sink.

Deciding to ignore the girls, I shifted my attention back to Kane and Connor…and I noticed Connor was sniffing at the air around me. Did I smell gross? It was like he was trying to catch my scent while wondering what the cat had dragged in.

Chapter Three

Deeper Than You Think

8:42 A.M. MDT, Monday, September 13th

Kane shot Connor a nasty glare.

"Dude, back off," he ordered. Connor looked a bit confused. Intimidated, I backed away from them, feeling like I was in one of those horrible teen movies where at any moment someone in a fancy sports car would drive by and throw an egg at me.

Baby Doll was still staring, a.k.a. glaring. *Wonderful.* She had seen my strange exchange with Connor. Her round eyes had opened wide, and then she dramatically turned her back on me. The cold shoulder was body language I knew too well. *We're going to be the best of friends,* I thought sarcastically.

"Forget Emma-Lynn. She's territorial." Kane looped his arm in mine, apparently not fazed by Emma-Lynn's early disdain for me.

"I'm sure she's awesome. Just off to a rocky start." I swallowed.

Kane tilted his head toward me. "She likes to think so." I could smell the forest scent of his cologne. If I did smell terrible, as the look on Connor's face had suggested, Kane did not seem bothered.

"I would never have guessed." The beginnings of a smile tugged at the sides of my lips.

"Dude, like I said—ignore her."

A boy approached with a mess of wiry auburn hair and dark skin—and more ridiculous muscles. Were most of the guys in Canmore steroid poppers?

"Hey, Connor, Kane," he said, nodding toward me. "Who's this?"

"Teddy, these are my buddies, Connor Ferguson," Kane said and punched Connor in the arm, "and John Bengal." Kane pretended to punch John in the shoulder. Both Connor and John were staring at me like I had lettuce in my teeth. I ran my tongue over my teeth just to be sure.

"Hi."

John and Connor? My half smile erupted into a full one. I'm sure both boys had heard the *Terminator* comparison before. I waved slightly at them.

"John and Connor—nice to meet y'all."

"I heard you were from Texas," Connor said, catching onto my slight accent. He was still looking at me funny. "Wait until you feel -30 degrees. You might want to go home."

Minus 30? No one had warned me it got that cold here.

"I wanted to take up skiing," I said dully.

"You came to the right place." Connor relaxed enough to exchange a laughing expression with John and Kane. Then a bell rang out and my heart did a nervous flip-flop.

Kane pulled me toward the main entrance.

I heard Connor whisper to John, "There has never been a chick...quite like *her* in Canmore before."

"You noticed too?" John whispered, twisting his neck around to see me.

What was everyone noticing? I wished I'd brought my underarm deodorant with me.

Kane held tight to my arm.

"Dudes—cool it," he warned. "We can hear you."

John cast another creepy yellow-eyed glance in my direction. Honestly, for a split second it looked as though he was angry with me.

"Alright, man—whatever—we'll chat later," Connor said as he and John disappeared into the crowd of kids spilling into the school through multiple entrances. The steady stream of students rushed up a pair of metal staircases to a second-level courtyard.

"Connor's right about one thing, this isn't Texas," Kane muttered, mistaking my shivers to be from cold.

"Not even close," I said, trying not to remember the hateful expression in John's eyes.

"Don't worry. You'll acclimatize like the rest of us."

I took my arm back.

"I'll live."

"You will," Kane agreed. "We all do."

"It snowed once over Christmas in Corpus," I explained, "but I was in Houston with Angelique."

"You've never seen snow—that's unheard of around here!" Kane's eyes opened wide in amazement. He grinned as he held the door open for me. "The only thing I like about winter is hockey season...you know what?"

"What?"

"You have this weird energy about you."

"I have a weird energy about me?" I choked on my words. "Ugh, thanks?"

"Don't worry—it's a nice energy," he quickly assured.

A few minutes later I was checked in as a new student at CCHS. Kane managed to nab me the locker two down from his. The hall was emptying of students as we headed to our lockers. "Look at this," a snide voice said. "Kane is being the school ambassador for a day."

"I didn't know Kane was a school ambassador?" the sidekick said.

"He's not!" Emma-Lynn snapped back at her. The sidekick cast a scowl in my direction. "Staring problem?"

"Don't listen to them," Kane instructed.

As we passed, both girls slammed their lockers shut and stared. Emma-Lynn stomped one foot. "Kane Piers," she sneered. "Who are you? *Her* personal keeper?"

We stopped five lockers down from Emma-Lynn.

"Em, that's enough—back off," Kane growled.

Emma-Lynn turned her nose up. Her sidekick whispered something I couldn't hear. Emma-Lynn's eyes opened wide with surprise.

"That's...not cool," she said, sucking in a sharp breath as her nostrils flared.

In frustration, Kane leaned his forehead against the locker. "Whitney," he groaned, "did you have to— why don't you shut up?"

"It's true!" Emma-Lynn screeched to Whitney. "Why would they let someone like *that* come here? They attract trouble like—"

"Whit, where did you hear about it anyway?" Kane groaned, interrupting her. *About what?*

"Sorry, Kane," Whitney flushed. "My mom told me about it."

"This shouldn't be allowed," Emma-Lynn said with a trembling bottom lip.

Kane's head was still leaning up against the locker.

"Em," he begged. "Please can we talk about this later—the bell already rang for class."

Straightening her back, Emma-Lynn closed the small space to Kane in three strides.

"Oh we *will* talk later." Emma-Lynn leaned in so her glossy lips were only an inch from Kane's cheek. "I will do *you* a favour during our talk *later*. I will remind you how this ends."

"Em, just chill out. Dude, you're going to make a big deal out of nothing—I know you." Kane's fists were clenched at his side.

"Emma-Lynn, let's go," Whitney urged. "Kane's getting mad."

"Fine." Emma-Lynn twirled around motioning for Whitney to follow. I could smell the scent of her flowery perfume as they both sashayed down the hall. I hated her even more for smelling good.

Upset, it took Kane three attempts before he opened his combination lock. "Your locker is this one," he said, finally opening his lock. He tapped a locker two down from his—thank goodness, farther away from Emma-Lynn.

"That was weird," I said. He stuffed a book under his arm with unnecessary force. I stood awkwardly holding my backpack and jumped as he slammed his locker shut. "What did the Whitney girl say? I couldn't hear."

"Forget about Em and Whitney," Kane sighed. "Trust me."

"I'll try." I looked down at the blue Post-It where my locker number and combination was written. *Locker #240, Combination: 8-7-14.* Miraculously, I managed to open it on my first attempt. "Kane, those aren't the kind of girls I want to be friends with anyway." I stored my backpack in the locker, crinkling my smell as I noticed the scent of rotten bananas inside.

A flash of charming dimples temporarily blinded me. "By the way, I like your hair."

I pushed a strand behind my ear. "Yeah, the red dye was an experiment gone wrong."

"You look great either way."

"Obviously you couldn't see well the other night." I flushed.

Was he trying to flirt?

"You're too modest, Teddy." Kane put his arm on my shoulder. "Mrs. Jordan's class is this way." He guided me down the hall. "Did you know she's Mrs. Abasi's daughter?" he reveled.

"No, but good to know." I shrugged off his arm. "Kane, is Emma-Lynn your girl—"

Kane put a hand up. "Please don't finish that question. Emma-Lynn Weldon *was* my girlfriend—two months ago."

"Why did you break up?"

"It's a stupid story," Kane shrugged. "Em kissed some guy at the *Calgary Stampede* on the Ferris Wheel. Connor was there with some girl he was seeing. He took a picture on his cell phone, then like a good buddy, sent it to me."

"That's terrible!" I said, but was really laughing inside.

"Now she wants to get back together," he said and shook his head. "She won't like you because we're friends."

"I will get mad at her eventually."

"Let me know if she's bothering you," Kane said gallantly. "I can deal with her."

"I can keep care of myself." I scrunched up my face. "Also, you don't have to...be my friend—I'd understand if it's too much trouble."

"They think you're competition. I'm hoping Em will soon find another guy to play fetch with."

Under Kane's math textbook I noticed he was holding *Romeo & Juliet.*

"I wouldn't take you for a Shakespeare kind of guy?" I pointed to the book under his arm.

Kane glanced down. "Maybe I'm deeper than you think."

"Maybe you have English after Math class?" I laughed.

"Smart ass." He grinned and nudged me lightly with his elbow.

Was that another attempt to flirt?

"Do you think you have me all figured out?" he asked, tilting his head to the side.

I shook my head. "Honestly, Kane, you're the person I haven't figured out."

"I haven't figured myself out yet either," Kane said. We slowed as we approached a classroom door. He reached for the doorknob and leaned over with his lips close to my ear.

"For never was a story of more woe than this of Juliet and her Romeo."

His words sent shivers up my spine.

"Act five. Scene three," I said weakly. *Maybe there was real substance beneath the cool-guy swagger after all.*

"Dude, you've read it...apparently a few times," Kane said looking surprised. "The ending is unfortunate." He knocked once and then opened the classroom door. I stumbled in feeling woozy.

"Come in, Kane … you're late," a female voice near the whiteboard said. The teacher's marker paused on the whiteboard. "If this was a regular occurrence, you'd be served detention," she warned.

"Sorry I'm late, Mrs. Jordan." I had my hands stuffed in my jacket pockets, just like a shrinking violet. He gestured to me. "She needed my help to find her locker—this is Teddy Owens."

Mrs. Jordan peered at me with intelligent eyes over Kane's shoulder.

"Hello, Miss Owens … glad you could join us."

She wore an artsy skirt all the colors of a rainbow and her dark hair was pinned back in a messy bun. The woman didn't need makeup, because her skin had an enviable blemish-free olive tone.

"Hi," I said.

I felt like nothing more than a viral specimen meant for inspection—an outsider. These kids had probably all been going to school together since kindergarten, except for maybe Kane. I'd learned from Ms. Lillian he only moved here two years ago and somehow had already managed to fit in like cream in coffee.

Mrs. Jordan put the top on her whiteboard marker. With a quick flick of her wrist, she snatched up the extra math textbook and approached me wearing a friendly expression.

"You'll need this," she said, handing the book to Kane, who reached over to hand it to me.

I took it. "Thanks, Mrs. Jordan."

"Kane, help Miss Owens find a seat." Ms. Jordan turned to continue speaking to the class, business as usual.

Kane slipped into a seat closest to the doorway. "Sit here, Teddy." He pointed at the empty desk behind him. I managed to take my seat without meeting any of my new classmates' curious gazes.

"I feel like the twinkling star on top a Christmas tree," I whispered.

Kane winked back at me then turned to open his text.

A few minutes later, I was already bored and studied Mrs. Jordan. She was an exotic looking young woman, maybe in her late twenties. I'd bet she was a mix of several ethnicities and couldn't help but wonder where her height came from—considering her mother was so short. Moving on from Mrs. Jordan, I noted there was a girl wearing a crazy hat, sitting near the classroom window. It was impossible not to notice her because she was dressed in bright colors…and intensely staring at me with a friendly smile.

"Hey, Teddy?" Kane rushed after me as I pretty much ran out of class when the bell rang. "Wait!" I continued to hurry away down the crowded hall. "Wisely and slowly—they stumble that run fast," Kane warned as he caught up with me.

"Okay, I get it," I jested. "You know Shakespeare—good job."

Kane's eyes twinkled. "What can I say—his words come in handy. Do you even know where you're going?" Already lost, I stopped.

"Actually, no," I admitted.

"What's your next class?"

"Art."

"Dude, turn around and go the other way." He pointed over his shoulder. "Let me walk you to class?"

I was going to say he didn't have to, but Kane was stopped by a group of three guys headed past us.

A short guy said, "Kane, *the Grizzlies* were totally rocked by your crazy hot slap shot—man, you got sick hands."

"Thanks." Kane smacked hands with him. "I'll talk to you guys in a few," he said. "I'm showing my friend to her class."

The short guy smiled brightly at me. "Sure—we understand," he said with a suggestive tone. I rolled my eyes at him.

"Hotshot, you don't need to walk me to class," I teased as the boys walked away.

In Art, I worked with watercolors while watching Alyssa Vallas—the girl I had noticed in math class. I found her quirky-girl attitude refreshing. She laughed *a lot* and seemed to enjoy standing out like a sore thumb. The girl was daring enough to wear a florescent blue jump suit, yellow runners, and a purple hat similar to the one from Dr. Seuss's *The Cat in the Hat*.

Wanting to avoid the lunch hour crush, I ended up hiding in the Art lab with Al—she had introduced herself—who seemed bent on making me her new best friend. We both ended up laughing hysterically the whole time.

After the final bell I headed back to my locker to find Kane talking to Whitney and John, and they all looked agitated. Kane's shoulders were bunched up and his neck was held stiff.

"Mind your own business—you too, Bengal," he said, pointing a threatening finger at John.

"You know, this is trouble for all of us," John replied, his face flush with anger. "Mr. Owens must be going wacko in the braino." He twisted a finger in a circle around his temple.

"Bengal, I will punch you in the face." Kane raised a fist in threat.

"You know what—pretty boy Piers," John egged Kane on. "I want you to *try* and punch me." John stuck his chest out. He and Kane were standing almost eye-to-eye. "You won't be walking out of a fight with me without bleeding."

Where were teachers when you need them? I thought, looking around.

"Chill out, you guys!" Whitney bravely pushed them apart, putting a hand on each boy's chest. For a moment her blue eyes flashed with the same animalistic glint. She lowered her hands only to clap them together to keep the boys' attention. "You two need to stop—this topic is closed," she said, pulling John away from Kane. "John," she lowered her voice another octave, "it doesn't matter what you think. Remember—both of you—we're at school." She looked back and forth between them. "You can go at each other's throats later."

A deep growl rumbled out of John's throat, and the sound made me shiver. Seriously, John freaked me out in the worst way.

Whitney's palm flattened on John's chest as she turned to glance over Kane's shoulder. "Teddy, how long have you been standing there?" she asked.

"Not long," I said curtly, and walked past. John and Kane both stood rigid and shifted their gazes to stare down at the floor. My appearance was like a bucket of cold water on a bonfire. I opened my locker and dropped my binder in. The silence was deafening.

"It's over—okay," I heard Whitney say to John. "It's time to go."

"Fine," John replied with a raspy voice, running a hand through his hair as he and Whitney walked away.

"Bengal!" Kane shouted down the hall. "Dude, we'll talk more about this at practice tomorrow." He pushed his back flat against his locker, looking smug.

"Whatever, Piers," John snapped back. "At this point I doubt talking will do much." Kane stared after them with an expression that was the epitome of annoyance.

"What were y'all fighting about?" I asked, pulling my backpack from the locker as John and Whitney disappeared around a corner.

"I looked for you at lunch—you disappeared," Kane said, still angry. "Wow," he sniffed. "Your locker stinks."

So that's how it was going to be. Him, ignoring my question.

"I'll bring deodorizer spray in tomorrow..." I closed my locker. "Look, sorry if you were looking for me at lunch. I didn't want to follow you and your friends around all day—plus, I made a new friend."

"Awesome. People around here are nice." Kane's arms were crossed tight across his chest. "Most of them." He clenched his jaw.

"Can I ask you something? But you have to promise to be honest."

"I don't know..." Kane said with hesitation.

"Do I smell?"

Kane's head snapped to attention. "What kind of question is that?"

"Seriously, Kane," I pleaded. "Please be honest! I noticed people sniffing the air around me...like I smell funny."

"That's absurd, what's next?" Kane threw his hands back in frustration. "Teddy, what if you don't have a smell at all?"

"I should smell like green apples. It's this wicked body wash in my shower at the manor," I rambled.

Kane lowered his hands. His mouth had fallen slightly open. "I'm sure you do."

"What are you trying to say, Kane? People around here are acting strange because they...can't smell me?"

"Precisely."

L.A. CADIEUX

Chapter Four

Far From Alone

3:40 P.M. MDT, Monday, September 13ᵗʰ

I was staring at Kane like he was ludicrous.

"You're saying I don't have a smell?"

"Just saying," Kane shrugged again. "No smell is better than smelling rank." His gaze lingered on my face. I had the distinctive feeling he wanted to say more, but he didn't.

I inhaled my regular scent. I definitely didn't smell awful.

"Very funny—you had me for a moment." I laughed.

"You didn't say how your day was." Kane was not laughing as he knelt to pick up his binder.

"Actually...it wasn't so bad." My smile turned into a frown.

"Let me guess. You thought you'd be stuffed in a locker?"

"No, because I promise—if I was stuffed in a locker—I'd be asking for a ticket home to Texas. I'd take my chances with the foster care system."

"Are you going to show up again tomorrow?" Kane shifted his feet, the rubber soles of his shoes squeaking. "Pinkie swear?" He held up a pinkie.

I couldn't help but laugh again. "I *pinkie* swear." I wrapped my pinkie around his. "I'll be back."

We broke our conjoined pinkies.

"Great," Kane said, then he surprised me—okay—downright shocked me by reaching over to hold my hand.

"So...do you have hockey practice tonight?" I asked, trying to play it cool, but wanted to grin like an idiot.

"Nah, I have practice tomorrow." Kane let go of my hand. "*The Eagles* are playing *Camrose Kodiaks* again this weekend." He stuffed both his fists swiftly into his jacket pockets.

"Are you going to win?"

"Yeah, we will," Kane said, matter-of-factly.

"Maybe I'll come watch the game…" I said, waiting for a personal invitation.

"Maybe another time," he said vaguely. "Don't come by yourself, eh."

"Eh, I don't need a babysitter," I said, making fun of his Canadian accent.

"Okay, then please don't come," Kane snapped.

What's his problem? Hello, we're having a moment here.

"Fine." I crossed my arms across my chest. "I won't go."

The worst part of the day ended up being Kane's scalding public displays of anger. I couldn't help but wonder what made him so angry?

****

After my first day at CCHS, Kane volunteered to drive me to and from school—if he didn't have hockey practice. I wasn't going to argue. His extreme concern for my wellbeing was cute.

Indeed, Al Vallas had swiftly become my new best friend, even though we were like oranges and apples.

Nothing alike, expect for a round shape. I liked spending time with her because she was always cheerful and carried our conversations. Her favorite hobby was millinery: basically, designing hats the Queen of England would wear. You know, the kind with an ostrich or peacock feather sticking out of the top. Along with designing hats and fascinators, Al was *obsessed* with multi-color tights and leg warmers. I'm not talking earth tones—nope—I'm talking Pippi Longstocking.

"I'm a hol-ly-wood diva in the making, baby!" Al liked to say. She was lovable, quirky, and thrilled to take me under her charismatic wing. The best part was, she made a point of avoiding Emma-Lynn and Whitney like the plague. Honestly, I needed Al's friendship more than I wanted to admit.

"Kane, do you like Al?" I had asked. I'd noticed he was easily annoyed by her flamboyant personality.

"Teddy, if you like her—I like her. I'm neither *for* nor *against* her," he replied. "I like whoever makes you happy."

"Not everyone has to like each other." Al was my friend, not his. I had to let the matter go.

"Teddy Bear!" Al screeched in despair the day she figured out I was crushing on Kane—hard. "My friend," she said dramatically, while twirling around in a circle. "You're looking for heartbreak like white on rice." Al often came up with head-shaking comparisons.

"Al, he's not a player," I said valiantly. "Kane's not a *Connor*. Think about it, other than Emma-Lynn he hasn't dated anyone."

"The fact he dated *Emma-Lynn*," Al would argue, "for nearly *two years* is enough to label him the enemy. You don't even know him."

After several disagreements we ended up deciding Kane was an untouchable subject, "like the flame on a propane stove," as Al had so eloquently put it.

"Teddy Bear," Al insisted after watching Kane and me flirting after the final bell one afternoon, "come to your senses, girly, and *forget* him." She brushed away his importance to me with a flick of her wrist. "Girly, there are so many better fish in the aquarium."

Fortunately for Al, and unfortunately for me, Kane was often busy with hockey. Even though I hated to admit it, our drives to and from school were often plagued by an impenetrable silence. When we were alone we'd taken to holding hands in the car—and even after many weeks of pretty much no other progress, I still had hope. I wasn't a great conversationalist and Kane wasn't the kind of guy who was uncomfortable with silence. To me, it was perfect.

I felt safe when his hand closed over mine during our commute…his thumb rubbing the inside of my wrist. The way he smiled at with his eyes, stealing glances over, it made my stomach twist nervously. He must feel the same way I did. Maybe he was too shy to admit it?

In other news, my uncle had arrived home at the beginning of October from his twice-extended business trip. I desperately wanted to meet him, if only to assure myself I hadn't created him in my mind. But it wasn't to be. He flew in around noon on a school day and stayed two full hours before heading back to New York for *another* meeting. I tried to ignore the tugging feeling he was purposefully avoiding me. My heart continued to insist he was a really busy man.

****

4:30 P.M. MDT, Sunday, October 31st - Halloween Day

The weather was overcast and nearly everyone from school had been invited to a Halloween dress-up party at Emma-Lynn's tonight—of course, except for me and Al. Kane was the only one who decided not to go, sweetly claiming he had to help his grandfather fix a water heater. Annoyed, I tapped my pen against the windowsill in my room. There was still no snow in Canmore and I was told no snow this late in October was almost unheard of.

"Teddy?" A voice interrupted my thoughts. "Can I come in?" Ms. Lillian peeked through the open door.

"Sure." I looked up. "Have a seat, Ms. Lillian." I gestured for her to join me at the window seat.

She came in, and moved a cushion out of the way to sit down next to me.

"How is your studying going?" Ms. Lillian asked, glancing down at my closed Chemistry textbook.

"Fine. Just studying." I set down my pen and closed my binder.

"We miss you downstairs. You've been holed up in your room all weekend. Are you feeling alright?"

I sighed. "I guess...I have been wondering why I haven't met Uncle Delmont yet?"

"He's tied up with business in New York."

"It's just..." I grumbled. "I've gotten the impression he doesn't want to meet me."

Ms. Lillian's Chanel No.5 scent wafted past my nose. For all her perfumes and fancy clothes, my uncle must pay her well.

"Dear, don't worry." She patted my hand. "Your uncle will meet you soon enough—he desperately wants to."

"Whatever," I muttered.

"Is there anything *else* bothering you?" she asked softly.

Yes, Kane Piers. He is acting weird, and also, I'm convinced everyone is keeping my uncle's secrets on this estate.

"Ms. Lillian, did you ever get married?" I asked, avoiding what was really on my mind.

Ms. Lillian stood and leaned against the window pursing both her lips together, as icy splatters began to fall from the sky.

"One summer," she tensely swallowed, "I dated a much younger man from England." She touched the glass with all five of the fingertips on her hand. A trail of water ran through the middle. "I have fond memories of him." Her blue eyes were glassy. "This young man was handsome—and charismatic. If he was an evangelical preacher he'd have followers to his every word." She lowered her hand and clenched her palm. "When we first met he was working with his brother at a river rafting shop in town."

"What happened? Did you two get in a fight?" I pushed my binder off my lap, interested.

Ms. Lillian looked weary as she rubbed her dress pants with her palms. "No, in the fall he left with his brother to drive across the U.S." She clenched her side as though in pain.

"Did you love him?" *I can be such a snoop.*

"It was impossible not to fall for him." Ms. Lillian laughed to herself. "God, I adored his intellect—there was so much of it. And, yes, he was smart, a gifted man." She shook her head and turned her back on the dreary weather outside. "At summer's end he had to go. Canada was my home—not his. I never wanted to leave."

"Did he ask you to leave?" I leaned forward, intrigued by Ms. Lillian's love story.

"He never asked me to, dear." She continued, "It was only an innocent summer romance and could never be—none of it."

"You don't have to say...but what happened to him?" I stared down at my pen.

"It doesn't matter." Ms. Lillian snapped out of the past. "My girl, eventually he fell in love with someone else." She stepped away. "After all these years, it makes me a fool, I suppose, for never finding love again."

"That's so...sad." The guy was stupid not to marry Ms. Lillian. She would make the perfect wife. "It must be lonely, being alone," I lamented for her.

"*Don't* put all your life's happiness in the hands of men," she scolded. "You should be happy—even if alone. There are people who have lost *everything* they love in this world. I certainly have nothing to complain about. And I have been *far* from alone in my life."

"I should think before I talk—this is a chronic issue for me." I stood up to join Ms. Lillian. "I'm sorry."

"I wouldn't say if I didn't want to." Ms. Lillian waved off my concern. "You do know how glad we are to have *you* here?"

"I know."

"Good." Ms. Lillian crossed her arms across her chest. "Shall we head down for supper? Mrs. Abasi has been slaving away on her special zucchini lasagne."

"Awesome. It's my favorite." Although, I was not sure about the zucchini part...

"She will be glad to hear it," Ms. Lillian said, trying to smile over at me. However, I knew it was only a sad attempt to cover up a troubled frown.

****

5:20 P.M. MDT, Sunday, October 31st

The drizzling rain had stopped and there was only a sliver of light left in the sky from the setting sun when I decided to go for a walk. The orange and purple glow from the setting sun was straining to peek through a break in the clouds creating a luminescent effect over the frosted estate. Overhead, the pathway lights were flickering on for the night. The days were getting shorter.

I pulled my winter coat tighter around me, feeling the skin on my cheeks tighten and my lips dry from the crisp air. Tonight, the weather broadcasters reported, it would again dip below freezing…a big snow would arrive soon. We'd already had several days of sporadic flurries.

With no real objective I walked down the path heading toward the north side of the property. Subconsciously, I'd hoped to run into Kane, but the chances were slim tonight. I found myself searching for the fairytale-like stone walls I'd seen once—Ms. Lillian had suggested I stay away from them. I was not one to follow such orders and naturally headed for the wall. As I searched I felt like Mary Lennox from *The Secret Garden,* although I was more a Lois Lane than a Mary: On a quest, to unearth the secret underworld in Metropolis—but without Superman to save me.

After finding the off-limits wall I searched and realized there wasn't any magical door hiding behind a thick hanging of vines. There was no door at all, but there was an old birch tree growing up and over the southern-most wall. I studied the lazy tree branch resting over the wall: it looked sturdy enough for someone of my weight.

Stuffing my mittens in the kangaroo pocket of my jacket I approached the base of the trunk. The tree was a good forty or fifty feet high with the nearest branch low enough for me to jump up and grab hold. I furrowed my brow before jumping up to wrap my arms around it. My boots braced against the trunk. Leveraging the strength of my limbs, I pulled myself up to sit on the first branch. The branch bowed slightly. It took a concentrated effort not to teeter off. Once balanced, I supported myself by clinging to the trunk and pulled up to the next branch, then the next. Wrapping myself around the branch draped over the stone wall I thought to myself, *don't look down...don't look down...don't look down.* I knew there was a chance the branch could break. If it did I would fall. If I survived a fall it would not be without a couple of broken bones and a severely bruised ego.

Unless I was extremely lucky Fred and Barney were probably already running over on their way to deal me a stern retribution. *Ugh, if only I could fly? Flying! Yes, that skill would help immensely.*

Each movement forward was slow and steady as I crept along the branch like a caterpillar. I did it, but even better, I did it without falling or sustaining serious injury. In my books a couple of scratches don't count. I carefully pushed myself upright and shifted to straddle the stone wall. *I must be going crazy to do this.* Shaking my head, I examined my finger. A sliver of blood had beaded on my forefinger. Sucking at the tip of it, I looked into the garden and blinked twice.

Was this a joke?

L.A. CADIEUX

Chapter Five

Attached

6:20 P.M. MDT, Sunday, October 31ˢᵗ

"What the heck?" I squinted. "Where are the flowers?"

Instead of the unkempt secret garden I had expected, there was a mowed field of grass. In the center of the field a helicopter was parked on a landing pad. The helicopter pilot and passengers weren't anywhere to be seen.

Why was my uncle's helicopter pad walled up? I had a bad feeling about this. The only building was built off to the east side of the cement—a small metal hut with a metal door. As I considered crawling back down the tree, I saw a flashlight slicing through the night.

"Some spy I turned out to be," I groaned. Frantic, I searched for an escape.

Nearby was a long metal pipe screwed into the side of the stone wall. I shimmied along the wall until I could reach it with my feet. Shifting onto my stomach, I braced my feet and carefully worked my way down the cold metal. My arms ached with the weight of my body. It took all my concentration not to lose hold. About six feet off the ground I reached the bottom of the piping.

"This might hurt." I clenched my teeth, closed my eyes, and then let go. I dropped into a roll on the frozen ground.

"Miss Owens!" A gruff voice shouted on the either side of the wall. "Are you out here?" It was an estate guard.

I opened my eyes to some good news—nothing was broken. Afraid the guard would climb over the wall after me, I crept towards the helicopter and I saw a machine gun affixed to the outside. *Who did my uncle think he was—Rambo?* Standing on my tiptoes, I looked inside. Indeed, there were two more handheld machine guns.

"A successful investor? More like Al Capone." Whatever Uncle Delmont was doing was illegal and violent. Not wanting to hang out with the killing machine, I continued to creep towards the metal door. "Please...please," I begged, "be unlocked." I pressed my back to the small metal building. "Whoa," I whispered as the doorknob turned easily. Apparently my uncle kept his secret building unlocked. The door was swiftly caught by a gust of wind and banged into my shoulder. I stifled a loud curse. Rubbing my shoulder, I peered into the outbuilding, only to discover a steep metal staircase descended into a dimly lit tunnel.

"Teddy Owens!" The guard shouted again. "Miss Owens! I saw you come this way. It's Garret—with manor security—I only want to make sure you're alright."

Not wanting to be found out, I stepped into the ominous but well lit stairway. The door closed behind me. Before I could take another step I heard a loud popping noise outside similar to a balloon bursting. *Was it a gunshot?* I had never heard one before so I couldn't tell. *Why couldn't my uncle be some old guy who lived in a bungalow and worked as an accountant? Was he involved with drugs? OMG—what if he's a drug lord!*

The stairs creaked beneath my feet as I made my way down into the humid tunnel. When I reached the bottom I channeled my inner Lois Lane and sidestepped along the wall. Up ahead were four metal doors. Exposed copper and metal pipes were dripping condensation into puddles on the cement floor. Directly over my head I could hear liquid rushing through a pipe.

Heavy footsteps clomped down an intersecting hallway. I froze. "Have the others been informed?" asked a deep male voice. "The President is adamant we protect the *One Life.*"

"How did they manage to locate us—through Lynette?" a female voice asked.

"I don't know." The tone of the male voice was troubled.

"The civilians are angry," the woman warned. "They feel Mr. Owens has put them in danger for personal reasons."

To stay hidden, I pressed in behind a mass of pipes, which travelled vertically up the cement.

"Do they consider protecting the fate of our heir a personal reason, or one of national interest?" the deep male voice pondered. Their footsteps paused. "The civilians must understand this is a particularly difficult situation for Delmont to be in. The President and Paul both are invested."

"I don't think they do...understand," the female voice replied. "You know they are frustrated right now— the campaign and election are next year. They want a choice."

"Nevertheless, I have it on good authority Mr. Owens is considering all options," he revealed.

"When is Paul arriving?" she asked. "He should be dealing with this matter."

"He was held up in Amsterdam yesterday," the man said. "Believe me, he's not happy with the delay."

"Won't she start to ask questions?" the woman asked.

There was a long pause. "She might, Maria," he admitted.

Maria?

"We need to protect our interests, Francis." A door creaked open, followed by retreating footsteps. The door clicked shut.

Francis? What was going on around here?

Just then a rolling growl vibrated through the exterior door to the helicopter pad. Though distant…I would have sworn there was a bear out there. The growl was followed by the bark of a dog and then a sharp yipping noise.

All animals with teeth. I'm not hanging around to find out what's happening.

Trembling, I sprinted down the tunnel and turned at the intersection. I reached for the first door and rushed inside. My eyes were closed as my back pressed up against the inside of the door. The room was silent. I opened my eyes to find I had entered a brightly lit infirmary room, which smelled like rubbing alcohol. Metal cabinets with glass doors lined a white cement wall. The cabinets were filled with clear canisters, many stocked with bandages. A stretcher in the middle of the room was covered with a white sheet, and next to the stretcher stood an IV stand. A surgeon's tools had been carefully laid out on a counter near a sink. *Let me guess,* I thought. *Guns = Injuries. Injuries = Surgery.*

What was this *One Life* drug? Feeling nauseated from the smell, I carefully opened the door a crack, plotting my escape. Going back outside was not a viable option considering there were rabid animals out there. *Is it possible to be cursed with bad luck?* I knelt on the floor inside the infirmary door as I heard more voices and running footsteps.

"There's been a breach!" Maria shouted with panic. "A mob of civilians—they've come—they want to take away the *Lifer*."

"Maria, stay calm," said Francis. He was starting to sound vaguely familiar. "Renaldo, is the target located?"

"No, Francis, she's still missing," said a different male voice, presumably Renaldo. "The last Garret and I saw she was snooping around the wall. I find her extremely difficult to track with no smell."

"Renaldo, are the H.A.S. here too?" Francis asked.

"Nope," Renaldo said with assurance, "KP should be here any moment. I think he will be able to talk some sense into these shifties—at least for the time being."

Shifties?

"Renaldo, I don't want KP involved," Francis said shortly.

"I've been around the block a time or two—it's too late—the kid's already involved."

"Francis, Renaldo is right," Maria agreed. "It's clear he has grown attached—much as he tries to hide it. You know well, his attachment will be a conflict of interest."

"You know, we shouldn't have allowed them to become so close," Francis said wearily. "We should have thought up a contingency plan for a matter such as this." He sighed.

"This is a very rare situation," Maria said supportively. "Please, don't blame yourself, Francis."

"I'll have a talk with KP. I'm sure everything will be fine," Francis said with assurance. "Now, change and do an intensive ground search." The tone of authority returned to his voice. "Don't return without good news— I'll do a fly over."

I heard another loud pop and stifled a scream.

"Renaldo, you could at least wait until we are outside," Maria scolded. I heard their retreating footsteps but the creepiest part was not all the footsteps sounded human. One set sounded like claws clicking against a cement floor. A door opened and there was a lot of shuffling and banging, then the tunnel was silent again.

Where was Superman when you needed him? All I wanted to do was forget I had ever found this bunker. I wanted to forget about playing Lois Lane. It felt like I had opened Pandora's box.

"Teddy?" Off balance, I fell into the hallway when the infirmary door was thrust open. *Perfect, I've been caught by my uncle's underground mafia. Now what?* I was pulled onto my feet by my captor, but found myself staring into Kane's eyes. Kane was doing a marvellous job managing to look intimidating and worried—all at the same time.

"Let go," I said and slapped away his hands, after it dawned on me that I was not about to be kidnapped by some psycho drug dealer.

"Good to see you too." Kane released me.

"I'd be happy to see you," I said, "*If* I knew what the heck is going on with y'all." I straightened out my jacket and then stepped into a corner of the infirmary. "There's some weirdass stuff going down."

"Teddy, just..." Kane's eyes closed until they were slits like he was fighting a headache. "You need to come with me."

He reached over and grabbed hold of my forearm and then led me into the hall.

"Kane," I demanded, "—stop!" I tried to dig my fingernails into his arm.

"You need to go back to the manor," Kane ordered, still holding my arm. He stopped only when we were in the tunnel. "Dude," he whispered. "What were *you* doing down here?"

"Do not call me *dude*." I pulled my arm away and glared. "I could ask *you* the same thing."

"Keep your voice down." Kane placed a finger to his mouth. "Believe me. You don't want the others to find you right now."

"I heard people talking," I whispered, obeying Kane.

A profanity slipped out of Kane's broad mouth. "What did you hear?" He swung open a door, behind which was another metal staircase.

"I don't know." I struggled to keep up with his swift pace up the stairs. The guy was as agile as a leaping gazelle. "I couldn't figure out what they were talking about." I whispered loudly, "I heard wild animals— fighting."

"Did you hear names?" he asked, "—see faces?" Kane didn't seem the least bit concerned rabid animals were running around the estate.

"No faces," I admitted as I clung to the stair rail. "I heard some guy…Francis." I frowned and tried to remember.

"Anyone else?" Kane put a frustrated hand to his forehead.

"He was talking to—or about—Maria, Garret, KP and Renaldo. They also mentioned a guy in Amsterdam– –Paul." We reached the top of the staircase. I pulled on Kane's sleeve to stop him. "Do you recognize those names?"

73

"Teddy, shh." He put his hand to my mouth listening for anyone following us. When he took his hand back he buried his face into it in despair.

"This isn't something we can sweep under a rug," I said, growing more agitated by the minute.

Kane lowered his hands and stared at me with great intensity. "Think hard—tell me everything."

I stumbled through my memories of the conversations. "I do remember there was other stuff said...but I didn't know what they were talking about." I stepped down one stair as a horrible thought dawned on me. "Please tell me you aren't involved in this—" I threw my hands up and stepped down another step, "—this operation!"

"Stop freaking out." His fists were clenched as he stared down at me. "You can trust me."

"If I can trust you—tell me what's going on around here." I scowled at Kane, expecting him to lie. "What is my uncle doing *and* how illegal is it? I've never met the guy, so I certainly will not go to jail for him."

To calm me Kane dropped onto the same step as me and gently placed both hands on my shoulder.

"Ouch." I winced.

He dropped his hands, horrified. "Teddy—you're hurt?"

"I banged my shoulder coming in." I reached up to touch my shoulder, shrugging painfully. "It's minor, considering everything."

Kane reached for my hand, clutching it protectively. "Forget anything you heard and saw tonight." My heart started to beat faster. "Go back to the manor. You're not listening." Kane studied my face. "I can tell," he said with more urgency. "Listen—this is important. When you get back to the manor you must say you were lost. Say it took you a while to find your way back."

"Kane, nobody will believe I was lost," I shot back. "The estate isn't exactly a Longleat Hedge Maze." My frustration was escalating. "Also, I have a lot of questions for you."

"They will believe you—if I play along."

"Why would you do that?" I asked. I was enjoying standing so close to him, smelling his earthen scents.

"You need to try and understand." Kane kissed my forehead. I blinked twice in surprise. *What was the kiss for?* "If anyone finds out you know anything *they* will make you leave. I don't want you to leave."

"They?" I asked, all too aware Kane had wrapped an arm around my waist… His lips were close, so close to mine. I'd never kissed anyone before, but it would probably be amazing with all the adrenaline running through me.

"Trust me—just play along." Kane pulled me into a hug instead. "Go back to the manor. Go back to school. Forget what you saw and heard. Do this, if not for me, then for yourself. I don't want you to go away."

"Go away?" I didn't want to go away.

"Trust me." Kane pulled my mittens out of my pockets and carefully put them onto shaking hands. I felt like a lost child. "You ready?" He looked me up and down. He seemed to decide I was presentable enough for this charade.

"No," I said earnestly.

"You better get ready." The door pushed open and Kane led me out an exit that looked like the backdoor. The door was attached to a small log cabin, a cabin I had not seen during my walks on the estate. "I'm going to head back to the manor with you." Kane linked his arm with mine.

"Is the manor safe?"

"The manor *should* be one of the safest places in the world for you." Kane wore a tense expression. He led me past a dense thicket of bushes and down a paved pathway.

"Look, no offense, but I don't feel safe."

"Didn't it occur to you that maybe all those names you learned down there—that maybe they might be trying to protect the estate—protect you?"

Chapter Six

Act Normal

7:40 P.M. MDT, Sunday, October 31st

"I don't know what to believe," I said under my breath. "What does H.A.S. stand for?" I asked, taking my hand back.

"No more questions. Just assume everyone is trying to keep you safe—we're supposed to be acting normal."

Arm-in-arm we walked along in silence. When the manor came into view many of the interior lights were on. As we headed for the front door a group of worried staff came spilling out to meet us.

Still linked with Kane, I stood and faced the gardener-cum-maintenance man, the cook, the housekeeper who didn't really clean anything, my math teacher who must be visiting her mother, and the butler.

"Hey, y'all," I said bewildered.

Ms. Lillian rushed past the group. "Teddy, my girl," she scolded. "You nearly gave us all heart attacks."

"You were gone an awfully long time, Miss Teddy," Mr. Green said, coming up behind Ms. Lillian with a worried expression. "Are you injured? Shall I call for medical assistance?"

"Really, I'm fine. I was out for a walk."

"You had me so worried." Ms. Lillian came over and gave me a tight hug. "Where were you? Fred and Barney looked everywhere."

Kane cast a sideways glance toward me, which I knew was a subtle reminder to lie through my teeth. Luckily I didn't need award-worthy acting to feign being surprised. "I was walking—like I said. I got turned around and tried to find a way back to the main pathway. Fortunately, I happened to meet up with Kane." I added quickly, "He was out for a walk too."

"This is an awful lot of walking around the estate after dark," Mrs. Abasi said, directing a frown at Kane. "Kane, is this true?"

"It's true." Kane's lips twitched at the side as he forced a smile. "I found Teddy wandering around." He spoke more to his grandfather than to Mrs. Abasi. "She'd left the path and was lost." Relief flitted across Mr. Piers' face.

"I'm sorry." I hugged my chest. "I would have found my way eventually. I didn't think it would be a big deal."

"You are well—no harm was done, Miss Owens." Mrs. Abasi gestured with her petite arm for me to come inside. "Come in, girl, before you catch cold. I'll make a tea." She waved toward the front door. "Kane, you also come in, young man."

I cast a fake smile at Kane. "Tea...great."

"Sure. Thank you, Mrs. Abasi," Kane said, ignoring me.

Mr. Piers and Mr. Green were the only ones who didn't opt to join us for tea. While Mrs. Abasi steeped the tea it was more than obvious everyone was on edge. They were all acting overly happy but any laughter was forced. The most uncomfortable part was that Mrs. Jordan hung out trying to engage in small talk with me. At 10 p.m. Ms. Lillian reminded Kane and me we had school the next day.

"Teddy, see you tomorrow," Kane said as he waved goodbye with his brows knit together.

"Later." He retreated out the door in the kitchen.

****

I woke up the next morning with a sore shoulder and a mood sharp as a machete's edge. With less than four hours of sleep, I felt and looked terrible.

"Stupid sunshine," I muttered to myself. I had an arm over my head in an attempt to try and block out the insistent rays. "Can someone please tell me last night was a nightmare?" I spoke to the ceiling. *Would I be able to follow Kane's directions and pretend I hadn't seen—or heard—anything out of the ordinary?*

Wincing, I sat up and noticed the cat curled up in a ball at the foot of the bed. Sensing I had awoken, she stretched out her legs and arched her slender back. Koko's amber eyes narrowed on me. A creepy shiver ran up my spine. I leapt out of bed and headed for the bathroom, meeting Koko's shutter-like gaze again. The ciliary muscles in her eyes contracted—it was beyond creepy. *I should never have watched 'Pet Sematary' when I was twelve.*

I took a shower until my feet and hands were wrinkled. With a tired sigh, I gave up trying to wash away all my apprehensions. I was running late and Kane would be waiting for me outside. *The guy had some serious explaining to do.* After rummaging through a pile of recently worn clothes, I found my favorite pair of jeans—success.

I pulled on my jeans and grabbed the nearest shirt I could snatch off a hanger. The shirt turned out to be a white blouse—a blouse I had never worn before. "It works," I shrugged. For old time's sake I rummaged through my shoes and quickly located my Converse sneakers. The sneakers were still in good shape, minus the mud stains. "They'll do the job," I said aloud again.

I rushed over to my make-up vanity in the bathroom. It took a few more minutes to blow dry my hair in a rush. I applied a dusting of pink eye shadow shimmer and rolled on clear lip-gloss to finish. "Darlin'," I drawled, trying to sound important and worldly. "We'll call this the understated look," I said to my reflection. "It will be all the rage in Milan." I laughed at myself as I grabbed my backpack before hastily throwing on my scarf and winter jacket. Koko hadn't wavered from noting my every move.

Downstairs, Mr. Green was waiting for me in the parlour wearing a sullen expression.

"Good morning, Miss Teddy," he greeted me. He was holding a silver tray with my morning bagel and a hot drink—in a take-along cup. "I do hope you had a good night's sleep."

"It sucked, actually." No need to lie. "Worst sleep in a while."

"Is that so?" Mr. Green raised a white eyebrow. "Do tell me if there is anything I can do to help?"

"You have enough to worry about. Don't add my insomnia and nightmares to an already long list." I snapped up the bagel and took a big bite. "Thanks for the offer, though."

"I'm sorry to hear of the nightmare." Mr. Green held the silver tray out to offer the drink—more green tea. "Mrs. Abasi had suspected you were running behind this morning," he said. "She instructed your breakfast be of the takeout variety."

"Tell Mrs. Abasi she's a mind-reader."

"I shall repeat your praises word-for-word, Miss." Mr. Green turned up his chin and looked very dapper and professional. Right then he reminded me a lot of that butler from *Batman*, Alfred Pennyworth.

"Great." I turned to leave with tea in hand.

Mr. Green followed me out of the parlour. "Let me get the door for you." Somehow he reached the front door while balancing the tray.

"Thanks." I pulled on my backpack.

"Good day, Miss Owens." Mr. Green bowed his head slightly.

I waved. "Later, Mr. Green."

As I had expected, Kane was parked outside waiting. He was leaning against his black Ford Explorer while staring down at the driveway and twirling keys around his thumb. Even though Kane's hair was a mess, to me he looked h-o-t. Like Ms. Lillian, how did the guy manage to never have an off day? As I walked closer it became apparent Kane was unusually tired and had black lines around his eyes. His suede jacket and blue jeans looked rumpled.

"Hey." I waved.

Kane took a step away from the car. "Morning."

"You look tired."

"Thanks." Kane pointed to the car. "Ready?"

I headed for the passenger seat. "I guess."

The passenger side door creaked open as I climbed into the car. Kane climbed into the driver's side, shaking his head. As we drove past the estate gate he waved at the dark-haired guard—the Fred Flintstone look-a-like. I slumped into my seat focusing on the spruce tree lined road ahead.

"You know what, Teddy?" Kane reached for my hand, squeezing it.

"What now?" I asked, grinning to myself, glad to feel his strong grasp.

"Sometimes you really could be nicer—like, wave back to Fred."

"I didn't see him wave." I lied. "Plus, I'm tired today. It's exhausting trying to act like last night never happened."

"Last night you weren't *trying* when Mrs. Jordan tried to talk to you. Look, everyone here is working hard to keep you happy. All I'm saying is—you should try to return the favour."

"Don't be unfair. Kane, you know darned well what I found out last night." My gaze narrowed. "I didn't feel like chit-chatting with y'all—if you catch my drift."

"Just try not to take people for granted," he reminded. "You don't know how long they will be around."

"I don't take people..." I considered pursuing this argument further but decided I was too tired. "I'll try to be nice," I agreed.

Kane turned up the oldies rock station on the satellite radio and Bon Jovi's *Always* blared through the speakers. The love song made me feel depressed. After we drove through town I turned down the music.

"Kane?" I turned to look behind me. "Are you half asleep? You missed the turn-off—and we're already late."

"We aren't going to school today." Kane's knuckles turned white as his hold on the steering wheel tightened.

"We're skipping?" I stared at Kane like he was losing it.

"One day of skipping will *not* destroy our high school careers," he said. If I missed my chemistry exam then my GPA would be affected, which would ultimately ruin my chances of being accepted into an Ivy League school. I supposed this was not the right time to talk about my higher education. I sighed and leaned back in my seat.

"If we are going to be rebels I need to at least know where you're taking me."

Kane adjusted his rear-view mirror. "Calgary."

"Why are we going to Calgary?"

"There are a few things we need to talk about." Kane put a hand on the automatic stick shift between us. "I'm not in the mood for school."

"What do you want to talk about?" I asked.

Kane turned his music back up at the chorus.

"Kane!" Frustrated, I shouted above the bass a moment later. "Who were those people I heard talking last night?"

Kane clenched his jaw and I swear his eyes narrowed not quite the right shape, or way, a human eye would. Koko's eyes had done the same thing this morning. Again a shiver ran up my spine.

"Staff." Kane turned down the music.

"Staff of what kind of operation?" I lowered my voice.

"I can't tell you everything." Kane sighed. "I wish you would have left well enough alone," he said sadly. "I wish you hadn't gone digging around."

My voice raised an octave. "What is this *One Life* stuff my uncle is selling?"

"What kinds of ideas are rolling around in your head?" He cast a sideways glance at me. "What do you think? That your uncle is selling street drugs?"

"Yes," I nodded. "Drugs or illegal weapons—isn't he?"

"No," Kane snorted, shaking his head he ran a hand down a cheek. "I can't believe you'd even *think* that."

"If it's not drugs or weapons—what is he doing?" His grip on my hand tightened.

"Not telling you."

"Of course you're not." I didn't bother to veil my annoyance.

"The truth is...I don't know what will happen when you find out," Kane said nervously. "It is better if you don't know."

"It should be up to *me* what I know and don't know. I want to know how this all pertains to me," I said stubbornly.

"This is not only about you. There are others who ca—" Kane stopped himself short.

"If you won't tell me more about this *One Life* then can't you tell me who the other people were—the attackers?"

"What do you want me to say?" His frustration was growing. "I told you my hands are tied."

"Just tell me what happened. Who's Garret, Renaldo and—"

"Forget about Garret and Renaldo," Kane ordered. "They are on *your* side."

"Wait." I put one hand up in surprise. "*My* side— there are sides?" My hand went to my chest.

"Last night there were people from town, angry ones, looking for you beyond those on *your side,*" Kane explained. "That's why it was so important I find you," he added. "The others trying to track you down wanted to tell you to leave Canmore—to leave Canada. They don't want the trouble."

"They were looking for *me*?" I croaked. "How did they get onto the estate?"

"You aren't the only one who can scale walls," Kane said, his tone dry.

"I climbed a tree. I didn't scale the wall. Anyway, why would *anyone* want me to leave—do I even know them?"

"Some you know," he said.

A light bulb lit up above my head. "Was one of them Emma-Lynn—what happened to her party?" I asked. "How did it turn into a 'track down Teddy and haul her out of town' party?"

Kane didn't reply.

"It totally was her!" I threw my hands up in disgust. "She hates me, Kane. She thinks something is going on..." I motioned between Kane and me. "Between you and me."

Isn't there?

"Em has been acting irrational," Kane grumbled. "I swear it must be something in the water," he said under his breath. "And yes, she was there last night."

Grimly, I pressed my lips together.

"Em was there with a few others from school— and their parents. You were in danger."

"From what?" I buried my face in my hand. "Murder by nail file?"

"Not funny." Kane bit the inside of his cheek.

"What? Was she leading an angry mob of angry aliens?" I asked. "Or maybe they were aliens with supernatural powers disguised as high school students?" I wiggled my fingers toward Kane in mock fear. "This could explain a lot." Maybe all alien creatures are drop-dead gorgeous with black hearts.

"Don't make me explain." I noticed Kane's tan complexion had paled. "Whatever you're thinking—it's wrong."

"What *can* you explain to me?" There was definitely a green tinge to his skin now. I leaned over, concerned. "Kane, are you feeling okay?"

"You ask a lot of questions." Kane's frustration was more than apparent. "Can we talk about something else? Please. I heard you're turning into a wicked actress—Al must be rubbing off on you."

"Al's helped me out a ton." I was still studying Kane's face with concern. "But acting is only a hobby or something to do in drama class. Hollywood is Al's dream. I hope to major in sciences at university."

"You're planning on going to university?" Kane persisted on changing the subject.

"Pre-med, but only if I can get an academic scholarship." The way things were going it would be a stretch.

"You have lofty goals," he noted. Was there something else in his eyes—regret? *Don't be excited for me, or anything, Kane Piers.*

"Lofty goals?" I repeated, insulted. "You don't think I can get in, do you?"

"I definitely do." Kane caught the edge in my voice. "Honestly, I think you would get accepted anywhere. You work really hard at studying. It's just..."

"Too much money?"

"No," Kane shook his head, "Mr. Owens would pay for whatever university you wanted to attend." I saw him struggling to find the words. "It's only…well, some people like *us* don't get a choice."

"'Us?'" I frowned. "What do you mean, 'us'?"

Kane groaned. "This is all so stupid. You should be able to do what you want."

"Yes, not explaining yourself *is* stupid." I was about ready to make Kane turn around and go back to Canmore.

"It's stupid to keep you in the dark," Kane said bitterly. "Clearly, you need some time to adjust your expectations."

Anger blared in my eyes like a burst of green flame. "Thanks for the lack of support." I sat back in my seat, taking my hand back.

"Hey, dude, don't get mad at me," Kane pleaded.

"Don't call me *dude!*" I shouted, crossing my arms.

"Listen, you can *still* be a doctor. There's always a need for medical doctors in the field. The president will just need to approve your university. Maybe he will let you complete studies by correspondence?" Kane suggested.

Let me? "What President?" I was completely taken aback. "*The field?* What the hell are you talking about? I'm not joining the frickin' army!"

"Forget it! Forget I said anything—I shouldn't have."

Angry, I smashed my fist into the dashboard of the car. Surprised by the emergence of my almost non-existent violent side, Kane looked down at my hands with concern. "Teddy—don't!" he said, horrified.

"Kane, this isn't fair." I was near tears. "You can't say vague things suggesting my future is plotted out for me and then leave it at that." I put my hand on the door handle, seriously contemplating jumping out of a moving vehicle. "I hate to break it to you, Kane, but I don't think I can *forget* about what I saw last night and act *normal*."

"Teddy, calm down." Kane reached over to touch my arm gently. "You're tougher than you think."

"Don't tell me to calm down!" I knocked his arm away and unclipped my seatbelt. "Do you know how insane this is making me? I was on edge around Koko this morning—Koko—the housecat! I kept thinking she was a super feline who could spy on me." I pointed dramatically to my temple. "All this is making me lose my mind. You're the only person who can help me sort this all out—so start talking now. May I remind you, mental illness does run in my family. I really could be going loco."

Kane veered sharply off the highway and screeched to a stop in a rest area. Leaning over, he took my face in his hands and then slowly turned my head so our gazes met. Even with him angry, staring into Kane's eyes was like getting lost in sickly sweet and addictive honey.

"Teddy, don't ever say that again." The tone of his voice was dangerous. "You. Are. Not. Like. Angelique. To have gone through everything you have—you're a strong girl. You're well-rounded and intelligent." Kane's fingers were now wrapped up in my hair. "I know you're mad right now."

I had to stop myself from running my fingers through his gelled strands. *His breath smells like peppermint gum.*

"No matter what you find out in the next few days, remember: I know you can deal with it."

All I could do was numbly nod my head in agreement. As I tore my gaze away from his luscious mouth his thumb rubbed my cheekbone and tilted my head back slightly. Naturally, his gentle touch was making me feel a bit lightheaded.

"I'm here for you no matter what," he said with a softer tone. "Okay?"

"Huh." My response sounded fuzzy and faraway.

"Are we clear?" he asked.

Staring at his lips, I inhaled peppermint again. "Crystal clear."

Kane was so close...too close...terrifyingly close.

Wow, he totally had a smouldering passion in his eyes. You know, the kind of passion the hunky guy in the movie would get right before the big kiss. Maybe I should kiss him? Maybe this shouldn't happen—wait—why not? I'm allowed to kiss guys, even the hot-shouldn't-be-looking-at-me-like-that ones.

My own indecisive nature gave Kane enough time to take the to-kiss-or-not-to-kiss decision into his own hands. He closed the small space between us and kissed me. Kane's hands and lips guided me as if aware of my inexperience. After a heated moment his lips parted mine, and the kiss deepened. I felt like a ship capsized at sea, a total goner. I was falling for Kane, really hard. It was an intense fall—nope—no little baby, 'first love' jumps for me. I had leapt from an airplane and I was in a free-fall diving headfirst for earth.

Kane peeled his body off mine as he suddenly drew away. "Teddy." He cemented his head to the steering wheel. "I just took a really crazy chance. We're both asking for a whole lot of heartbreak."

"Don't be a moron." I gasped, taking two deep breaths and wondered if I would ever feel my legs again. "For two minutes can you forget about what we should—and shouldn't do?" Maybe I should take my own advice.

"You're right." Kane raised his head and reached over to pull me to his chest. "What am I going to do?" he asked himself. He spoke into the top of my head, "This wasn't supposed to happen."

"You regret—?"

"No." Kane put his finger to my lips. "I wanted to kiss you for a while now."

"More than you want to kiss Emma-Lynn?" my petty jealous side asked.

Kane laughed. "Teddy, kissing you isn't even in the same stratosphere as kissing Em."

"Really?" I smiled—must be beginner's luck. Kane held me for a few more minutes in silence. As my senses returned so did more questions. I sat back in my seat with a sigh.

"Put your seatbelt back on," Kane said as he drove out of the rest area. I complied and clicked it back into place. He reached for my hand and didn't let go until we pulled into a parking stall at the shopping mall.

A couple of girls in their early twenties exited the mall as we entered. They smiled at Kane and ignored me.

"What is the plan for today?" I asked, trying to hide my grin in my shoulder.

"To be honest, I didn't have much of a plan." Kane shrugged. "I just need to talk. Are you hungry?"

"Food would be good."

Smiling, we walked toward the food court. Kane pulled his cell from his jeans pocket. "We can grab a bite in a few minutes. I need to phone my grandfather to tell him where we are." Kane pointed around a corner. "I'll be right over there—don't go far. I'll be right back."

"I won't be far."

He had to hide in order to talk to his grandfather?

Kane hit a speed dial button. His grandfather must have answered on the first ring. "Hey, Grandpa—"

As I turned to check out a nearby shop I ran right into the broad chest of a man. "I'm so sorry." I jumped back. The man blocked my escape with his body.

"Hello, gifted one," a deep voice greeted me, a voice so deep and intimidating it reminded me of James Earl Jones. He was a short man of first nations decent with a big voice and was definitely a chip off the old Allysa Vallas block, wearing a lime green vest with florescent beads in the shape of the rock singer Bono sewn into the chest pocket. He had raven black hair with streaks of blue. A braided ponytail was trailing down his back, tied-off with a strip of purple leather.

"Do I know you?" I asked, nervous.

"I know your gift." For his size the man put a shockingly broad hand on the left side of his chest. His skin looked worn like aged leather, but not from the sun, it was as though he'd been to the tanning beds too much. "I'm Mr. Feathers."

"What do you want?" I asked, plotting my escape route. The man gestured towards a small black tent. It was a simple kiosk set up in the mall, oddly simple for such a flamboyant personality. A wooden sign leaned against a column outside the tent entrance said, in fading magenta writing, *"Feathers: A Friend and Gift Seeker"*.

I glanced behind me. Kane was still out of view, on his cell.

"I want to talk about your gift," he said.

My gift?

I bit my lip, studying the flimsy opening to the tent in serious contemplation. I *could* scream if anything shady went down. We were in the middle of a mall and surely Kane would not be gone much longer. Plus, I didn't get the sense Mr. Feathers was a serial killer.

"I'm intrigued...you have five minutes," I relented.

Following Mr. Feathers inside I expected to find a psychic orb or something to indicate this man had a travelling fortune-telling business. The nature of his business was not indicated except for a simple folding table and a pair of plastic folding chairs on either side.

"Have a seat." Mr. Feathers gestured toward one of the chairs. He rested a hand on a large leather bound book on the table. The book had worn edges, and a symbol I recognized but couldn't name, etched into the cover.

I took a seat and folded my hands in my lap. "Mr. Feathers, why do you think I have a...gift?"

He waved away my question, taking his seat. "One cannot give away all his secrets." He leaned back in his chair, his hands folded on the table. "Young one, you're easy to read. I saw your power—your gift from the creator like an aura surrounding you in a golden glow."

I looked behind me through the tent flap. Still no Kane.

"What gift?" I asked with a whisper.

"Your gift—*One Life*—a very rare gift indeed." I had to stop myself from jumping out of my chair. This man knew about *One Life*? "I also saw your friend's gift—not as rare. That boy has the energy of the shiftie warriors who are strong and brave." Mr. Feathers shook his head and put a hand to his chin. "But there was a chasm of darkness between the two of you...your future is uncertain."

What makes this guy know about my future?
What's a shiftie?

"His name is Kane." Annoyed, I took a deep breath. "Can you tell me about this *One Life*?"

It was Mr. Feathers' turn to look surprised. "You don't know about your gift?" he asked.

"If I did I wouldn't still be sitting here—please hurry. My friend will be back soon."

Mr. Feathers studied me as though I was a prize to be won. "You're very special, but your gift is often abused by others—those with selfish intentions." He leaned forward shaking his head. "Sadly, young one, I sense it's too late for you. Your arrangements have already been made and you will need to make your choice soon." He frowned. "In return for my good fortune in finding you, I'll offer some advice: in times of need, remember to love who you want to love."

Love who I want to love?

"Your gift is...you're able to save a life—any life," Mr. Feathers revealed proudly.

When our eyes met he became instantly serious. I was too stunned to look away, but my instincts said I should because it felt like he was looking into my soul and siphoning out my darkest secrets. As though momentarily in a trance, I too leaned forward and saw his jaw fall slack.

"Amazing. You have no scent. I didn't realize..." Mr. Feathers sat up straight with a look of shock. "This is very rare indeed...young one...your blood is strong because you're like me." He tapped the symbol on the leather bound book with two fingers.

"What?" I asked curiously. "Am I cursed or something?" It would not have surprised me in the least if I were cursed.

"Not a curse by definition." The gift seer shook his head, breaking the trance. "No. There is *more* inside of you. It has not risen to the surface yet—it needs help." Mr. Feathers looked at me with the adoration of a treasure seeker who had found his treasure trove. "Activation."

"What is this *other* gift?" I asked, afraid of the answer. *Like being able to save one person's life wasn't enough.*

"I've only heard of a few other cases—like ours. Most end tragically, but for the first time I need to seek advice on this matter." His voice lowered. His expression of awe and amazement turned to concern. "You're not from here."

"From Texas."

"How do you *not* know?" he asked, starting to sound frantic. "You need protection. If they figure out your burden it could cost your life—you must stay hidden," Mr. Feathers ordered as his fist closed around his odd book.

"Pro...protection?" *Hide? Burden?* I stuttered. Mr. Feathers' eyes opened wide as he looked past me. I screamed in alarm—jerked out of the tent by my forearm. A strong hand covered my mouth before I could scream again.

Chapter Seven

Hello, Miss Owens

10:30 A.M. MST, Monday, November 1ˢᵗ

"Teddy." The hand over my mouth tightened. People passing by in the mall stopped to stare. "It's me." The hand slowly relaxed. I pulled out of the strong grasp.

"Nice entrance," I scowled.

"What were you doing?" Upset, Kane turned on his heel and started to walk away from me. Worried, I followed after him. He stopped and jerked his thumb over his shoulder towards Mr. Feathers' tent. "Why were you talking to a gift seeker? Never mind *that* gift seeker."

A gift seeker? "Kane, what are you freaking out about—it's probably all hocus-pocus. He just wanted to tell my fortune."

Kane looked grim. "What did he tell you?"

"Not much. He didn't have time." *He only said I had a power to save someone's life. Oh, and I might have some other unknown gift—and—there are people called shifties who know about it—in addition—I needed protection. Yes, it was just a regular old conversation.*

"Good," Kane said. "Don't listen to him."

"You think Mr. Feathers is dangerous?" I wondered, thinking about the spooky trance.

"The guy's been around forever and is mainly harmless, actually… he's a respected gift seeker." He shook his head and glanced over my shoulder. "I should have smelled him there."

"If he is harmless—what's the big deal?" I asked.

Kane put his arms around my waist and slowly backed me into a wall, putting one hand on either side of my head. The people passing by would probably think he was leaning in to kiss me. "You aren't telling me something." I could feel his warm breathing against my neck, and it felt good.

I didn't reply. I had lost my train of thought.

"I can tell, Teddy. You're hiding something." He whispered close to my ear, "You haven't asked me what gift he was seeking in you."

Kane knew that I knew about *One Life*. Guilt was written all over my face.

"Dammit, Teddy." Kane clenched his teeth. He backed away a few steps and slammed his fist into the wall. "You weren't supposed to find out *yet*—I'm never met someone who needs protecting from themselves," he muttered to himself. "Did he tell you about the *other* thing?"

My instincts told me to lie through my teeth. "Mr. Feathers didn't mention any *other thing*."

"Good, let's go eat." Kane straightened out and ran his hand through his locks. "I'll explain this whole *One Life* gift."

I stuffed both my hands in my jacket pocket and relaxed my shoulders. "Eating sounds good."

Fifteen minutes later we sat in the food court with our fries and Cokes. There were only a few people seated, all a few tables away.

"Tell me about *One Life*," I asked tentatively, taking a sip of my Coke through a straw.

Kane ate some of his fries. "The first thing you need to know is—you don't know anything." He lowered the fries.

I swallowed. "Why? Because I'm a girl?"

Kane took a sip of his Coke. "You know I'm talking about *the gift*."

"Just get this over with. Come on—tell me," I said.

"This is hard to explain...you're one of only a handful of people who have been born with this particular preternatural gift." Kane emptied his lungs of air, and inhaled sharply. "Your gift provides you with the opportunity to bring *one* person you care about back from death's door. Once used, this gift is obsolete."

"Alright...wow—that's weird." My face scrunched up. "How did I come by this gift?"

"It's hereditary." He took another bite of fry.

Hereditary? "Okay...does Angelique have it?"

"No, but your father does."

My eyes opened wide. I put a heavy palm down on the table and leaned forward. "How'd you know if I inherited this gift from him—why not Angelique?"

"Shh!" Kane glanced around. I took another sip of my Coke and turned to smile politely at an older couple taking a seat next to us. Indeed, the couple had turned to stare.

"Get to the point, Kane." I breathed out in frustration. "What does my father have to do with this?"

"Stay calm," he said, slumping in his chair.

"I hate when people tell me to stay calm—clearly this is a surprise."

"Listen. First off, Angelique and Mr. Owens are not brother and sister."

"What!" I screeched, and then covered my mouth. "That's insane. How would you know?" I lowered my hand, shocked.

"My grandfather told me." Kane again reached for his Coke. "Promise you won't freak out."

"I'm not making any more promises."

"You will make more…promises," Kane said with an edge of bitterness. "Really big promises."

"Of course—but you know what I mean," I said with exasperation.

"Delmont Owens...was your *father's* brother." Kane took a sip. He warily considered my expression as it transformed to despair. "He's still your uncle, Teddy. He's just not Angelique's brother."

"But...Angelique said she didn't know who my father was," I croaked.

Could this week get any more bizarre? I think not.

"From what I've been told Angelique and your father used to be involved in an organization called the H.A.S. Your dad left the H.A.S. because he was actually a double agent for the A.O.G.—an opposing organization." He ran his finger in a circle near his temple. "Even back then Angelique wasn't on her rocker. She felt like your father had stabbed her in the back by jumping ship. My grandfather claims afterwards she disappeared—taking you with her."

"Sounds like her."

"Dude, your uncle searched everywhere for you," Kane said solemnly. "Grandfather said Angelique knew how to cover her tracks well, and back then the Internet was a baby itself."

"Why did Uncle Delmont take me in?" I pressed my thumb and forefinger to my temples. "And where's his brother?"

Kane shrugged. "Grandfather never told me the whole story, but I do know that your uncle was glad to have found you—before the H.A.S did."

"Why would they want me? And what does that acronym stand for anyway? H.A.S?"

"*Humans Against Shifties.* Sometimes they are also called: *Humans Against Shifters.* Generally, they hate everyone with abilities."

"And they are?" I asked.

"An organization bent on eliminating anyone with what they consider 'unnatural' gifts. Most non-gifted people who know about them think they are a radical cult—a bunch of nutcases who believe in the supernatural. Kinda like what most 'normal folk' think of ghost hunters, or those people who spend their whole lives searching for the lost city of Atlantis."

Of course, a terrorist group cult, that could be the only explanation. Angelique hadn't imagined all her carrying on about human mutations, after all.

"Well, such news won't help me to sleep at night—knowing there are a bunch of crazies like that in the world." I searched the food court, growing nervous. "Mr. Feathers mentioned something about shifties."

"You'll understand soon enough." Kane cast a glance around the food court again. "After my mom and dad—" he winced.

"I already know...someone at school told me your mom and dad died in a car accident. I'm really sorry."

"Yeah, well, they are wrong. The story about a car accident was a cover up." Kane squeezed my hand and stared down at his fries. "In truth both my parents were shifties. The two most important people I remember were killed during an undercover operation for the A.O.G—it stands for *Alliance of the Gifted.* It all went down in Calgary." Kane sounded tired. "After, I came to live with my grandfather."

"That is so sad," I whispered. "Is anything around here what it seems?"

Kane refused to meet my levelled gaze. "Look, I can't say anymore."

Annoyed, I pushed my tray away. "Look—what happened is horrible—but what do you mean you *can't*?"

"I've already said too much."

Forlorn, I let go of Kane's hand and sat back in my chair. "I don't want to get you into any trouble."

Kane piled his tray on top of mine and then stood up. "We need to head back anyway, Teddy." Holding both our trays in one hand, he offered me the other. "You need to pretend you're none the wiser when we get back to Canmore."

Taking his hand, I stood. "You aren't off the hook for owing me a better explanation."

Kane emptied our trays into the garbage before we left.

For the rest of the day, Kane was careful to keep our conversations focused on school and gossip.

Halfway back to Canmore I finally managed to bring up gifts and shifties again. "Is my uncle a shiftie?"

"Your uncle is a *very* connected man." Kane glanced over at me apologetically. "His connections make him powerful...and he does have a gift, but more importantly he has multi-national support to defeat the H.A.S."

"So basically the H.A.S are the bad guys?"

"Dude, the H.A.S definitely are the bad guys. They could also be considered simply well funded terrorists of the gifted. The A.O.G could be considered like a chapter of the secret service—the good guys—in our case." He glanced over at me then back on the road. His dimples deepened.

"Are these organizations—the good and bad—only in Canada?"

Kane was no longer smiling. "The A.O.G headquarters are in New York City. Like I said, they are multi-national—and extremely organized, and also more than adequately funded. To some extent most shifties and other groups of people with abilities are involved with the A.O.G. The Canmore shifties are one of the largest and organized civilian groups in North America. It'd put many lives at risk if the H.A.S...were here."

"Scary," I whispered. "I don't want anyone in trouble...this all sounds complicated."

Kane stared straight ahead. "Yeah, it is...scary."

"Are you a shiftie?" I asked. We fell silent. "Well?" I asked again.

"Teddy, yeah." He clenched his jaw again, taking a deep breath. "Yeah, I am."

"What does it mean?" I asked, my instincts told me not to push the subject, but as usual I ignored them.

"It means I can change into an animal—okay." Kane's fist tightened on the steering wheel. "Enough with the questions."

"What animal are you?" I asked, surprised not to be more shocked. Considering everything else I'd found out earlier...I suppose anything is possible now.

"Teddy, I'll tell you later."

****

We were back at the manor by the end of the school day and Ms. Lillian seemed oblivious of our decision to skip. Kane dropped me off but not before brushing his lips softly against my cheek...even though I went in for a kiss. Still, I knew our connection was intense. What I couldn't understand was why he was in a battle with it.

"Remember, you're none-the-wiser." He squeezed my hand. "And don't be afraid of me, alright?"

"None-the-wiser—and don't worry—I'm totally not afraid of you." I was currently too busy being disappointed about the non-kiss. Yep, not afraid.

I was in a sullen mood at supper that night. What annoyed me most was that I knew Kane had purposefully avoided telling me what animal he was. My sleep was filled with images of ominous shadows with luminescent eyes. The most repetitive image to emerge from the shadows was of a lion with silver eyes.

****

The next four days during the drive to and from school Kane avoided my attempts at any conversation that pertained to our trip into Calgary. It also sucked that I didn't get the impression our relationship had gone to the next level of officially dating. For some stupid reason Kane was convinced he was breaking my uncle's trust by being romantically linked to me. Of course, he refused to explain *why* he felt this way. I pictured Kane's heart as having a metal cage over it—like one of those old-school chastity belts. His heart was closed for business, or at least closed off from me. It frustrated me because I knew he cared too.

On Tuesday my chemistry teacher had been kind enough to let me write the exam a day late. I didn't have to provide much of an explanation for my absence. Emma-Lynn and company spent the week pretending I didn't exist—no surprise there. Both girls were busy planning another house party at Emma-Lynn's for Friday night. My hope was it wouldn't turn into an angry mob party again. Emma-Lynn continued to be blatantly obvious she was working overtime to get Kane back—and continued to fail miserably.

Al, thank God for Al, was my sole refuge. Unfortunately it took her only about two minutes before she called out my fib—not at all convinced I had been sick Monday. I had to repeatedly claim it was only a coincidence Kane was sick on the same day.

"Teddy Bear!" she'd pestered me. "Girly, what's up? You look like your best friend moved away—hey look—I'm still here."

"I've been down lately, Al." I leaned up against the door of my open locker and peered past to watch as Emma-Lynn tried to pull Kane down the hall. God, she was leaning in too close again. Kane cast a hesitant glance my way. I knew he felt trapped because Emma-Lynn's backup, Whitney and John, were boxing him in. That girl had her whole crew in stealth mode, busy trying to reconnect the broken-up lovebirds. *I wonder if she knows what he is?*

"You've been feeling down?" Al had followed my gaze to Kane. Al dramatically put a hand on her hip. I knew she was preparing to lecture me. The blue peacock feather in her hat fluttered as she turned and glared. The rest of the top hat was covered in a blue organza. In her typical style Al wore bright orange leggings, a lime-green skirt, and a bright purple sweater. I was almost certain an astronaut would be able to see the girl from outer space.

"Teddy Bear, you're so far *down* I'm afraid no one will be able to reach you without a deep-water submarine." As she shook her head, the feather fluttered back and forth.

"I'm pretty sure my problems are the last thing you want to hear about." I shifted my gaze to stare down at my holey blue jeans, white running shoes, and black t-shirt. My outfit was typically boring.

"Guess again, girlfriend." Al crossed her arms across her chest. "I want you to spill *the truth*." She pointed a red painted nail at me. "I bet most of your problems stem from a certain boy. This boy can often be found in a sugar cane field." Al whipped a thumb in the direction Emma-Lynn and company had headed. "My guess," she said. "Girly, you're still pining over yesterday's dessert?"

"Don't hate on Kane right now." *You have no idea what secret he's been hiding.*

Al lowered her hand. "It's hard not to hate on the guy. He's been breaking your cute little heart ever since you moved here. Even worse, at school he acts like you don't even exist."

"He hasn't meant to. Please, just try and believe me." I slammed my locker shut. The smell of my latest spray of twice-daily deodorizer still lingered. Leaning against the closed locker, I held my binder to my stomach. "Kane is purposefully trying to put distance between us."

"Why would he do that?" Al's hand was still on her hip.

"He feels bad about some issues we talked about."

"Issues?" Al's eyebrow rose in a perfect arch. I have tried to make my eyebrows do the same thing—and failed. I always ended up looking like one eye was open real wide, and one squinting. "Why don't you spill, little miss bear? What kind of issues did you talk about?"

"Al—"

"—No more *Al* from this point forward," she cut me off curtly. Remember, until the drama production is over you should call me *Hermia*. By taking on her name I'm better developing a bond with my character."

I felt like hurling my binder at her. We had found out earlier in the week that we'd both been cast in *A Midsummer Night's Dream*. I had shocked myself and won the part of Helena. *The last thing I wanted was for people to start calling me Helena.*

"Sorry, *Hermia*." It took all my strength not to roll my eyes. "Someday I hope you realize you're totally wrong about Kane."

"I'm never wrong," Al said stubbornly. "The boy has an alternate agenda written all over him."

"Alternate agenda—like what? You think he's tryin' to take advantage of me?" *More likely I have wanted to take advantage of him.*

"Look, bear, that boy has a secret."

"What do you mean?" *Well, he is a shiftie, so yeah, he does—big deal.*

"Mr. Sugar was accepted far too easily by Emma-Lynn and the rest of that group when he moved here." Hermia readjusted her hat. "It was weird. You know that group is like a pack of wolves that don't accept people into their folds without a proper initiation. Isn't it odd how Sugar Kane moved to Canmore and within two weeks he was dating Miss Emma-Lynn Weldon—their leader. Now, the problem is Miss Weldon is a real stickler about a guy's..." Hermia coughed, "heritage, if you catch my drift, Miss Bear." She patted her bright red purse.

"They need to have a lot of money?" I asked, confused.

'Hermia' nodded. "Then, lo and behold, Mr. Sugar Kane moved to town in the second semester of ninth grade. Before anyone could say 'dibs' Miss Weldon was stuck to him like butter to a biscuit. Mr. Kane, as you know, is a gardener/maintenance man's grandson—not exactly the heir to the Hilton fortune." She tapped a finger to her lips. "Someone like Miss Weldon has a list of *must have* qualities. The most important quality on that list helps to line her precious Prada with a lot of green." She rubbed her fingers together like she was holding a wad of cash. "Other than looks, and maybe athletic skills, your sweetheart, Mr. Sugar Kane, doesn't have the *Em* qualities. He's more American Eagle Outfitters—rather than Armani."

"Maybe she really does *like* him." I sighed. *Is this really happening? Am I really standing up for my arch nemesis? I need to have my head examined.* "And, they aren't dating anymore. He's not interested in her."

"Yet. I agree that she probably does really *like* him." *Bring on the conspiracy theories.* "Miss Bear, if she does that means there is something about Sugar Kane she knows, that we don't—the truth. Don't you want to find out what the truth is?"

Leaning forward, she said, "We can make it our secret mission for the school year. You live near him, which is all the better."

"No—just stay away from Kane. Let his secret stay buried, will you," I begged.

"You admitted it." She grinned in triumph, a smile stretching across her heavily glossed lips. "There *is* a secret!"

"Look." I glanced around to be sure no one was listening. "Trust me on this, sometimes finding out other's secrets can come with all kinds of trouble."

"I love trouble." She smiled. "Even more—I *love* the truth." She clapped her hands together with glee. "Now tell me, girly, do *you* have any truths to be told?"

"Al I've told you my life story and my upbringing sucked—remember? My friend, I think you've been watching too many spy movies." I grabbed her by the arm and started to lead her down the hallway. My runners squeaked on the waxed floor.

"Hermia," she pointedly reminded.

"Sorry." I sighed. "Forget about the truth and let's go to English. We should conserve our energy so we can survive the wrath of Miss Queen of the School and her loyal pawns."

****

4:00 P.M. MDT, Friday, November 5th

"Em has pissed me off again," Kane claimed angrily. "Teddy, I can't believe she didn't invite you and Al to her party. *Everyone* was invited." Kane shifted the car into park after we pulled up in front of the manor.

"Do you really think I would go to Emma-Lynn's party anyway—even if someone offered to pay me a million dollars?" I opened my car door. Mr. Green stuck his head out of the manor door and waved. We waved back. "Don't be so mad about the party." I moved to climb out, then paused. "Would you like to come in?" I asked, shy.

Kane's nostrils flared and for a moment his eyes widened in alarm. "*Wait*," Kane ordered.

I froze. "What's wrong?"

His shoulders sagged in relief after a moment of staring at the manor. "Sorry, it was nothing. I can't come in anyway. My grandfather is expecting me at home to help make supper." He leaned forward in his seat to stare past me again. His eyes narrowed like a cat's, the pupils more diamond than round. With a death grip he kept both hands on the black steering wheel. "How about you come over to the cabin, for some hot cocoa later—my treat?" He paused. "Will seven o'clock work for you?"

A hint of nervous laughter escaped me. "Are you asking me out on a date, Kane Piers?"

"Maybe," Kane said, trying to sound mysterious. He blushed.

"Sure." I tried not to grin like an idiot. "Seven o'clock will work for me." Kane shifted into drive, which I took as my queue to climb out and close the passenger door. With a goofy grin plastered on my face I barely held in my glee as he drove away.

Once the Explorer was out of sight, I walked into the manor and waved cheerfully. "Hi, Mr. Green." I felt like shouting, *I have a date tonight!* Al was going to *hate* hearing about this on Monday.

"Good afternoon, Miss Teddy," Mr. Green greeted me. He closed the door. "Please, Miss, let me take your bag."

The butler helped me to remove my backpack. "Thanks, Mr. Green." I turned around to hug him. "You really are the best."

"You are too kind, Miss Teddy." Mr. Green straightened up and stole a glance toward the parlour.

"Miss Owens, please come into the parlour." I froze. An unfamiliar voice had floated through the foyer. Mr. Green placed my bag in a hall closet and at record-breaking speed he disappeared down the hall, headed toward the kitchen.

Who had just called my name?

Hesitant, I walked toward the parlour. Within, a man in an expensive navy business suit was sitting in an armchair like he owned the place. His legs were crossed and he was reading the newspaper as flames busily crackled in the fireplace. The room smelled of peppermint tea and pine firewood. In front of him on the parlour's heavy wooden coffee table rested a steaming teacup. I could imagine him taking a deep drag of a pipe because the man had such an aristocratic air. He could easily have passed for an English Duke or Earl.

The man lowered the paper slightly. "Teddy? Do you mind if I call you, Teddy, or Theodora?"

"I prefer Teddy," I said quickly, but instead of meeting his gaze I studied the tile in the hallway.

"Are you my Uncle Delmont?" I asked shyly, looking up. I took a few more tentative steps into the parlour.

Wow, we really did look alike—minus the gray streak in his shoulder-length hair.

"Please do join me." He had an English accent to rival Mr. Green. "Do you want a brew?" He gestured toward his teacup.

"If you mean tea—no thanks." I was still staring at my uncle like he might disappear in a puff of smoke.

Uncle Delmont thrust his chiselled chin toward an armchair across from him. "Sit—stay a while. I've much anticipated this meeting. I do apologize for my long absence and hope the staff made your stay more than comfortable."

"They did." I smiled a weak smile.

"There were—still are—a number of business matters which needed my serious attention."

I walked slowly towards the chair. "That's fine...I understand."

"I've heard you're not one to talk the hind legs off a donkey." My uncle smiled. "An old British saying."

"I suppose that is true." Still hesitant, I unzipped my jacket and took a seat in the silk upholstered armchair, not sure where to place my hands. After a moment of fidgeting I settled on folding them in my lap.

"Thanks for letting me stay here," I said, trying to raise my voice above a whisper. "Thanks for everything—the clothes, and all the other stuff."

"All my pleasure, Teddy." Uncle Delmont carefully folded his newspaper twice, making a thick crease down the middle and placed it onto the coffee table. "We're glad to have you." He let go of the paper. "I understand you're doing exceptionally well at school."

"I guess." I was about to be interrogated—I could sense it coming.

"You joined the Drama club?" he asked, leaning back in his chair.

Holy, he must have been briefed by Ms. Lillian. "I did." I stared at my hands, intimidated.

"You're also good friends with the colourfully dressed girl—the one with the hats. I believe her name is, Alyssa?"

"I'm friends with...the girl with the hats," I nodded.

Al would get a kick out of being called 'the girl with the hats'.

"Do you like the dramatic arts?" he wondered.

"I guess." *Okay, is there a point to all these questions?* "Enough that I tried out for the school play." I lifted my elbows to my ears, uncomfortable.

"I did hear that." My uncle smiled and I relaxed slightly. "I understand you were cast for the part of Helena—in *A Midsummer Night's Dream*."

"Yes," I said.

My uncle pursed his lips for a moment, a smile tugging at the sides. "Ms. Lillian also mentioned you've developed a close friendship with Kane Piers."

"We're friends." *For now, but it might be more very soon.*

My uncle's hand was gripping now at the edge of his armrest. "The old saying is true, I suppose: birds of a feather do flock together."

"Sorry?" I frowned.

"I've known Kane his whole life." He loosened his grip and stood. "He's a special boy, brave and strong—like a warrior." He stood next to the opulent silk drapes and stared out the window, clasping both hands behind his back. His stance reminded me of a prosecution lawyer on *Law & Order*. "I've known Kane's grandfather even longer." He glanced over his shoulder. "Since Antoine Piers' unfortunate end, Kane has become like a son to me...he may not realize this because I'm so often away."

"Antoine was Kane's dad?" Seriously, I needed to take a toastmaster's course or something. It felt like I was nervously asking these questions in front of a crowd of thousands.

"He was. Did Kane happen to mention my friendship with Antoine?" my uncle asked.

"No."

What did Al say about secrets—maybe Kane did have a few more loitering around in his closet?

"Kane doesn't care to discuss what happened to Antoine and Victoria. I believe the topic still bothers him quite deeply." Uncle Delmont shook his head. "Victoria—Vikki—was Kane's mother, and my friend. We went to secondary school together in London. When she came to visit me in Canada one summer I introduced her to an acquaintance, Antoine. It didn't take long before Vikki moved and they tied the knot, and then started a family. Due to medical issues Vikki was certain she would never become pregnant—Kane was her miracle."

"That is so amazing...yet sad. I mean because of the way everything turned out."

"Yes...sad." Delmont considered me for a moment.

My foot tapped nervously against the wood floor. "So, umm, Uncle Delmont, why did you move to Canada?"

"I moved onto this estate fourteen years ago and hired Antoine's father as my summer gardener. He has since been a loyal and trustworthy friend ever since—like family."

"Mr. Piers seems like a good man. It was nice he took Kane in after the crash."

My uncle's eyes narrowed in the same way Kane's often did. "I have a friend coming in tomorrow." Uncle Delmont changed the subject, his gaze shifting again from the window to me. "His name is Paul—a business partner of mine. I apologize in advance, for I will not be readily present."

"I understand." I flexed my fingers and pretended to study my thin nails. "Y'all do whatever you need to do."

"Teddy," my uncle's voice lowered, "I want you to stay here on the estate this weekend."

"Why?" I stopped examining my nails.

"Trust me." All these requests for trust without explanation were making me extremely frustrated.

"I don't have plans anyway," I said glumly. *Why do I feel like this has something to do with those H.A.S. crazies?*

"Good. Now, shall we eat?" My uncle took a deep breath and smiled. "If my nose is not deceiving me I smell Mrs. Abasi's roasted chicken..." He took another deep breath. "And rosemary potatoes."

"I'll take your word for it." I stood and followed my uncle as he turned to leave the parlour.

"The woman's cooking would be rated five stars at some of the best restaurants in New York City."

"Her cooking is phenomenal," I agreed, casting a curious glance over at my uncle.

"Do you have something to tell me?" he asked.

My foot's heel probably ground a huge skid mark into the marble as I stopped.

"Should I?" I stared up at him.

"You don't have any questions about Angelique?" he wondered, studying my expressions like a professor would his undergraduate apprentice.

"Actually, I do..." I sighed, exhausted that I even had to think about my troubled mother. "Why haven't we met before today? Angelique never spoke of a brother."

"Angelique was always excellent at leaving out the important details." Uncle Delmont crossed his arms across his chest and his golden cufflinks glinted in the dimly lit hall. "Have you heard the latest news?"

"I don't think so—what news?"

"Sadly, Angelique has been removed—without the necessary permission—from the institution in Los Angeles. The authorities have been turning over every rock in their search for her."

"She's broken out?" My mouth dropped open. "Is she coming for me?" I asked, fearful.

"Don't worry, Teddy." My uncle placed a broad hand on my shoulder.

"How did this happen?" I choked back tears.

"We are particularly concerned Angelique was freed by an organization which she has past ties to." By the H.A.S? Uncle Delmont really did sound concerned.

"Does she know where I am?" I asked. "Will I have to go with her?"

"We don't want to let that happen. We believe she may have been told, but nevertheless she'll certainly use the resources of her past organization to search for you. I have it on good authority that they will gladly support her efforts to reclaim you. You can understand why I'm asking you to stay on the estate."

"How long do I need to stay put?" *Hello, have you heard of high school?*

"A few days, but in the meantime if you hear from her...do let me know." He looked contemplative for a moment. "I know she's your mother, but do try to remember she could be a danger to you and others."

"Look, uncle, I don't want to be involved in this—whatever it is," I said, lifting both hands in the air.

"I'm sorry, Teddy. There is nothing I can do to change your involvement."

****

After supper I ran upstairs to change before heading to the Piers' cabin for my seven o'clock date. Standing in my walk-in closet, I pulled a couple casual dresses off their hangers and then chucked them into a pile on the floor. It was too cold outside for anything but pants. Anyway, Kane and I lived on the same estate for two months—it shouldn't be a big deal he finally invited me over.

I stared at a perfectly folded cashmere ruby red sweater, which had been beckoned to me for days now. "What the hell," I said snatching it and then pulling it over my head. A perfect fit. "It's my first date, might as well be dressed well," I said, trying to be brave as I stared at a pair of brand new dark wash skinny jeans.

"Only I could be at the best—and worst—point in my life all at the same time." I laughed to myself as I reached the bottom of the staircase on my way out. I paused in the foyer and was met with silence. Where was everyone?

"Mr. Green—hello?" There was no answer. "Hello?" I called out again. After a moment of standing and listening to nothing at all, I went into the library to find a pen and paper. I then proceeded to scrawl a quick note to explain where I was headed and made sure to add: *PS, don't wait up for me.* I carefully placed the note in a visible place on the table in the foyer. With a final glance around the eerily abandoned manor I pulled on my boots. I contemplated calling Kane to walk me to his cabin but I didn't want to seem childish. The Piers' cabin was only a few minutes' walk away and I didn't need a babysitter. My cell phone started to vibrate and ring in my pocket. "Perfect, *now* they decide to answer me." Ignoring the persistent ringing, I headed for the back door in the kitchen.

The security system beeped as I opened the door and I knew my departure had been reported. Closing the door, I met the frigid wind outside. The air felt particularly cold and the night particularly dark. Where was the moon? My cell phone vibrated and rang again, startling me. I never used to believe in supernatural things people conjured in their minds—you know—things that go bump in the night. But this had changed recently and it made me wonder what else had as well.

Shivering, I looked around, trying to calm my irrational fears. Instead, I became more terrified. I broke into a sprint, bent on getting to the Piers' door as quick as possible. The familiar sound of a screeching eagle pummelled through the darkness, sending me ducking for cover. I ran along with arms covering my head as suddenly the night erupted with the barking dogs and people shouting in the distance. Then, the strangest sound I'd heard in my life ripped through the frosty air—it could only be the horrific roaring of angry bears attacking. I broke into a sob. The carnivorous battle noises were followed by a trio of screaming jaguars—or maybe panthers. Definitely not the sounds of a house pet…and definitely not animals you'd find in the Rockies.

As I ran, my cell phone continued to ring in my jacket. I tried to concentrate on reaching the porch light beckoning to me from the Piers' house. I would be safe in just ten more yards, but I found myself screaming in terror as the horrible, agonizing wail of a man being ravaged rang out. This was followed by consistent popping, what I assumed to be multiple gunshots.

After the shots pierced the night the ghost of a golden retriever with glowing blue eyes bounded out of the forest, just a few steps behind me. My scream started deep in my belly and spilled out of my mouth as a stifled wail. I'd never experienced true terror until that moment. I practically flew up the front steps and with super-human strength burst through the door, slamming it shut, struggling with the deadbolt for good measure. When the bolt was in place, I pushed my back up against the door, trembling. Everything was quiet and dimly lit inside the cabin. The loudest noise was my frantically beating heart and ringing ears. It all felt too quiet and too dim—not safe like I desperately required. Outside, I could hear the ghostly golden retriever's paws, patting along the front deck like it was pacing back and forth.

"Kane?" I whispered into the cabin.

L.A. CADIEUX

Chapter Eight

Snowflakes

7:03 P.M. MDT, Friday, November 5th

"Kane?" I called again louder. "Is anyone home?"
I tried to rub my arms to stop the shivers. "Mr. Piers?"
Tentatively, I took a step further into the cabin.
The walls were made of horizontally placed logs. Several
oil paintings of blue jays and Rocky Mountain landscapes
were placed sporadically on the walls. Separating the
living area from the kitchen was an overstuffed dark blue
sofa. The cathedral ceiling in the living room was
constructed with timber frames and supports. Out of the
expansive windows I could see thick clumps of white
cotton balls floating down from the night sky.
"Snow?" I whispered, still too racked with fear to
be excited. I just stood at the window, staring until I
heard a door slam from the lower level. Still trembling, I
crouched down to hide between the armchair and
window, searching for a weapon to defend myself with.
As I reached for a bronze table lamp, I could hear the
intruder bounding up the basement staircase.
"Teddy?" The intruder shouted. "Teddy! Are you
here?"
"Kane?" Slowly, I exhaled a shaky breath. "Is that
you?" Kane burst into the living room through a door,
which must lead to the basement. The moment he saw me
peeking over the chair he rushed over and pulled me to
stand.

"Whoa...what's wrong?" he asked frantically, looking me up and down. "Are you okay—I heard you scream."

"You're kidding, right?" I said with a scowl.

"I'm so glad you're safe," he said with relief, loosening his hold only to nuzzle his face into my shoulder. Water and mud were dripping from the bottom of his jeans into a puddle on the floor.

"What's going on?" I asked, pushing him away. "Enough lies—alright. I'm a big girl, I can handle it."

"I called your cell," Kane said, clinging to me. "When you didn't answer—then you screamed. I thought the worst." I felt his heart racing through his shirt.

"Where are your shoes and socks?" I wondered.

Kane closed his eyes. "Forget my feet—I'll explain the mud, later."

Of course he would—later—what else was new?

"I'm sick of later," I snapped. "Plus, I had already left when you were calling. I didn't want to answer the cell in case it was Ms. Lillian or my Uncle Delmont—because I didn't want to be ordered to stay at the manor tonight," I explained.

"There is such a thing as caller ID," Kane said staring down at me, his expression full of loving concern. "I was worried they had broken through our lines and found you. Hurt you."

"I heard gunshots...and animals." I shivered again. "I'm fine, but was anyone hurt?"

He shook water droplets from his hair. "Dude, there definitely were a couple close calls tonight, but we got lucky."

He had a strange look in his eyes, there was more. "What else is wrong?" I prodded, not sure if I wanted to know the answer.

"I have a guilty admission," he said sheepishly as his expression softened.

"A guilty admission?" I asked, preparing myself for the worst.

Kane glanced away. "I don't really want to be *just* friends," he said softly. Kane gently put a hand on my shoulder and kissed me lightly on the cheek, starling me. "Teddy, I liked you the first moment we met."

Al would not like this, not one little bit.

"You had a crush on me?" I asked astonished. "Kane, I was in my pyjamas."

He moved to hold both my arms, his cheeks flush with emotions. "I was sure my feelings were more than obvious." He paused. "Are you mad?" Kane asked, wearing an expression of uncertainty.

"No ... of course not," I stammered. "I…I totally feel the same way." *Did I really just admit it?*

"That's what I was hoping to hear." Kane reached up to touch my cheek. "There are some other things I need to tell you."

"What is happenin' outside?" I stared up, my expression pleading for everything to be okay.

"The H.A.S attacked the estate," Kane said simply.

I gasped. "Those H.A.S crazies are here?"

"They won't come back tonight—they lost a few of their people. Don't worry, we chased them off."

"Thankfully!"

"But they will be back," he warned.

"Why won't they leave us alone?"

"Because they know this estate is supposed to be a place of protection for shifties. They shouldn't have known how or where to find us—but it's amazing what people will do when they are looking for a fight."

"Angelique," I groaned, smacking my forehead.

"You think she would do this?" Kane asked.

I nodded. Inside I was screaming at the top of my lungs. "My Uncle Delmont told me earlier."

"Your Uncle Delmont was talking to you about Angelique...and H.A.S?" Kane looked shocked. "Why?"

"I don't know why," I admitted.

Kane put a hand to his forehead. "Please say you didn't."

"What did I do?" I exhaled the breath I was holding in.

Kane eye's narrowed. "I hope you at least *tried* to act surprised when he mentioned H.A.S?"

"I *was* surprised." I was hurt by his change of tone. "There was no act."

"If Delmont doesn't *know* we've talked," Kane stepped away and sat on the couch with his elbows on his knees, "He probably *suspects* I have told you classified information. Did he notice you have no smell?"

"What? I doubt it!" I replied. "Don't worry, Kane." I sat down next to him and put a supportive hand on his shoulder. "I didn't say anything to get you in trouble." At least I had tried not to. "My uncle didn't seem upset at all," I said hopefully.

"We're going to have to face the music eventually," Kane said with a sigh. I lowered my hand. For a long time we sat side-by-side in silence. I listened to the creaks and groans of the house as a furnace turned on in the basement. *Why doesn't he kiss me already?* Outside, the thick clumps of snowflakes tumbled down to the earth, blanketing the trees and ground with white. From the inside looking out I felt like I was in a snow globe.

"At least the snow is peaceful," I said, trying to sound happy.

Kane stared out the window with a blank expression. I could tell he was still fuming about my conversation with Uncle Delmont.

"Most people around here get depressed when it starts to snow," he said tritely.

"Those people need to open their eyes." My forced smile was fading. "Snow is miraculous."

"It's alright," he muttered.

"I've always wanted to make a snow angel," I said, "but it's probably too dangerous out there tonight."

"Of course you can," Kane said; his bad mood dissipated as he reached for my hand and pulled me to stand with him. "It will be safe here. The grounds are being patrolled." He handed me my mittens.

"But I saw a dog outside—a golden retriever—it scared me half to death."

"The golden retriever is helping to protect you...and they are hardly scary," Kane explained.

"What about the bears? And I know this is crazy but I swear there was a jaguar."

"You're going to have to trust me." His dimples deepened in the way I loved. "It's the perfect angel-making night."

"Only if you come with me," I said as the responsible part of me warned this was really the kind of night where you stay inside.

"Give me a minute." Kane returned a moment later wearing boots and gloves. We walked out the back door a moment later.

"Holy coldness," I whispered as we took our first steps outside. "The temperature has dropped a few *hundred* degrees."

"Like I said, around here," Kane scanned the yard, "most people don't welcome the snow like you do." He motioned for me to follow. "It's safe."

He supported me under my arm as we descended the slick deck staircase. When we reached the bottom Kane lifted me into his arms.

"What are you doing? Put me down," I whispered near his ear.

"You wanted to experience snow," he said playfully. "You haven't experienced it until you've had your face washed."

I tried to wiggle free. "You wouldn't?" I gasped.

Kane took a few more steps and managed to keep hold of me while reaching for a fist full. There was a deviant sparkle in his eyes.

"It's a Canadian right-of-passage. You are truly not one with Canada until you've been face washed."

"Don't Kane." Testing the waters, he pushed a smudge of flakes onto my cheek.

"Kane!" I screeched in surprise. Kane emptied the rest of the snow from his palm onto the ground.

"You're right." Kane grinned, loosening his hold and placed me gently onto my feet. "I wouldn't."

"Not cool." I punched him in the arm and turned around. "Now, if you will excuse me I'm going to fulfill a lifelong goal and make a snow angel." I smiled over my shoulder. "Would you like to join me?"

"It's been a while—" Kane hesitated, "—I'd love to." Holding hands, we crawled onto the nearest patch of snow and lay on our backs. All around us snowflakes were on a quest for world domination. The occasional tiny flake would become trapped in my eyelashes. I opened my mouth and a few flakes gently settled in. I savoured each icy crystal as they melted on my tongue and lips.

I turned to face Kane. "Hey, what's wrong?" I asked. He was staring at me oddly.

"I've never seen anyone look at snow the way you do." His dimples appeared again, to my great pleasure.

I bit the inside of my cheek, uncertain whether I should ask the question on my mind. "Kane?" I said.

"Yeah?"

I looked away, blushing. "Was this a date tonight? Are we...dating?"

He met my question with a troubled gaze. I could tell he cared—a lot—but why fight it? "Teddy, make your angel," Kane said softly, but I sensed he'd wanted to say, yes. He captured a few snowflakes in his mouth. "We should head back in soon."

What was the big deal? To me it already felt like we were dating. I knew he was a shiftie—I was totally fine with it.

"Okay, we make our angels on the count of three," Kane instructed as he blinked away a few snowflakes trapped in his eyelashes. His cheeks were red from the cold and his eyes shone brighter and more alert. Maybe all the fresh air helped but tonight that eerie wildness inside him...the animal.

"Ready?" I asked, clouds of breath formed with each of my words. "On three," I said, "One...two..." I took a deep breath. "Three!" On the third count we spread out our arms and legs and moved them quickly to and fro. Laughing, we swiftly stamped the ground with the image of our bodies.

"There." Kane said grinning ear to ear, his dimples blaring. "Now you have a check mark on your bucket list. Miss Owens, you have officially made a snow-woman." Kane's words were preceded by a cloud of air.

"Snow angel, genius," I corrected him, laughing.

Kane reached over my head to draw an oval in the snow above my head. "Every angel needs a halo," he said, then gently brushed the melting snowflakes off my eyes and lips.

"I'm going to kiss you," he warned as our eyes our locked. In his eyes I interpreted a troubled adoration…it was the only way to describe happiness and turmoil mixed together. "You can say no," he whispered.

"Yes," I said instead, wide-eyed. When our lips came together he pushed my hair out of the way, shifting to kiss me passionately—it was like he too had been waiting a long time. My lips tingled as we melded together with the cold air and snow. Breathless, with my fingers in his hair, and his hand under the back of my head we clung to each other as though it could be the first and last time. The kiss lasted longer than I would have expected. To say the least, I was supremely disappointed when Kane pulled away and sat up—as though startled—and listened intently in the direction of a nearby barberry bush.

"What's wrong? Is something there?" Putting a finger over his mouth, he motioned for me to stop talking. Alarmed, I sat up.

"Show yourself," he directed his voice toward the bush. His head tilted as he listened closely. "Not good," he whispered to me.

"What's wrong with you?" I asked, afraid. Was he changing? His body was shaking and his skin was starting to crack like soil in a drought.

"Go to the cabin—now," he ordered through chattering teeth and with a pained expression. His skin was now cracked and turning manure brown.

"Your skin!" Stubbornly, I planted my feet to the ground.

"I have to deal with *her* on my own," Kane pleaded. "Listen to me for once."

"Teddy, watch out!" Kane leapt up, pushing me aside. Caught off guard, I fell and sadly ruined the imprint of our angels. But the worst was yet to come, because when I looked up a pit bull was snarling at me from a foot away.

"Kane!" I screamed, terrified. I crawled backward on my hands. The pit bull took a ferocious step forward then lunged at me. Kane dove swing his arm around to knock the crazed animal out of the air like a leaf. The dog flew back into the snow with a yelp of pain. Determined, it jumped up and circled back to me. Its beastly brown eyes were focused on me saturated with a deadly intent.

"I think it has rabies!" I shouted in horror. Kane fell forward onto his knees, his eyes glowing golden in the night. "What's wrong with you?" I asked with alarm. A rolling growl erupted from his throat as the pit bull took a tentative step back. Kane's chest was heaving up and down, and there were popping noises like bones moving out of joint, then suddenly it sounded like they were cracking apart.

"Not. Rabies," he struggled to say with a raspy voice. "Stay. Away," he warned me and the savage animal. Kane struggled to pull off his jacket as he stumbled toward the snarling dog. The pit bull took this opportunity to bypass Kane—only making him angrier. As I stared at its bared teeth, a loud popping noise like gunfire shot through the night.

"Get away!" I screamed, kicking at the dog's rock hard head as it clamped down on my foot. As I flailed in panic I felt the jerk of long canine teeth tearing at my boot—my new boot—which really pissed me off because until recently I rarely had new things. "Let. Go—stupid mongrel," I warned through gritted teeth, smashing a foot into its nose. The dog yelped and let go. *Really, that works?* Then the dog was lifted off the ground and thrown several yards into the air, until its body smacked against the side of the cabin with a thud. It slumped to the ground with a pained whine. What just happened? I scrambled to my feet and sharply inhaled. I found myself staring into the golden eyes of a brownish-tan cougar. The cougar broke hold of my terrified gaze and leapt toward the pit bull, which was trying to get up again.

"Kane?" So he was the cougar? "Kane!" I screamed as a bald eagle screeched a warning cry overhead—it had to be the same bald eagle I had seen two times before. "Oh...crap," I whispered. My heart was falling into my stomach as several more, low growling animals approached—they were followed closely by more popping and cracking. I stared in horror, completely at a loss as to what to do when two glowing eyed grizzly bears came rambling around the corner of the cabin. *Well, this is officially my worst nightmare.* Both the grizzlies were glancing back and forth ferociously, teeth bared. Their beady gazes settled on me and they took a tentative step back. Behind them I noticed a white panther and the ghostly golden retriever approach, although this time I realized they were not ghosts.

"No way," I said, too stunned to run. The cougar growled in frustration and let the pit bull go, leaping to stand between me and the newest group of predators. The retriever's appearance calmed the others while the pit bull whined in fear. With a single warning snarl from the panther the creatures turned and disappeared into the night, leaving me with the pit bull and cougar.

What the hell was that? And had I seen Koko trotting along below the panther's haunches...?

On a positive note, at least the pit bull did not seem so scary now. Another loud pop echoed into the night—startling me—yet again. In an amazing and horrifying scene the pit bull's fur fell out by the root onto the ground, then its skin began to crack as Kane's had changed to manure brown, then slowly the cracks disappeared. The nude tone of pale human skin appeared around the pit bull. A shivering woman appeared from within the mass of fur and her bones were popping but when the transformation was complete she lay against the wall sobbing, buck-naked in a pile of fur and holding a bleeding calf muscle.

"Holy Joseph and Mary," I said. Color me shocked, but Emma-Lynn's baby doll face was hidden behind her bare knees.

"I'm sorry—I'm sorry," she sobbed. The cougar cast over the epitome of a look that could kill. "I don't get it!" she cried out, tears streaming down her face. "Please explain how she's better than *me*," Emma-Lynn's voice broke. Her expression was full of a mixture of self-pity and loathing. "You little tramp!" Her dark gaze shifted to mine. "Since you've arrived, you've ruined my life. You've put us all in danger—you're selfish—you only think about yourself!"

"Excuse me!" My head snapped back as though she had walked up and punched me. I knew she was angry because she lost the object of her affection but that psycho had tried to kill me.

"Emma-Lynn, if I've wronged you—I'm beyond sorry." I stared directly into her eyes. I was surprised how steady my voice was. There was another loud pop. My fear depleted as the cougar became a mass of fur and shifting. When the skin was no longer cracked and bones were all in their proper place the stomach churning noises ceased. Kane was standing next to me shivering while standing in a mound of fur...naked. He quickly bent down to reach for the winter jacket he had thrown aside. I noticed his boots and jeans were off to the side as though they had been kicked off upon transformation. After zipping up the jacket he reached out to hold my hand.

"Em," Kane said in a low and measured voice, "go home to your party—now."

"But..." Emma-Lynn sniffed, still fighting back tears. "I love you, Kane."

"Em," Kane's hold on my hand tightened. His voice softened, "We've been through this before."

"You know this girl comes with a load of trouble. Put your head on straight," she snarled and sprang onto her feet with unnatural finesse. Without further argument, she dashed off into the night.

"Em!" Kane shouted after her. "At least take my jacket! You're going to freeze." *Keeping the psycho warm was not high on my concern list.*

I stared daggers after her. "She's a shiftie too," I said, shocked.

"Yah," Kane sighed. "Surprise." He glared in the direction Emma-Lynn had disappeared. "Now do you wish you *didn't* know about shifties?" Kane asked softly. He shifted back and forth on bare feet sniffing the air. The sniffing motions were a little uncomfortable for me but seemed second nature to him.

"No, actually I'm glad," I said honestly. "It's pretty spectacular to see, that's all."

Kane put his hand on my lower back. "My grandfather is home now. We should head inside." He looked down at his naked legs. "I need to have a shower and find some clean clothes."

"Okay," I agreed trying not to feel overwhelmed.

"I still owe you some hot cocoa if you still want to stay," Kane said with hesitation. "We shouldn't let Em ruin the rest of the night." *Yeah, she'd love that way too much.*

****

9:00 P.M. MDT, Friday, November 5th

What I wouldn't do to take a piece out of Emma-Lynn right now.

Mr. Piers stirred sugar and cocoa powder into a boiling pot of hot cocoa. Once the cocoa was boiling he flavored it with vanilla then carefully lifted and tilted the pot, pouring the contents into two waiting mugs. With a smile, he popped a couple of marshmallows on top.

"Watch out," he warned. "These mugs are hot." He placed a mug in front of me and handed the other to Kane.

"Thanks." I returned the smile.

Mr. Piers followed my gaze as it shifted to stare out the window. He squeezed Kane's shoulder. "Let me know if you need me. I'm headed to bed." He added sweetly, "In the next room."

"Have a good night, Grandpa," Kane said. "Thanks." He held up his mug.

"Goodnight, Mr. Piers," I said. He nodded and then retreated down to his bedroom. Kane took a sip and grimaced.

"Careful," he mouthed to me. "It's hot."

"Thanks for the warning." I blew on my hot cocoa. I stared out at the snow again. I was replaying the incident with Emma-Lynn over in my mind.

"You know…" Kane followed the direction of my gaze. "Everything dies in the winter."

"It doesn't die—it hibernates," I reminded. "Speaking of hibernating. Why are the grizzly bears still awake?"

"Dude, shifties don't hibernate," he explained.

"So what are you, a human...or a cougar?"

"Actually...I'm not sure." Kane shrugged. "I feel more human, but our old legends and history lessons claim Neolithic Europe and Asia was once fairly populated with gifted folks—including shifties—who stayed mostly in their animal forms. However, whole lines of people with gifts were wiped out by a weird bubonic plague. This plague originated in rats, and for whatever reason specifically brutalized the systems of the gifted. In a way, it's as though the sickness unveiled a weakness in our genetic makeup and then capitalized on it. The result was hundreds of thousands dead within four days of contact—all their bodies were ordered burned."

"That's horrible!" I let the new information sink in.

"Yeah, bet it was." Kane paused to think. "Anyway, in 3500 B.C.—back when non-gifted humans used to know about our kind—a great battle broke out because of the fervent belief the plague was actually a sign from God. A sign we were deficient and needed to be eliminated. Naturally, the non-gifted started a war with the gifted because they believed the survivors had to be purged from the earth."

"*Naturally*, they forgot to mention this in history class," I said dully.

Kane nodded. "Seriously, they don't talk about the Neolithic period much at all. It gets worse: after thousands of years at war, a chunk of those with abilities now think *they* are genetically superior to the non-gifted—whom they call parasites."

"Geez, someone needs to raise the white flag on this war. How many more thousand of years will it go on?" I wondered.

"Forever, if the haters have their way. Our strategy is to keep a low profile—or avoid fighting all together—but it hasn't worked in the sense we are no longer anything more but movie-fodder-myth to the typical human."

"How did the H.A.S. people find out about y'all?" I asked. Puzzled, I stared down at the handle of my mug.

"The H.A.S. is like a secret society whose members obtain knowledge of our kind through family inheritance or recruitment."

"Why don't they just tell the rest of humanity about those people with abilities?" I contemplated the illicit responses that would happen in reaction to such news.

"Teddy, plenty of powerful people who don't have gifts *do* know about us. It's to their benefit to use our unique protective services…and in return help keep our secrets."

I looked up to meet Kane's gaze. "Do you want to be a…cougar…more often?"

"I've been warned that if I stay in shiftie form long enough I'll eventually begin to connect more with my animal instincts." He laughed. "As I'm sure you can imagine a human with too much cougar instinct wouldn't fly with the non-gifted—it can change a person's personality."

"How many shifties are there left in the world?" I took a sip. The cocoa ran smoothly down my throat. "This is really good."

"It is," Kane agreed. "Not enough, when compared to the non-gifted human population of billions."

I put my elbows on the table and leaned forward in interest. "So we are both pretty rare birds in a sense."

"Yeah, we are," Kane agreed glumly. "Those with *One Life* gift are super-rare because a long time ago a bunch of you decided to be heroes and wouldn't promise to save the lives of some oppressive, but prominent, world leaders and their families. As a punishment, they arranged to have the *lifers*, as we call them, handed over to the H.A.S. They were imprisoned or slaughtered as witches during the witch trials in Europe and North America in the 14th-17th century. Luckily there were several who escaped death—with help—and a couple of weird cases claimed a few vanished while burning on the stake or being drowned. It sucks, but those escape artists managed only to make the haters stronger in their beliefs that we were possessed…or worse, devils."

"H.A.S *has* been around a long time," I said in amazement.

"Oh yeah," Kane confirmed.

"Can y'all—shifties—change into more than one form?"

"I don't," Kane said. "Most of us only ever master one."

"Will your children be cougars?"

Kane picked up a teaspoon off the table and stirred his hot chocolate. "Anyone with abilities has a hard time to procreate," he frowned.

"How do you...procreate?" I blushed. "You know...can shifties have babies with only the same species?"

"Awkward question." Kane stopped stirring and blushed scarlet.

"Oh—you don't have to tell me," I said quickly.

"Well..." Kane swallowed and stared into his mug. "We can have a physical relationship in our animal or human form, but most prefer to mate in our human form." Kane couldn't help grin at my relieved expression. "If the parents of a baby are a different species the baby will usually possess the species of the more dominant form. For example, a lion is genetically dominant so basically a lion usually only makes a lion even if they mate with a grizzly—whose genes are dominant over a cougar or black bear."

Twisted pictures flashed through my mind. "That's sick," I said with a disgusted expression. "What would happen if a shiftie tried to have a baby with someone with *One Life*?"

"First off, if a *lifer* hooked up with a shiftie it would obviously be in human form, and the shiftie gene is dominant, so..." Kane looked up and blushed again.

"I can do the math." I added quickly, "In the super unlikely case a baby resulted it would be a shiftie with a small chance of *One Life*." I sighed. "Is there a chance the baby could still be a non-gifted human?"

"That's a possibility as well—unlikely—but it could happen, especially if one of the parents isn't gifted."

"Were your parents both cougars?" I noticed Kane's grasp tighten around his mug.

"They were." Kane said warily, "But Grandpa is one of the special ones who can turn into two different species."

"Are Emma-Lynn's parents both pit bulls?"

Kane hesitated. "Yes…"

"Cool," I said. I couldn't help it. My expression was immediately downcast. We were far from compatible.

"Don't look so sad," Kane said as he reached over to squeeze my hand. "Teddy, don't worry about the future—I try not to."

He probably just didn't want to think about a future, with me.

Chapter Nine

Promises You Can't Keep

10:02 P.M. MDT, Friday, November 5th

Junior, you can turn into a cougar—please don't tell the kids at school.

"Sure, right now you don't care if you ever have children," I said, unconvinced. "But what about the future?"

Would I make a choice to start a serious relationship with him if I was a few years older and wiser—would Kane?

"Think about the future—in the future," he suggested with a reassuring voice. "Try to be happy right now." Kane let go of my hand and then pushed his chair back, and it scraped against the wooden floor. "Anyway, do you want to play a game of *Guitar Hero*? It's fun." He leaned over my chair to whisper, "Winner gets a kiss."

****

11:44 P.M. MDT, Friday, November 5th

"You're letting me win," I accused Kane. "Is this game rigged?" After two matches of *Guitar Hero* there was more laughter in the living room than serious concentration. Kane was not lying—it was fun.

"Teddy, you won fair and square," Kane hit the power off button on his PlayStation 3. "Unfortunately," he grinned, "I should walk you back to the manor before your uncle sends out a search and rescue team—and I'd like to deliver your winnings." We exchanged a shy smirk. A glance over at the Piers' microwave clock claimed it was exactly 11:45 p.m.

Fifteen minutes later we clambered arm-in-arm onto the deck at the backdoor of the manor. "Anything wrong?" I asked as Kane pulled me into a tight hug, resting his chin on my shoulder.

"Nothing," he said. "It's been a long day." Both his gloved hands were wrapped around mine…and I loved this feeling. I'd never connected with a guy before and felt such a primal draw to everything about them. Everything.

Only the occasional wild glint in Kane's eyes would give away any indication there was another scarier form hiding beneath the surface. Since my first meeting with Kane I had learned *typical* in itself was an illusion. Whatever made Kane so appealing to me, it could not be cloned because it had nothing to do with buying the *right* clothes or hanging with all the *right* people—it didn't even have to do with self-esteem. He did not understand himself so no one else was going to unlock the door to his secrete allure either.

What if I had to make my difficult choice soon? What if I had to try and save someone's life?

Kane knocked me out of my thoughts by running his thumb over my lips and softly kissing me. I leaned into the kiss, savouring the moment. I found the spot where I fit perfectly in his shoulder. Feeling safe in his arms, it was a long time before we begrudgingly broke apart.

"Kane," I asked weakly, kissing him once more. "Who can I talk to about my gift? I need to understand it."

"You should ask your uncle." Kane kissed my forehead. His breathing intermingled with the cold air was a wonderful sensation.

"Why can't you tell me?" I asked.

"Teddy, it's not my place. Plus, I don't have your gift and your uncle will want to explain." Kane played with the hair sticking out of my toque.

"Fine," I said reluctantly. Kane kissed me again before we begrudgingly broke apart, then opened the door. The security system beeped in warning.

We squeezed hands. "I'll see you tomorrow."

I waved. "Tomorrow."

Kane softly closed the door behind me and then walked into the night. A layer of snow covered his head and shoulders like a dusting of icing sugar. The moment he disappeared I was overtaken with an intense feeling of longing. Tired, I shook the snow off my jacket and began the long walk down the hallway. Halfway up the marble staircase a voice from below called out to me. I stopped and turned.

"Teddy—please come into the parlour, dear," the voice was urgent. Ms. Lillian was staring up at me wearing a troubled expression...and her winter jacket. Her hands were tightly clasped in front of her. Worry lines were deeply etched into her forehead.

"Ms. Lillian," I said concerned, "What's wrong?" If I had a sixth sense for trouble that sixth sense would have warned me to keep on walking up those stairs. It's safe to say my sixth sense sucks. After a slow and painful descent down the stairs I stood facing the housekeeper—a housekeeper who never cleaned. I had come to identify Ms. Lillian as my uncle's Business Manager.

"My girl, your uncle will explain," she said. Warily, I followed Ms. Lillian into the parlour and zeroed in on my uncle who was standing in front of the fireplace. His long arms were resting on the cherry wood mantle. Judging from his stance, I could tell the man was stressed out.

"Teddy," Uncle Delmont turned to face me. "Please sit." He motioned to one of the armchairs. With one even exhale, his worried features transformed into that of a controlled businessman. A woman I did not recognize was sitting in the opposite armchair. She was a small woman with ebony skin, short dark hair, and a tense expression. She remained silent as I obediently sat down.

"Uncle Delmont—what's wrong?" I asked nervously. The tension in the room could have cut through a diamond. As though on cue Mr. Green, Mrs. Abasi, Mr. Piers, and Barney—the light haired security guard—emerged from the hall that led to the library. They crowded into the room and all stood near Ms. Lillian. Mr. Piers nodded to my uncle. Like Ms. Lillian, the rest of the manor staff had dressed for outdoor weather.

"What is this?" I swallowed tensely. "A staff meeting?"

My uncle fiddled with the black iron handle of a wood poker. "No." He shook his head. "We had a staff meeting earlier in the evening." He gestured to the silent woman sitting near me and I noticed she had a friendly smile as our gazes met. There was something about her strange yellow eyes that made me feel like we had met before. "Teddy, I do apologize in advance for Koko's silence—she cannot speak," my uncle informed.

"Koko?" I asked. "The cat?" The woman nodded.

"Alright," I said under my breath. "That news is no stranger than anythin' else I've learned tonight." I managed to tear my gaze away from Koko. "Why do I feel like the guest of honor?"

Uncle Delmont stepped away from the poker and put a foot up on the ledge near the fireplace. "I understand tonight you learned about the shifties and—" my uncle's gaze shifted to Mr. Piers, "—you may have managed to obtain knowledge on a little-known phenomenon, *One Life.*"

"I did," I said confidently. "But don't worry—I'm not goin' to tell anyone's secret."

"Humour me," my uncle's voice hardened. "Do you understand the existence of those with abilities is a carefully guarded secret?"

"Like I said," I met his gaze bravely, "I'm not going to tell anyone's secrets."

"Your new knowledge has put you in a precarious position—a dangerous position. Now we must ensure you are safe." He stressed the word 'safe'.

"Are y'all offering me protection?" I looked around at the solemn faces.

"You've had our protection for months now." My uncle cleared his throat. "With new knowledge comes new responsibilities," he added. "A clear line of allegiance must be drawn."

"That's easy, Uncle Delmont... my allegiance is with you."

"Are you prepared to serve our alliance—the A.O.G?" Uncle Delmont asked. "I understand you've heard of them." There was an edge to his voice. "If necessary, are you prepared to battle our mutual enemies?"

"Yes...and maybe." I sighed. *Why was my life never simple?*

"Are you prepared to use your gift as directed?" My uncle certainly was not one to beat around the bush— as cliché as it was to think of that.

My jaw was slack as words bulldozed through my mind. "Wait, one second." I put a hand to my forehead to fight back the beginning of a headache. "Am I getting dragged into some sort of secret government program?" *Would this be like joining the army, or maybe the FBI? Would I have to carry a gun? I didn't want to carry a gun.*

"I am only asking to be polite." My uncle's voice remained hard. "Sadly, there is little choice in the matter."

Geez, Uncle Delmont sounded like he was signing off on an employee paycheck.

"First, I want to speak with another like me," I said, with a hard edge to my voice. "I want to understand my gift," I said with conviction.

"Mr. Green, if you will." My uncle turned to Mr. Green. "Inform Paul we are ready to see him, please."

"Yes," Mr. Green bowed politely, "Mr. Owens, right away." The butler took several long strides down the hall and headed for the library. Did my uncle even know what it was like to be told no—ever?

"Who is this Paul?" I asked, meeting my uncle's steady gaze.

"He has flown to Canada from Europe to help you," Uncle Delmont explained.

On cue, Mr. Green entered the parlour followed closely by another middle-aged man. I stared at him and felt my stomach flip in apprehension.

"You're twins!" I jumped up. I gaped back and forth between them, noting they both had long hair, but Paul's was a bit longer and less well kept.

My uncle cleared his throat and gestured toward his eerie likeness. "Teddy, I would like to introduce you to my brother, Paul Owens." They were mirror clones of each other—identical twins. The only difference was Paul looked a lot more uncomfortable than Delmont. Hell, Paul was even wearing a similar expensive suit.

Paul's gaze landed on mine and he smiled. With uncertainty he stepped forward to reach out and shake my hand.

"Hiya," he said, his British accent thicker than crude oil. "Miss Owens, I've heard nothing but complimentary things about you." Was there something else in the way he looked over at me…confused devotion, maybe?

"You don't sound like your brother," I said dully.

"We hear that quite often," my Uncle Delmont replied.

"Call me Teddy." I numbly shook Paul's hand. We both stared each other up and down.

Geez, lose the crazy expression, buddy—I'm not Julia Roberts.

I quickly let my arm drop limp. "I guess you're my uncle, Paul?" I asked, realizing I had more family than I thought.

"No," Paul said. "I'm your father." He nervously twisted his black leather gloves in his hand, but may as well have slapped me right across the face.

"You're lying," I gasped, staring at Paul with utter disbelief. My head felt like it was exploding inside as my eyes widened and my heart started to beat faster. I suddenly had to fight a strong urge to sob. Not from the happiness I'd always thought I would feel if I'd had a father, but from confusion and mistrust. "You're supposed to be dead," I cried out. I managed to take control of the tears only to battle a crashing wave of exhaustion. I couldn't take any more news, good or bad.

When Kane came running into the parlour a moment later I was standing there, staring in a way that suggested the neurons in my brain for controlling movement and adequate thought process had stopped firing.

"We cannot do this," he said with a shaky voice, "—this decision is not fair to her." He stopped to address the room, despair drenching him from head to toe.

"Kane, I see you received my text." Mr. Piers squeezed his shoulder in warning. "You mean this decision is not fair for you," he said. "We all must make sacrifices for the good of—"

"Francis." Uncle Delmont interrupted. "KP may need to step outside for this discussion." Mr. Piers and Kane closed their mouths at the same time.

Francis? KP?

The realization hit me like a bag of waterlogged cement mix. Why hadn't I figured out the connection earlier? All the people in this room had purposefully left out a few very important truths, but the worst part was there was *one* person in this room who had abandoned me. There was one person in this room who had hurt me with his lifelong absence. One man who knew I had been in Alberta for over two months but had failed to come for me. This man was my father and I knew him the *least* of any person in this room.

When Mr. Piers, nor Kane, responded, my Uncle said, "I'm glad that matter is settled." He smiled at his brother. "Now Paul, as we discussed you will take Teddy with you to New York."

"New York!" I screeched in alarm. "I'm not going anywhere."

"Do not worry, Teddy," my uncle said like a hard-line army general attempting to show compassion for his troops, "Ms. Lillian already packed your things."

I wasn't worried about my things.

I cast a look of contempt over at Ms. Lillian, who was staring guiltily at the floor.

"My pilot has suggested my personal jet not fly in this terrible weather—but commercial flights are still taking off out of Calgary," Uncle Delmont explained.

"Why are you doing this?" I glared at my uncle, feeling very much like I was being taken captive.

"The higher powers have requested your relocation," he answered simply. "This is the way things are done with the gifted—you best get used to it."

I don't want to move. What about Kane?

"Excuse me, but there is no way I'm moving to New York," I snapped, my eyes blazing with anger and there was a quiver in my voice. "What about school? What about social services?" I remembered and felt a spark of triumph. "They won't allow this."

"Of course," my uncle said with a deteriorating measure of patience. "I've already made the necessary arrangements with Mrs. Rivera. I do agree your education should continue to be a top priority. You certainly will continue high school at our institution for the gifted—in addition to the typical apprentice agent training."

I made no attempt to veil my anger. "*Apparently* I don't have a choice."

"I know you're an intelligent and brave young woman." My uncle's voice softened. "With a few minor alterations to your current expectations your goals are all still achievable—in New York."

"Teddy, dear, you will soon understand how a medical profession, with your gift, could be especially...difficult?" Ms. Lillian piped up.

"I told you about that in confidence," I snapped back. I'd told her about my desire to enter medicine on one of our walks a month ago. "This is kidnapping." Not wanting to be angry with Ms. Lillian I instead cast an angry stare toward Paul. With his hands stuffed in his pockets and shoulders slumped, he looked like a man stuck in a situation he didn't know how to fix.

Yes, father dear, to be stuck with me, for God knows how long, might as well be a prison sentence.

"You are going to live with your birth father in New York—you are not being kidnapped," Uncle Delmont ordered, losing his patience.

"I don't even know him," I argued while trying to keep my voice level.

"You will know Paul when you have to live with him," my uncle insisted. "I'm done being diplomatic with you, Teddy."

"He is nothing to me," I shouted, losing grasp on my hair-thin strings of control. It felt like I was yelling at my school principal. *Who does Uncle Delmont think he is?* I only felt mildly guilty as Paul's shoulders slumped with defeat. "Haven't I been through enough?" I pleaded.

"Darling," Ms. Lillian approached and bravely pulled me into a hug. I felt like a child as I hid my face in her shoulder, seething with anger. "Dear, sweet girl," she smoothed down my hair, "I know it's hard to understand right now, but going to New York is for the best—we wouldn't let you go if it wasn't." She whispered in my ear, "Give Paul a chance."

"This can't be for the best." I broke free from the hug. As I whirled to glare at my uncle again I caught

Kane's eye. He looked torn between wanting to support me...and being loyal to his grandfather—who wore a stern expression. "Kane?" I begged for help, any help.

Kane took a step forward with a clenched jaw, his eyes burning with wild emotion.

"Mr. Piers, shall I help you to escort Mr. Kane out?" Mr. Green asked Kane's grandfather, and as if anticipating a battle Mr. Green smoothed down the front of his jacket while his polite, but careful, gaze never left Kane.

"I'm fine," Kane assured before his grandfather had a chance to answer.

"Are you certain?" Mr. Piers asked Kane. I could tell Mr. Piers and Mr. Green were preparing to physically haul him out if necessary.

"Yes," Kane said curtly, but his balled up fists were saying otherwise. "Mr. Owens, may I have permission to go with Teddy to New York?"

"I'd like Kane to come," I replied immediately, offering him my support.

"Try to understand—both of you." My Uncle Delmont shook his head. "I'm only the vessel. This decision has been made by a power much higher than me." He softened his authoritative tone, "I'm deeply saddened by both your hurt, really. This does not change that KP is needed here to protect the estate if the H.A.S attack again. Teddy will go, with Paul," my uncle said, sternly.

"Yes, sir," Kane agreed, sounding beaten down. "I do my duty."

"It's not our place to protest any of the President's decisions," Mr. Piers reminded. Tired of keeping my 'place' I swiftly turned on my heel and ran into Kane's arms—to his great shock. I hugged him as tight as I could manage and took in a deep breath of his scent. As he recovered he bravely hugged me back.

"It's selfish," Kane whispered, but he knew as well as I did everyone could hear. "You should know I was falling in love with you."

"I was too," I admitted. "I wanted you to be my boyfriend."

I have flipping bad luck, if you ask me.

"No matter what happens in New York," Kane suggested as he kissed my forehead, "—don't forget me, because I'll be thinking of you."

"I'll be back soon, okay," I promised. "We'll have our chance." We hugged once more.

"Teddy," Kane pulled back, "Don't make promises you can't keep."

"Kane," I said. "Don't make it seem like I'm dying."

Uncle Delmont reached gently for my hand. "I'm sorry, goodbyes are over." He patted my hand. "Your ride is waiting outside."

"Wait." I tugged my hand back and kissed Kane's cheek. "Doubt that the sun doth move, doubt truth to be a liar, but never doubt love," I quoted *Hamlet*.

Kane nodded and I saw tears forming in his eyes as he released me. He looked away abashed.

Chapter Ten

New York, New York

10:18 A.M. EDT, Saturday, November 6th

My uncle wasn't exaggerating when he said our flight would be leaving *early* in the morning. Here I was, miserable and heartbroken with only two hours of sleep, stuck on a flight bound for New York City.

Against my will I had been forced to leave my home, again.

I was being forced to live with another person I had never met—again.

I was acting like a moody teenager. Again.

I was with an absent parent...again.

I held a mini bottle between my forefinger and thumb, lamenting my losses. I'd come full circle and didn't like it one bit.

"Teddy!" Paul whispered loudly. "Put that away—you're not old enough to drink voddy!"

Voddy?

Paul snatched away the mini bottle with a stern expression. He stuffed the 'voddy' in the seat pocket. "Don't be daft, Teddy," he scolded. "You're old enough to know better."

"So I've been told," I said dryly. "Even though I'm old enough to know better—clearly I'm not old enough to make my own decisions."

"We have discussed this matter to no jolly end." Frustrated, Paul put a hand to his forehead and leaned forward in a poor attempt to focus on his laptop screen.

"Why don't you watch a film on the telly?" he suggested, noticing I was staring at him.

"Whatever," I grumbled, trying to be less obvious as I studied Paul out of the corner of my eye. I would not have been surprised to see 'CLASSIFIED' in blood red letters across the middle of whatever document he was studying. Taking Paul's unsolicited advice I sat back and changed the movie on my headrest 'telly' to a Hollywood blockbuster, some romantic comedy starring Sandra Bullock and that hot Canadian, Ryan Reynolds.

****

11:20 A.M. EDT, Saturday, November 6th

An hour later we began our decent into New York City, the city of dreams—*in my case not likely, because my dreams had been torn out of my grappling fingers by the Owenses.*

Oh yes, and I shouldn't forget to mention the five *Louie Vuitton* luggage bags full of clothing stuffed into the belly of the 'aeroplane'—a word Paul had used several times since we left Calgary. *Many thanks can go out to Ms. Lillian for the designer luggage.* I was long past the point of being shocked by my uncle's exorbitant spending habits, like Paul, the man did own Hartmann luggage and both wore William Fioravanti suits.

The Teddy Owens from the wrong side of Corpus Christi seemed to have existed a lifetime ago. Texas Teddy had certainly never understood romantic heartbreak until Kane had decided to smack into her heart like a mallet to a gong. I sighed dramatically. Paul peered over at me. *Ugh, the last thing I needed right now was his concern.* Tomorrow, Kane would be back at school and I knew Emma-Lynn would be again professing her undying love to him without skipping a beat.

Really, Teddy, I lectured myself, *it's not like you can't e-mail back and forth. If there was ever a time a long-distance relationship could work it was now—with the Internet and smart phones. Long-distance should be a cinch.*

As we drove along the tarmac at LaGuardia I stared out the window and made a mental note to phone Al later…I'd try to come up with some sort of excuse for my sudden relocation.

Welcome to New York City. There we stood waiting for our luggage at baggage claim, father and daughter, both waiting for our ride impatiently with arms folded tight across our chests. A woman with long black hair stood next to us. She put her arm around a little girl with the cutest light brown pigtails. "Jane," she said, looking over her shoulder at us, "This girl looks like her father—just as you look like your daddy."

That's a first.

"Where exactly are we livin'?" I finally asked Paul, breaking my self-imposed silence.

"My flat in Manhattan," Paul said. "Upper East Side."

"I don't know New York, but if you're like Uncle Delmont, I'm sure it's quaint," I said with a sigh.

"We'll share the flat while I'm in the city," Paul said. *Good, maybe he will be away on business 95 percent of the time like Uncle Delmont.* Paul pulled out his iPhone and hit a number on speed dial. I saw the name 'Leevi' flash up on the screen.

"Flat?" I asked. "Oh, you mean an apartment. Spectacular…" *That meant Paul and I would be living in close quarters.* I hoped my sarcasm was apparent.

"Leevi, hiya...yes," Paul turned his back to me while speaking into his cell. "Tell your father we have arrived safely."

The name Leevi sounded like "LEA-vee".

There was a long pause. "Yes, she was bloody well resistant to the idea. What did you think would happen?" Another long pause. "There's nothing else to report. Tell him...tell him to give her some time to adjust. I will ring him to arrange for an introduction in due time. All right...yes, we'll see you soon. Thanks, cheers."

Cheers? Was this an episode of Coronation Street?

Paul hit the 'End Call' button and turned to me with a frown. "Teddy, it's rude to eavesdrop."

"It's kind of hard not to listen when I'm only standing half a foot away," I said. My newest keeper didn't bother to snap back at me because the conveyer belt began to move and our luggage was the first to spill out. "Paul, after a sixteen-year absence, you don't get to teach me what is rude—it's hypocritical," I said, annoyed.

"You're right, Teddy." Paul reached out and grabbed one of my overstuffed bags and grunted as he moved it onto the luggage cart. "But do allow me at least one opportunity to explain my absence. I do feel terrible."

"Terrible? Sure, whatever." I reached over and then struggled to lift another of my bags onto the cart. Paul hurried to help me. "Paul, forget I said anything." Paul complied by not replying.

When we had finished collecting our baggage, Paul and I headed out of the claim area.

"Are you hailing a cab?" I asked.

"No, Branimir Balakov," Paul glanced toward a row of VIP cars. "A good friend of mine should be here with the limo to pick us up."

"Of course, the limo," I said, rolling my eyes.

"Here he is." Paul nodded toward an approaching man with slicked black hair. He was also wearing a designer suit and had a huge gold chain around his neck.

"Branimir," Paul called out to greet the man and they shook hands with wide grins. "Good to see you again, my friend."

"Paul, it's been months too long." Branimir smiled warmly past Paul at me.

"Branimir, this is my dau—" Paul stepped aside. "Miss Teddy Owens."

"Miss Owens, what a pleasure to finally meet you." Branimir reached out to shake my hand. His grip was strong and he made direct eye contact. I was instantly taken with his eyes, the color of coffee beans.

"Hey," I said to Branimir. Paul's eyes narrowed in on me warning me to be polite. "I mean...nice to meet you, Mr. Balakov."

"Branimir has a daughter your age," Paul explained. "Her name is Mila."

"We are also fairly new to New York. We moved here a year ago from Sophia, Bulgaria." Branimir smiled.

"I will have to introduce you," Paul said.

"Sure, sounds good," I said, not really caring either way.

Because of an accident and congested weekend traffic it took us over an hour to drive from LaGuardia to Manhattan's Upper East Side. Most of the way Branimir and Paul talked about the weather or the sights Paul had seen in Amsterdam. It was painfully obvious both men were working over-time to keep the conversation away from business matters. My assumption was proven correct only a few moments after we pulled up to a picturesque red brick condominium.

"Teddy, after you're settled in the flat Branimir and I have a pertinent meeting to attend elsewhere," Paul informed. I have arranged for a friend of mine to stop over and keep you company. Is this plan agreeable for you?"

And, can I trust you not to get into any trouble? I noticed sometimes Paul didn't say what was actually on his mind.

"Fine, I have to unpack anyway," I muttered, too tired to veil my annoyance.

"Good day, Mr. Owens." The uniformed doorman let us in with a greeting to Paul. "It has been a long time."

"Barry, good day, fellow. Yes, my visits have been too few and far between—I was away working in Europe," Paul said with a smile.

"You're home now," Barry replied as he started to unload our baggage onto a cart.

"We will take the lift up," Paul instructed. "Barry will bring our bags up when ready."

"The lift?" I asked.

"Yes—the lift," Paul said shortly.

"You'd call it the elevator, Teddy," Branimir piped up.

Branimir, Paul and I stepped into the elevator. Paul hit the last button: PH.

"What does the PH stand for?" I asked.

"It means penthouse," Paul explained.

"Oh." I stared again at the PH.

When the doors opened we stepped into a contemporary flat with clean lines and minimal clutter. Across a whole wall were floor to ceiling windows.

Outside I could see an outdoor barbeque area and an enclosed rooftop swimming pool.

"I see you live modestly," I said dully.

"Paul, I will be downstairs waiting," Branimir stepped smoothly back into the 'lift'. "Good day, Miss Owens," he said, before the doors closed.

"Branimir seems cool—I mean nice." I turned to Paul. "Is he a shiftie?"

"He is," Paul nodded as he rummaged through a pile of mail on a side table. I stared at the back of his head and glowered—*hello*—here I was his long lost daughter at home in his 'flat'. The least Paul could do before he disappeared again was kindly show me to my room—or at least explain his sixteen-year absence.

"What gift do you possess, Paul?" I asked the first question to pop into my head. "Do you have one?"

"I have the same ability as you." Paul was pretending to read the address on an envelope.

"That's what I'd assumed," I said with a huff.

Paul slapped the envelope back down on the pile then turned to face me. He looked pale and tired. I do suppose he had been travelling for days now and was jet lagged. Most likely he had not slept since he left Amsterdam. Paul opened his mouth and then seemed to change his mind.

"Teddy," he finally said after a long and awkward silent moment. "What have you been told about my relationship...with your mother?"

"Not much." I shrugged. "Angelique didn't talk about you."

"Well," he coughed, "we met a long time ago when we were both involved with the H.A.S."

"Would you fancy a glass of water, milk—maybe juice?" Paul asked, walking towards the kitchen.

"I'm not thirsty," I said curtly. "Why were you involved with the H.A.S?" I asked boldly.

"I was a nark." Paul leaned against the black granite countertop, his hands gripping the edge.

"Undercover?" Interested, I slid into one of the barstools at the island. "That's insane… for how long?" I asked.

"A while."

"Did the H.A.S know about your gift?"

"Those bastards did," Paul scowled. "I knew before I took the nark job that I would vow my *One Life* gift to a high-ranking member of the A.O.G—only they just didn't know that."

"Did they try to make you use it—the *One Life*?" I asked.

"Right around the time I left, when their leader had been critically wounded," Paul said, "I had to flee, in order to avoid using my gift."

"Where do I fit into this?" I wondered.

Paul stepped away from the counter. For a split second I caught an anguished expression flit across his face, and before I could blink twice he was at the elevator pushing the down button. Wow, the guy sure could move fast.

"Teddy, we can talk about this upon my return," Paul said without turning towards me. "I don't have enough time to get into the matter right now."

Way to avoid the subject, Dad.

The elevator door opened and Paul stepped in. He ran a hand through his hair and pointed towards the staircase off the living area. "Your room is upstairs at the end of the hall," he said.

"Okay...thanks…" I was a bit taken aback by Paul's abrupt departure.

"Don't be daft and let anyone into the flat," he warned. "Also, remember no one can come in unless they have a pass card or code for the lift. You should be safe until my friend Leevi arrives."

Paul waved and the elevator doors closed.

Now I was really alone.

I felt lost as I looked around the 'flat'. The staircase's steps were wooden and embedded in the wall, creating an illusion that they were floating. I walked slowly up to the second floor.

"Cool," I said at the top of the landing.

The second floor of the 'flat' was designed in the same contemporary style as the first floor. I poked my head into the first door on the right and saw it was decorated with pale blue and white tones offset by dark brown wood. A black and white palm leaf print hung from a brick wall above Paul's leather headboard. If curiosity killed the cat I would have used up my nine lives. On top of the wardrobe in a silver frame was a 5x7 photo of a much younger Paul. The boyish Paul was handsome, as he still was—in a more mannish kind of way. Young Paul was wearing a royal blue winter jacket and had his arms around two girls, both of whom, I'd guess, were in their early twenties. The background was snowy and the girls were also wearing winter gear: one of the girls—the taller one with long, platinum blonde hair—looked a bit like former supermodel Nikki Taylor. The shorter girl with chin-length dirty blond hair and gray eyes looked like Brittney Daniel from the *Sweet Valley High* movie.

"Who are *they*?" I wondered out loud taking a step toward the photo. "Are they Paul and Delmont's sisters?" *Does the reproduction issue also affect those with the gift of One Life? Maybe our family was particularly fertile?*

Freaked out by the old photo, I left Paul's room and found my bedroom at the end of the hall. The room was richly decorated in several shades of black and white. I stood in the doorway and my shoulders slumped, as I suddenly felt exhausted. I moved to sit down on a luxurious black chaise lounge chair at the foot of the platform bed, then pulled out my cell phone and powered it on.

"Please answer," I pleaded to the electronic device.

"Hello—Teddy?" After three rings a thrilled voice answered.

"Hi, Kane," I said with a smile and imagined his dimpled grin.

"I heard you made it to New York in one piece." He sounded relieved. "I'm glad to hear your voice."

"Word sure travels fast—I haven't even unpacked yet."

In the background I heard a few shuffling and whispering noises. "Yah," he said. Kane sounded annoyed with whoever had whispered to him. "Word does travel fast—especially around here."

"Where are you?" I asked, trying to identify what the male voice in the background was saying. *Was Connor with Kane?*

"I'm preparing to head out...on a mission," Kane informed me. He put a hand over the receiver. "Dude, seriously," his muffled voice said. "Can I have one private moment here?" I imagined him gesturing in annoyance, attempting to tell whomever the other person was to get lost. He put his mouth back to the receiver. "We've located...them."

"The H.A.S?" I asked quickly. "Try and be careful," I warned. "Y'all don't do something stupid."

"I'm really sorry," he said. I heard more muffled voices and counted at least three people talking at once in the background. "I want to talk with you so bad," Kane whispered. "I'll call you back on this number later? It sucks, but I have to go."

"I think so." I didn't bother to mask my disappointment. "Yes, call this number, unless Uncle Delmont shuts down my cell service—this is still an Alberta number."

"E-mail me if you get a new number," Kane suggested.

I was silent for a moment. Long enough to hear Kane's shuffling footsteps and nervous background chatter. It sounded like he was walking on a sidewalk—or maybe along one of the estate paths. In the distant background was a distinctive popping noise.

"Where are you?" I asked with concern.

There were several more distant popping noises.

"Kane?" I shouted in alarm.

"We have to run—like now," a familiar female voice urged.

"Who was that?" I asked. My jealousy metre was hitting an all-new high. *What was that mongrel doing there?*

"Teddy, I have to go—don't worry," Kane's words jumbled over themselves. "We have so much to talk about. I miss you, I love you," he said with a low voice. I could clearly imagine Emma-Lynn scowling in response.

"I mis—" The connection was cut off. "I miss you too," I whispered to myself.

****

11:40 P.M. EDT, Saturday, November 6th

Paul didn't return until nearly midnight—by which time I was freaking out with worry for Paul and Kane and seriously contemplating calling the cops. If Paul were any kind of responsible father he would have at least left me with a phone number to call him. Instead I had been left to my own devices all day and Paul's unreliable friend, Leevi, never did show up to babysit me. To kill time I had unpacked all my clothes, cooked myself lunch, and then supper, and watched four episodes of a *Beverly Hills 90210* marathon. Finally, at 11:45 p.m. Paul walked wearily through the 'lift' door.

"Where were you?" I jumped up off the couch relieved. "Why didn't you call?" I was too annoyed to bother masking my worry.

"Sorry I didn't ring you, luv."

Luv? That was new.

"The meeting went much later than any of us expected." The man was literally staggering into the flat, walking like a zombie he was so tired. "Where's Leevi?" he asked, glancing toward the kitchen.

"If you mean your tardy friend—the guy didn't show."

"Bloody hell—the bugger's not here?" Paul said, more concerned than angry.

"Nope."

"That prat." Paul rubbed the back of his neck. "You were *alone* this whole time?"

"Yes. I was worried."

"Blast." Paul took out his iPhone and hit a number. "Leevi—pick up the dammed ringer." He listened into the earpiece. After a moment he gritted his teeth and slammed his finger down on the End button. "Better call me back," he grumbled.

"What's going on?"

"I don't bloody well know," Paul said. His hair fell over his face as he stared down at his phone. The combination of his pale face and worried expression made me feel sick to my stomach.

I hope nothing bad happened to his friend.

"Paul, does this have anything to do with H.A.S?" I asked. "I talked to Kane and he said they were...on some sort of mission."

Paul tried to dial Leevi again. He was met by another no answer. "If Leevi was hurt coming here, I'll never forgive myself," he growled in frustration. "Bugger that, his father and mother will never forgive me, nor will his species." Paul put a hand to his forehead in angst. "*She's* going to know something is wrong."

She?

"Who exactly is this Leevi guy?" I asked.

"Leevi was the messenger in this case." Paul continued to stare down at his iPhone waiting for it to ring. "Haven't these sods ever heard—don't kill the bloody messenger?"

"Is Leevi a shiftie?"

"A lion," Paul nodded. "Give me a moment, Teddy. This really is a botch up," he groaned. "I'll have to ring the President—our services might be required tonight."

"*Our* services—tonight?" I added quickly, "But Paul, you're tired."

He shook his head. "Right now it doesn't matter how tired I am." Then a heaven sent sound disrupted our conversation as Paul's cell rang. "This is trouble," he said in frustration as his hopeful expression fell. He stared down at the screen in despair. "It's Leevi's mother."

"Bad timing if you ask me." I reached for the remote and turned off the 'telly'.

Paul turned his back to me while walking into the kitchen before answering his iPhone.

"Hiya, Jo—no, luv. I'm sorry," Paul said quickly. "Yes, I was pissed right off. Not about you...about something Teddy told me. We weren't having a row...yes she's well... She right does—almost identical. I'll arrange so you can meet her soon." There was a long pause and Paul leaned his back against the refrigerator. "Jo, is everything all right there? Good...give me a ring tomorrow, luv." Paul pulled the iPhone away from his ear and looked down at the screen. After reading the caller ID a relieved expression washed over his face. "Jo, I have to let you go. Yes, there is another call coming in. Cheers, Jo."

"You prat!" He answered the incoming call with a shout. "Are you well?" he asked, red-faced. "Don't skive around the question. Where in bloody hell are you?" There was a long pause. "That's a mad question, and yes I'm gutted...Teddy was alone all day. You're a lucky bugger—" Paul listened for a moment. "Glad the matter is sorted. It could have turned out a hell of a lot worse...of course I spoke with your mother. No, I didn't tell her— jut leg it over here, will you." When the call was over Paul stood at a kitchen window with his back to me. One arm leaned on the window and he looked both pissed and contemplative.

"Was the other call from your friend?" I asked.

"Yes," Paul said, "He's fine." He lowered his arm and took a step back. "He was held up and claims he had to haggle out of a bad situation," Paul explained. "The unfortunate part is the lad did a right piss-poor job by changing in front of a group of civilians."

"The guy's a lion. Big deal, so it will make the 6 o'clock news." I shrugged. "No one will identify him based on seeing a lion."

"Lion or not, he had to have the memory eaters brought in."

I put my hand up. "Wait—memory eaters?" I asked.

"Memory eaters are those who obtain their sustenance by feeding off memories," Paul explained, looking tired. "They eat memories—we save a *life*."

I put a hand on my waist and raised both my eyebrows in surprise. "Paul, will you tell me next unicorns really do exist?"

"Nah, unicorns don't exist." He shook his head wearily. "At least I don't think so." Paul rubbed his eyes. "Teddy, I'm sorry to be rude, because I know you have many questions...all of which I want to answer. However, I haven't gotten shuteye in forty-eight hours."

"Understood." I waved off his concern. "Go to bed." Paul complied and headed for the stairs. "Hey?" I called to him. "Can you do me a favour and ring Uncle Delmont tomorrow morning?"

"I can. Why?" Paul asked.

"I just want to find out if everything is fine in Canmore."

"No need," Paul said. "I spoke with Delmont earlier in the evening. He mentioned the Canmore shifties had succeeded in thwarting another attack by the bastards—the H.A.S."

"They did?" *Bloody hell, as Paul would say.*

"There were a few...setbacks, but nothing to mull over." Paul yawned. "Delmont is dealing with the matter."

"Did he mention Kane?"

"I'm sorry, luv, he didn't." Paul yawned even wider. "But do ask Leevi when he comes up. He might know more."

"It's twelve o'clock at night," I noted. "He's still coming over?"

"He intends to stay the night—he should be here soon." Paul rubbed the back of his hand over an eye.

"Guess I'll be the one to wait up for him." Paul was already up the stairs and I knew he would be asleep before his head hit his pillow. Waiting for Leevi, I busied myself by putting the dishes I had dirtied earlier into the dishwasher. I found the dish wash soap under the sink, filled the soap canister in the washer and then turned it on for a cycle.

Why hadn't Kane phoned to tell me he was all right? He must know I'm concerned? My fingers thrummed nervously on the island. I needed some air.

After pulling on my coat I unlocked and opened a sliding glass door off the side of the living room. The security system beeped in warning. The beeping noise made me miss Fred and Barney. I felt extremely sad and very alone as I stepped out onto the rooftop patio. Leaning against a cement wall as high as my chest I stared out at the downtown New York skyline. The city's lights cast a reddish orange haze into the sky above. The haze was beautiful but it was sad I could not see the stars. Far below a hum of vehicles and honking car horns disturbed the peace. I could just make out a young couple rushing to hail a yellow taxi. They were dressed for a night out and if I hadn't been so high up I am sure I would have heard the woman's high heels clicking frantically against the pavement. A few more minutes passed and the cold November air began to bite at the tips of my ears. I could hear a fire truck siren ringing in the distance, followed by a police siren. New York: the city that never sleeps.

"New York at night, amazing isn't it?" said a voice thick with a guttural foreign accent. Startled, I turned and grabbed my chest. A lanky young man with gray eyes was leaning against the open patio door staring at me with a smirk. He had shaggy blond hair the color of white sand, the kind you might find on an exotic, secluded beach. Those eyes were stunning—a sexy— nearly metallic gray.

"You scared me." I said, with a frog in my throat. "Who are you?"

"A friend," he said with a sideways smile. The guy looked like an attorney but he was too young to have already finished university. He was wearing black dress pants and a crisply ironed gray dress shirt—which was not tucked in. There was a nasty scar above his right upper lip like the actor Dermot Mulroney. He had the look and the sound of a person of northern European descent. "Do you like what you see?" He took a step away from the door.

"Excuse me?" Blushing, I looked away.

"I'll take that as a yes."

How dare he assume I was checking him out…? Okay, maybe I was...a little.

"In Helsinki," my arrogant companion said, "The architecture is contemporary mixed in with Old World. I suppose it is no surprise New York would have a different skyline and architectural influence than a city in Finland."

"Naturally," I replied. I swallowed the lump in my throat and attempted to tear my gaze away from the concrete rooftop.

"NYC is the epitome of all things American, don't you agree?" he asked.

"There is no place quite like it," I said weakly.

"Where else can you mix in Broadway plays, supermodels, and *Saturday Night Live*?" He smiled.

"Let me guess," I took a relieved breath. "You're Leevi?"

He grinned. "My name is, Leevi." Leevi walked out onto the patio with a smooth— almost regal—grace. Grace was an odd characteristic to see in a guy. Even when Kane played hockey it probably wasn't graceful. He was limber and fit—just not graceful.

Why am I comparing them?

Leevi sat in one of Paul's patio chairs. He seemed oblivious to how cold the chair's waterproof fabric must feel.

"You, fine lady, must be Miss Owens," he said gallantly.

Fine lady? Miss Owens? Dude, take it down a notch or two.

"Really, *please* call me Teddy," I insisted. "Also, don't address me as *lady* and it sounds weird if you call me *Miss* anything. How old are you anyway, twenty?"

Leevi laughed. "As you wish, Teddy Owens." He looked down at his hands. "I'm twenty—a good guess." Though Leevi did have a Scandinavian accent, he spoke very good English.

Stepping away from the rail, I stood uncomfortably for a moment with my hands in my pockets and shoulders to my ears. "Leevi, you're late tonight—and that's rude."

Leevi shrugged. "I was held up." He looked down as his palm opened and closed.

"I heard," I said, annoyed.

"If you heard, then why ask?" There was a smirking tone to his voice.

"Dude, I don't think it's too much to ask for an explanation about what happened," I pointed out. I was beginning to suspect Leevi could have a bit of an attitude. I hoped Paul didn't think we were going to be best buds.

"*Dude?*" Leevi asked. He stood, then pushed the patio chair out of the way.

"A guy from back home liked to call everyone 'Dude'," I explained. "It's catchy—you should try it sometime."

Leevi shook his head. "I think not. Though, I'm a fan of Michelangelo from the *Ninja Turtles.*"

"Let me guess, you're too cool to say *dude?*" I laughed. "Come on, say *cowabunga dude,*" I urged. "Like Michelangelo would."

"No ... *dude,*" Leevi said. His expression suggested he had just eaten a rotten sardine.

"Alright, you win," I laughed again. "When you said *dude* it just didn't sound right." I imagined the taste of rotten sardine and stuck out my tongue in distaste. It was Kane's trademark—and it was best kept that way anyway.

"I didn't realize we were in a competition?" Leevi met my gaze and I noticed his gray irises were shining bright in the city lights, leaving a silver line in the circle closest to the pupil. This guy was cute—like cute in a way that was totally different than anyone I had ever met. I couldn't even think of a celebrity to compare him to. "You're feeling sick?" Leevi asked. He looked at me with his sideways grin. Once again—cute—I had always liked a sideways grin.

"I'm fine," I said, looking away.

"I understand." He grinned widely and put a hand to his chest. "You find me startlingly attractive."
Honestly, I'd never met anyone so high on himself.

"Full of ourselves, are we?" I asked.
Unimpressed, I glared at Leevi. To do so I had to look up at him, as he was also quite tall.

"I prefer to describe myself as confident." Leevi's smile was toothy and when he smiled, it was impossible to ignore how his eyes closed slightly and his scar tugged on the side of his upper lip.

"You certainly have *confidence* in spades," I noted, folding my arms stubbornly across my chest. "Why don't you spill and tell me what happened tonight?"

"Can I give you a piece of advice, Teddy?" Leevi asked smoothly.

"Possibly..." I said with hesitation. "What kind of advice?"

"Get used to not being told *everything* you want to know. Secrecy is the way of the A.O.G. There are *many* things I still don't know—and *both* my parents have been involved for what feels like forever."

"Are your parents with you here in New York?" I tried to ignore how bossy and arrogant Leevi sounded.

Leevi turned his back on me and then headed inside, holding the door open for me. "My mother is back in Helsinki."

"It's probably none of my business, but—" I said, following after him.

"Then I would suggest you don't ask," he said smugly.

"Paul told me you're a lion." I rolled my eyes. "Are your mom and dad lions too?" How did being a lion from Finland work anyway? If any of the *normal* people saw a shiftie lion—and there weren't any memory erasers around—it would be breaking news.

"Maybe, and maybe not." Leevi headed for the kitchen.

Geez, lately I was pulling short straws when it came to finding answers to any of my questions.

"Look," I said, "I'm not going to twist your arm." With a hand on my hip, I clenched my jaw in annoyance.

"Then don't," he said simply.

"Fine—forget I asked," I huffed. "Anyway, Paul said you might be able to update me on something that occurred in Canmore?"

"What happened in Canada?" Leevi asked, dropping his attitude a pinch.

I shrugged. "Paul said the Canmore shifties battled the H.A.S. I was hoping you might know if Kane Piers—you might know him as KP—is alright?"

"I don't know anything." Leevi opened the fridge. When he found nothing to his liking, he closed it. "*Anyway*, what's it to you?" He grinned to himself as he opened a kitchen cupboard. "Is KP your boyfriend?" he asked.

"What if he is?" I found myself studying Leevi move around the kitchen. He sure seemed at home in Paul's flat. Pleased, he found a box of Oreos then turned around holding the cookie box. He opened the carton.

"Teddy Ruxpin, I don't know if anyone has mentioned this to you, but KP is a cougar." Leevi looked me up and down. "You're most definitely not." I had to stop myself from walking over and smacking him.

"Don't call me Teddy Ruxpin," I warned. "And what makes you think we are on a nickname basis?"

"If I recall, *Teddy* is a nickname." Leevi pulled out the inside Oreo carton and gave me a look of triumph as he selected two cookies.

It was like talking to a little kid.

"Also, for your information, I found Kane more *human* than *cougar*," I snapped back with growing irritation. Leevi separated two sides of an Oreo. In one bite, he ate the side with the icing. "Hasn't anyone ever told you—" I held my hands up in refusal as he offered the whole carton of cookies to me, "You're supposed to *enjoy* the icing?"

Leevi popped the icing free side into his mouth. "Thanks for the unsolicited advice, Miss Oreo Expert," he said, talking with a full mouth.

"What makes you an expert on my relationship with Kane?" I asked with great chagrin.

"Believe me, I'm not a relationship expert," Leevi said. He separated another Oreo and ate the icing side—again with one big bite. The guy had such a white, toothy grin. "But...since it's so important to you, I *could* find out if your boyfriend was involved in any altercation. Anything for *Miss* Owens," he said serenely.

"I don't think you're the next Adam Sandler, Leevi." I exhaled deeply.

He slowly chewed on the plain side of the Oreo. A bit of red on his knuckle caught my attention.

"Leevi!" I screeched.

"What!" Leevi asked, jumping slightly. "Good lord, woman, lower your voice."

"Your hand." I pointed at it. There were shallow gashes, still bleeding slightly across his knuckles. Also, peeking out from a blood spotted sleeve of his dress shirt was an ugly scratch down his forearm. "Your arm—what happened?" I asked, reaching out to grab his hand and study the damage.

"Injuries happen." Leevi pulled away like I had singed him with a lighter. "Please don't," he said. "These are only minor. I will treat them before I retire for the night."

"Sometimes—when you're not being sarcastic— you sound like Mr. Green." I shook my head, still concerned.

"I'll take that as a compliment," Leevi said, burrowing one hand in his jacket pocket. "Mr. Green is a fine man."

"He is." I paused. "Those who attacked you," I bit the inside of my cheek as I stared down, "were they trying to find out information about me?"

"Not everything is about *you*." Leevi studied the ugly scratch on his arm in disgust.

"This is ridiculous." I dramatically gestured with my arm. "They hurt you."

"They wanted to more than hurt me," Leevi said. "Teddy, this is the way things are for us. There are always dangers," his voice softened. "These cuts, they're minor."

"Fine. Be stubborn." I moved into the living room and went to stand near the couch, tearing off my jacket. I was so...tired. "Leevi, do you know of anyone else who used their gift—a gift like mine?" I lay my jacket over the back of the couch and sat down, curling my knees under me.

"At least a dozen people—why?" Leevi walked out of the kitchen and popped the last bite of an Oreo cookie into his mouth.

"Are we talking a baker's dozen?" I asked, tossing the number thirteen around in my mind.

"It's an estimate." Leevi sat down next to me and rested his feet on the edge of the glass coffee table.

"Look, Teddy," he said, "The majority of people with your gift would *never choose* to use it—unless they had to." Thoughtful, he gazed intently at the coffee table.

"Wait, this just occurred to me," I said, with building excitement. "Can someone with *One Life* choose to save another person with the same gift? For example, could I save Paul from death?"

"All I know is the carrier of the *One Life* cannot use the gift on themselves," Leevi said, with a shrug.

I yawned into my hand. My eyelids had grown awful heavy. Leevi surprised me when he put a hand on my shoulder and squeezed.

"Ted, you should go to bed—it's late," he urged. "You don't need to entertain me."

Ted? I guess somewhere between the patio and Oreos we *had* moved onto a friendship level. Maybe Leevi was particularly into creating a nickname from a nickname, which was actually sort of endearing. I grimaced as I ran my hand through my tangled and oily hair. I needed a shower—bad. I yawned and unfolded my legs to stand up and stretch.

"You're right, Leevi," I admitted. "I'm going to shower and then sleep." I paused. "Where are you sleeping?"

Leevi was studying me. "I have my own room," he said.

I yawned again. "Oh...you have a good night."

As I walked up the stairs, I heard him say, "*Hyvää yötä*, Ted. Goodnight," he whispered.

****

11:00 A.M. EST, Sunday, November 7th

"Theodora, wake up." Paul's stern voice knocked me out of a deep sleep. "You certainly zonked out," he said. "I've already called up here four times."

"Ugh," I gurgled into my pillow. A bright light had been turned on overhead making me feel like I was lying on a surgery table. I jolted up to a sitting position, having been woken from another nightmare involving lions. My limbs were tangled in the silk bed sheets and I was only wearing an oversized t-shirt and shorts. I squinted and noticed the curtains in my bedroom were drawn open, filling the bedroom with daylight. Paul was standing in the doorway wearing a similar designer suit from the day before. His long hair was tied back at the nape of his neck and he looked rested.

"What time is it?" I asked with a tired voice. It felt like I had slept all of ten minutes. "Is there school today?"

"It's 11 A.M—but the bloody clocks moved back an hour last night," Paul reminded. "And no, you'll start your studies again next week."

Next week?

"I don't want to fall behind," I croaked, sitting up straight.

"Surely you'll have no problem to catch up," Paul said. "Hurry up now, luv, Leevi has been up since dawn. The lad's been waiting patiently for us downstairs."

"Yay for Leevi," I grumbled. "Okay, Paul, just..." I put a hand to my forehead and winced at the beginning of another headache, "give me a few minutes to get ready." I lazily moved my legs to hang off the bed. The first thing I reached for was my cell phone, which was sitting on the night table. I flipped it open and blinked a couple times. "Not good," I groaned.

There was still no call from Kane. Something had to be wrong. I could feel it in my bones.

Chapter Eleven

Jiri Koivu

11:15 A.M. EST, Sunday, November 7th

It took enough energy to fuel a cruise ship before I could drag myself to the adjoining bathroom and wash my face. The reflection staring back at me in the mirror was a mess of hair sticking up in all different directions.

"Yuck." I stared with a look of disgust at my ruddy complexion.

"If I had white hair," I grumbled, "I'd look like Albert Einstein." I leaned over to examine a particularly heinous pimple on my chin. "Gross—I'm Einstein with teenage acne."

At least I had showered the night before. Plus, it was not like I would see Kane today—and I really couldn't care less what Paul or Leevi thought about how I looked. I rummaged through my make-up bag until I found a silver hair clip. Of course, the clip was hidden down at the bottom, somewhere between the blush and a small compact of pink eye shadow. Yawning, I pulled back my hair with my hands and clipped my hair half back.

"Not perfect," I said to my reflection, "but it will have to do." I wasn't in any mood to follow my usual morning routine. "It's definitely a hooded sweatshirt day," I murmured, rummaging through my mostly unpacked luggage to find a black sweatshirt. "Found it." I pulled the sweatshirt on over a plain white t-shirt. Next, I pulled on the first pair of black yoga pants I could find. A moment later I tied the laces on my running shoes and was ready for the day. "New York City," I said under my breath, "Here I come. The metropolitan fashionistas will be horrified."

"Teddy?" Paul shouted from downstairs. "How are you getting along?"

"Coming!" I yelled back. I stuffed my cell phone into my sweatshirt pocket and then made my way downstairs. I found Paul was distracted from his own impatience, having answered a call on his heavily used iPhone. Leevi was sitting on the sectional couch dressed in a similar suit to Paul. He had both arms resting casually across the back of the couch.

Leevi watched me walk down the stairs with a smirk on his face. "I see you are planning to go for a jog this morning."

"You look like you're going to a funeral," I said, smirking back at him. I headed for the kitchen.

"Fair enough." Leevi leapt up off the couch and followed me into the kitchen. He took a seat at the island. "If you want, Ted, warm up a plate of breakfast." He pointed to the microwave.

"You cooked for me—how sweet," I said sarcastically, opening the microwave. I found a covered plate inside. Removing the cover I was met with the aroma of a traditional American breakfast: hash browns, whole-grain toast, eggs, and sausages. "Smells good." I set the microwave for one-and-a-half minutes on high, then pressed the start button. The microwave powered up and the plate started to turn slowly in circles—the food was being zapped.

Leevi was watching my every move. He was making me feel insecure. "If you want," he said, "There's *ketsuppi*—ketchup—in the fridge."

I shot an uncertain expression his way, "Aren't you nice this morning?" I found the silverware drawer and took out a fork and knife. "You wake up on the right side of the bed?" After closing the drawer, I placed the silverware on the island. "If it wasn't for the comment about me goin' for a mornin' jog, I'd say we're off to a great start."

"Teddy, didn't you know?" Leevi leaned back in his chair and crossed his arms with a smug look. "I can be an *arka heppu*," he said. "*Arka heppu* means *nice guy* in Suomi," he explained, "the Finnish language."

"How do I say *thank you* in Finnish?" I found the '*ketsuppi*' in the fridge and closed the door, placing it on the island. I could see Paul out on the patio gesturing into the air as he talked. He sure seemed frustrated.

"*Kiitos* means thank you," Leevi said with his Fin accent, which became much thicker when he spoke his native tongue.

"*Kiitos* to you, Leevi," I said. "Thank you for breakfast."

"*Ole hyvä*," Leevi translated saying, "You're welcome."

I opened the microwave and took the plate out, then sat down next to Leevi. Hungry and rushed, I started to fork the food into my mouth barely bothering to chew.

"Slow down," Leevi laughed, "Eating isn't a marathon. Food is meant to be enjoyed—you forgot the *ketsuppi*." He pushed the ketchup toward me.

"This is coming from a guy who doesn't *enjoy* the icing in an Oreo cookie." I pointed my fork at him, speaking with a mouthful. "Leevi, for your information, I can eat however I want."

"*Jääräpäinen*," Leevie said under his breath. He took out his cell and looked at the time. "*Kaunis*," he said, "We need to go." He turned to the window and raised his arm up to point at the clock on his cell. Paul saw his gesture and nodded in agreement.

"*Kaunis?*" I glared. "What did you call me?"

"Until you learn Suomi," Leevi snatched a small piece of sausage off my plate and popped it into his mouth, "I can say whatever I want."

I finished the last bite of my eggs. "It's rude."

"*Kyllä.*" Leevi laughed at my humourless expression. "I said *yes*," he said.

If Leevi and I were supposed to hang out, I'd definitely have to pick up a Finnish-English dictionary.

As Paul entered the flat the security system beeped. He locked the patio door behind him.

"It's time to go," Paul said. "Branimir and Mila are waiting for us downstairs in the limo. The President just called me and said he's leaving for Washington for another pertinent engagement early this evening. He will only be in New York for the next few hours." Paul was speaking mostly to Leevi. "He wants to meet Teddy." Leevi nodded slightly, but I noticed he was quiet as we followed Paul to the elevator.

"Whom am I supposed to meet?" I asked.

"The boss." Paul hit the down button and repeated, "The President."

"Is he...anyone I'd know?" *Please don't say the President of the United States—not when I'm dressed like I'm going for a workout.*

The elevator arrived and the doors opened. "You'll see," Leevi said, snapping out of his quiet spell. The three of us entered the elevator and Leevi moved to stand unnecessarily close to me. I was about to shift away when he leaned over my shoulder, very near my ear. "Earlier," he whispered, "I said you're stubborn, and then called you beautiful."

"*Kiitos*, Leevi." I rolled my eyes. It was difficult to ignore the alluring sensation of his breath on my neck and ear.

"It's hot when you speak Suomi," he whispered again, making me blush.

"Bloody hell—stop teasing her, Leevi," Paul snapped. "Don't be daft, at least try to remember you're four years older than Teddy."

"Thanks, Paul." I edged closer to Paul and muttered back to Leevi. "A little reminder—I *do* have a boyfriend." In all honesty, Kane was only a sort-of boyfriend and we had never made it official. However, I did not feel like getting into those kinds of minor details. "My *boyfriend* wouldn't appreciate your comments," I added with a glare in Leevi's direction.

"I'll try not to think out loud," Leevie said. He stepped away from me and into the farthest corner of the elevator.

It was then I concluded it would be a long day.

****

Branimir and his daughter were waiting for us inside. The first thing I noticed was that she was the spitting image of her father, only way smaller. Her hair was the same wavy coal black, only longer. She was dressed modestly in a schoolgirl's uniform with a golden crest adorning the left side of her blazer. The crest featured a lion.

"Hi, Teddy." She greeted me with a shy smile. "I'm Mila."

"Hi." I smiled back and took the seat across from her. Leevi sat next to me, and Paul sat next to Leevi.

179

"Leevi," Branimir reached out to shake Leevi's hand. "As always, it's good to see you."

"Branimir, I can say the same to you," Leevi greeted Branimir with a firm handshake. He shifted to shake Mila's hand and she blushed. "Mila, I'm charmed as always," Leevi crooned, only making me want to puke. "It has been a while."

"I have been busy with my studies," Mila said. Her voice was thick with a Bulgarian accent. She looked away and folded both her hands politely into her lap. Paul gave Leevi a *behave* look.

Branimir punched a golden intercom button on his door. "Grigor, do head for Central Park South—*The Plaza*."

"Yes—*The Plaza*—right away," the limo driver's voice came through the speaker.

The Plaza? The first image that popped into my mind was Macaulay Caulkin in *Home Alone.*

Amused, Leevi was considering my expressions. "Ted, I take it you've never visited *The Plaza?*" he said.

"No, but I take it you have." I tried to sound cool or at best, unexcited.

"I asked you not to give her a hard time," Paul warned as he nudged Leevi. Leevi shrugged with an expression of mock hurt. "Leevi's father," Paul ignored Leevi, "purchased a few flats at *The Plaza* back in '98 and knocked them together. He *lives* in the hotel."

Lives in The Plaza? I didn't have to be a real estate expert to know a 'few flats' in *The Plaza* would cost one big expensive penny. "Lucky you," I said acting uninterested. Leevi would like it too much if I were impressed. "So Paul," I changed the subject without missing a beat, "What's this President's name we are meeting?"

Branimir shifted his gaze from Mila to me, then to Paul. "Paul," Branimir said with a tone of encouragement, "It is fine if Teddy knows his name—she's A.O.G now. She should probably be debriefed."

"I am? Don't I have to take an oath, or at least sign something?"

Paul leaned forward with elbows on his knees and had both hands clasped. "Teddy, you are automatically a member when it is confirmed you're gifted and onside with the A.O.G." Paul captured my gaze. "Do you remember an old fellow who is fairly hard to forget, Mr. Feathers?"

"Yes, of course."

"He is a gift seeker who works with the A.O.G. After you met with him, Delmont called to confirm your gift—a profitable venture for the seeker." Paul added with a nudge in Leevi's ribs, "The president of the A.O.G's name is, Jiri Koivu." The name sounded like K-OYE-vue. "President Koivu answers directly to a global committee of political leaders who are aware of the existence of individuals with abilities. These political leaders often use the services of the A.O.G in classified projects. Therefore, they have an invested interest in protecting our secrets."

Branimir folded his arms. "Paul—as usual—you're being far too modest. Miss Owens," he said to me, "this committee of politicians is led by the most powerful and prominent presidents, prime ministers, chancellors, and royalties in the world."

"He's my *isä*," Leevi added dryly, with an arm resting casually behind his head.

"What is that—your mentor?" I asked.

"President Koivu is Leevi's father," Paul translated.

"Your father is the President of the A.O.G?" My throat felt as though someone had run forty-grit sandpaper across my esophagus. Leevi had left out this rather important piece of information in our previous conversations. "Doesn't that make you the *first son* of the gifted?" I asked weakly.

"*Kyllä*," Leevi shrugged. "It's no big deal."

Paul shook his head at Leevi. "Bleeding hell, lad, don't be right cheeky—speak English," he urged.

"I'm trying to teach her my language," Leevi said, with a devious glint in his eye. "It will come in handy in the future. Paul, you know my *isä* would agree with me."

"Sorry, Teddy," Paul apologized. "Try to ignore Leevi's stubbornness. He doesn't know when to stuff it." Paul shot Leevi a pointed expression. "He always *thinks* he's right—it's a hereditary disability."

"Who is more stubborn?" Leevi grinned. "*Isä, äiti* or *minua*?" Leevi put a long fingered hand to his chest—an elegant hand—the hand of an artist or dancer. "*Minua* means me," he explained.

"Leevi." Paul exchanged an apologetic glance with Branimir and Mila. "Your father is stubborn but wise," Paul agreed. "And your mother, or *äiti*, certainly does give you a run for your money in the stubbornness area."

"I must agree with you, Paul," Leevi said. He removed his arm from behind his head and shifted closer to me. I attempted to push Leevi away, to no avail. "Mum's the word," he said with his trademark, tilted grin. "She has me beat by a long shot."

With Leevi's admission to *not* being the most stubborn in his family, Branimir and Paul started to talk A.O.G business. A couple minutes later the limo pulled up outside *The Plaza*—I was pumped to see Central Park was across the street. The driver, Grigor, opened the door and we stepped out. A doorman from *The Plaza* was waiting to greet us. "Mr. Koivu," the doorman said with a smile, "I hope you're having a fine day."

"I'm especially well, Wallace—*kiitos*," Leevi replied. The doorman nodded as we entered the hotel.

The Plaza's lobby was *Gorgeous* with a capital g. The floors were marble, the paint was a cream color, and *everywhere* there was gilding, yards of expensive drapes, and glittering crystal chandeliers.

"Nothing cheap around here," I whispered out loud to Mila. She nodded. I saw Leevi wave at a pretty brunette guest services clerk that he must have been intimately acquainted with because she blew him back a kiss. Annoyed, I glanced down at my outfit.

"Leevi, y'all could have warned me—I would have changed if I had time," I said with disgust.

"Ted, you're hilarious." He put an arm through mine. "I wouldn't trade seeing your face right now." Leevi gestured to his all black designer suit. "And, might I add, this also is not a funeral parlour."

"I'm glad you find this funny," I said gritting my teeth together. Leevi unhooked our arms opting to drape an arm over my shoulder. "I look like I just rolled out of bed."

"Did you—just roll out of bed?" Leevi asked like a smart aleck. I smacked him in the arm as he laughed at my horrified expression. "Ted, I promise the President won't care." Our banter drew curious stares from the rest of our entourage. "You throw a good punch." Leevi winced and rubbed his arm.

"Leevi," I yelped. "I forgot about your hurt arm—I'm sorry."

He removed his arm from my shoulder and flexed his fingers, staring down at his damaged knuckles. At least his knuckles didn't look as bad as I remembered. "Just *scratches*—not a big deal."

"Leevi, you bugger, what happened?" Paul interrupted, sounding particularly fatherly.

"Leevi was hur—" I said.

"I'm fine." Leevi levelled his gaze on me, clearly suggesting I stop talking. "Paul, it was nothing serious."

"Nothing serious my arse," Paul said, unconvinced. Wisely he didn't pursue the subject any further.

Our small group took the 'lift' up several floors, then followed Leevi down a bright hallway where we were greeted by the scent of all spice and flourishing bouquets of assorted aromatic flowers. Halfway up the hall, Leevi reached forward to push a doorbell but before he could actually do so it opened from inside. Standing in the doorway was a butler with a salt and pepper hairline that was receding somewhat. He was dressed exactly like Mr. Green.

"Good day, master Leevi," the butler said enthusiastically. He stood aside motioning for the party to enter. "Welcome home, sir—*mieluinen koti.*"

Leevi warmly patted the old butler on the arm.

"*Kiitos*, Mr. Park."

The Koivu's condominium was designed in a similar style as *The Plaza* lobby, although it was actually more exorbitant. In the middle of the grand living room, showcased by a white grand piano, was a man talking on his iPhone—these A.O.G types were always on the phone. As I had expected the man was dressed for high power business ventures. He had straight pure white hair, the length reaching to his waistline. He turned and motioned with one forefinger for us to join him in the living room. I stood with arms plastered to my side and my back straight, too afraid to touch anything.

"Have a seat." Leevi motioned towards the leather sectional couch. "*Isä* will be free in a moment. Mr. Park drinks, *miellyttää*—please," Leevi requested of the butler.

I took a seat and nervously glanced around. Mila cast a small smile in my direction, then came to sit beside me.

"Hi," she said.

"Hi Mila," I replied. "So...what kind of shiftie are you?" I asked. It was the first question that came to my mind.

"A wolf," she said, playing with a few strands of her hair. Mila was such a small girl with a kindness about her.

"I would have never guessed you were a wolf." I had a hard time imagining small and gentle Mila transforming into such a feared creature.

She shrugged. "That's what most people say when they find out." She added quickly, "But, I'm a normal wolf—we're nothing like the ones in scary movies."

"You mean no full moon changes and bloodlust?"

"Exactly." We exchanged a friendly grin.

Now Branimir must make a handsome wolf. He has the physique and intimidation factor. If he went to the gym regularly he could audition for a role in the next blockbuster action movie.

"How long have you been living in New York?" I asked, trying to continue the small talk.

"A year now." Mila stopped playing with her hair. I glanced around and noticed Paul was talking quietly with Branimir and Leevi near the piano. The President was still on the phone closer to the window.

"Do you like it here?"

Mila's gaze shifted to her father. "I do miss our home in Bulgaria." She sighed, as though resigned to a life in New York. "Teddy, where was your home—before you moved here?" Mila asked.

Where was my home? Right now I didn't know if I was coming or going. "For now," I said, "New York is my home. Before here I lived in Alberta, Canada. Before Canada, I lived in Texas."

"You've moved a lot," Mila noted. She folded her hands over her side-by-side knees. Her feet were crossed like a lady, at the heel.

"Before September, I'd never left Texas," I admitted. "Lately, I've moved a lot."

"Are you dating Leevi? If you don't mind my asking," Mila asked. She tilted her head toward Leevi and studied the Fin with a shy appreciation. I was not blind. I knew Leevi *was* attractive and surely any girl in her right mind could see that. Leevi also tried constantly to be suave, which managed to get under my skin for reasons I had yet to discover.

"No." I snorted loudly in disgust—much louder than I had intended. Mila looked at me startled. Leevi, Paul, and Branimir glanced over. "Sorry for that outburst," I apologized. Without questioning the men returned to their conversation. "Mila, no, I'm not dating Leevi. I have a boyfriend," —*sort-of*— "back home," I whispered. "His name's Kane. He's amazing."

"Oh," Mila blushed. "Won't that be awkward...after?"

The rosy color on Mila's cheeks spread swiftly to her ears and neck. "After what?" I asked suspiciously.

"Drinks?" Mr. Park asked, reappearing with a silver tray full of beverages. The butler had terrible timing. I wanted to dig deeper and find out what Mila had meant.

With Mr. Park's reappearance the men's conversation ended.

"Teddy?" Paul said, as he and Branimir approached. "Luv, President Koivu mentioned to me he would like to speak with you privately in the study." Paul knelt beside me.

"Why does he want to speak with *me*?" I asked.

I noticed Mila's mouth had opened as if to suggest she had a good idea why. Mila's mouth closed as swiftly as it had opened after Branimir cast her a warning look. She glanced away pretending to intently study Central Park through the flat's living room windows.

Paul took my hand and helped me to stand. He then guided me toward a shallow hallway off the side of the living room. The hall led to President Koivu's study. As we waited I stood awkwardly looking around the study. Instead of Andy Warhol replicas hanging in his office, the President had a single, fairly realistic, oil painting of a triumphant lion mid-roar hanging on the wall behind his oversized brown leather chair. The lion's mane was rippling as if wind was rushing into the room through the two office windows.

"We haven't had a chance to sit down and talk about...the past," Paul said softly. "Before President Koivu comes in I want you to know...it was the best moment of my life when Delmont rang me to say they'd found you." He took a deep breath and exhaled. "I wanted to leave immediately to see you. But I couldn't, you see, luv because I was held up by an assignment in Europe."

"It's fine, Paul." I patted his hand. "Don't worry, I get it—you're a busy guy."

"I don't think you do...understand," Paul said. "I left for Canada within moments of receiving clearance to leave my charge. I have immeasurable regret because it took so long for me to arrive. I feel like an arse—I let you down."

"I get it." I gave Paul an awkward side hug. "Don't feel like an ... arse." I smiled.

"Mr. Owens, excuse my interruption," a voice thick with a Finnish accent came from near the door. "May I have a moment with your daughter?"

"Yes, Jiri." Paul turned toward the voice. "I'll wait outside the door in case you need me," Paul said, all business.

"That's not necessary, Paul," replied the President.

Paul made eye contact with me. I nodded slightly to indicate I was fine. He exited, brushing past Leevi as he entered. Leevi closed the door behind him. He settled in one of the two chairs at the foot of the President's desk, gesturing for me to join him. I stayed standing.

President Koivu was slightly taller than Leevi and shared the silvery gray, highly intense, eye color with his son, but that is where their similarities ended. The father and son duo didn't have similar facial features. The President's were much more angular and harsh than Leevi who had a defined jaw line and a sweeping softness to his face and sandy blond rather than white hair. Everything about President Koivu was intimidating and scary. Even his measured strides. I suspected people who had tried to cross this man had met their demise the hard way—by becoming lifeless corpses in a dumpster. Leevi must have taken after his mother because his father could have played a Finnish Don Vito Corleone, Marlon Brando's role in *The Godfather*.

"Ted," Leevi was the first to speak, "This is my *isä*—my father," he introduced. President Koivu stood behind his desk with arms crossed behind his back and chest out.

"Miss Owens, words cannot express how pleased I am to make your acquaintance," said President Koivu with a raspy edge to his voice.

"I'm glad to meet you, President Koivu." The president motioned to the empty chair in front his desk. "Have a seat, Miss Owens," he ordered. I obeyed and took the seat next to Leevi. Leevi tried to lighten the mood by casting a supportive smile my direction. It would take a thousand such smiles to keep my knees from vibrating up and down nervously. *He's the President of the shifties—not Hannibal Lecter.* What I wouldn't give to be with Kane right now.

"Do you know *why* I asked to speak with you, Miss Owens?" The President asked, interrupting my reverie.

"No." I shook my head slowly and glanced over at Leevi—who was staring at the tile. "Mr. President, I don't know," I said again.

"We're going to assign you to an A.O.G leader," he said. The President took a seat in his chair and it creaked as he leaned back. He put one leg over his knee and pushed the pads of all ten fingers together.

"Assign me—to who?" I asked.

"To the person you will pledge your gift to."

"Pledge my gift?" I repeated, confused.

"You see, Miss Owens, I have a *second* gift called the Oath Binder's ability. When someone comes to me and makes an oath...their word becomes mortally binding."

"Mortally binding?"

"The oath taker must stand by their pledge until their last breath—or face immediate death," the President explained. Leevi grimaced.

Bloody hell! I felt sick to my stomach. *He wasn't talking a pinkie swear or innocent wish-oath on a star.* "*Today* you want me to make a mortally binding pledge—to whom?" I asked. It felt like the President was suggesting I had to give my right arm for this cause.

"It is unfortunate you've not been previously informed of your responsibilities to this person." The President's eyes narrowed on Leevi. "I had ordered you be informed upon first meeting."

"Well, I haven't been informed," I said, thinking back over the events of the last day. Paul must have forgotten to tell me. "President Koivu, I've been really busy travelling, and I only recently found out about my *One Life.*"

"Then there shall be no further delay." President Koivu pointed at Leevi. "You're being assigned to my *poika*—my son," he said.

Leevi avoided meeting my gaze as he lounged back in his chair. At least he didn't seem the least bit bothered by having *me* assigned to the task—one which could concern his life and death.

"What happens if I make this oath and Leevi lives to old age?" I asked, swallowing my shock in an attempt to seem braver than I actually was. "Would that mean I lose my *one* opportunity to use my gift?"

"You should only hope for such luck," President Koivu said with a frown. "Miss Owens, do realize if you make this promise to Leevi, you're eternally bound to each other. If you died...his chance to be saved by *One Life* would die with you."

"I see," I said nodding slowly. *But, I didn't see—this was all insane.*

"Do you understand what I mean, that you would be *bound* together?" the President asked.

I shook my head. "It would help if you could clarify further." I noticed Leevi was gripping the arm of his chair, revealing the true state of his nerves. It was the first time I saw Leevi nervous.

"If you made this oath and Leevi died—if you didn't get to him in time—you would also die," President Koivu reveled. He took a blue pen out of the canister and twirled it in between his thumb and forefinger, waiting for my reaction.

Nausea rolled through me as if a tsunami was in there on a collision course with land. I put a hand to my head and leaned over.

"Ted, are you alright?" Leevi asked, with concern. He was kind enough to put a supportive hand on my back.

"No." I shook my head weakly.

"*Isä*, hurry—*vesi!*" Leevi requested of his father. Leevi was probably the only person on earth who would dare shout an order at President Koivu.

The President stood and poked his head out the study door. "Mr. Park," he barked, "*Vesi*—now." He paused for a moment. "*Kiitos*," he added. The door closed and then I heard the top of a bottle of water being twisted open and a bottle pushed into my hand.

"Drink," Leevi encouraged.

"I can't. I feel sick," I said. Grasping the water bottle, I gripped President Koivu's desk with my other hand.

"Ted, take a deep breath," Leevi said with a soft voice as he knelt beside me. "There you go," he encouraged me. "Okay, now one more breath." I took another big breath. "Good job, now have a drink of water—it will help you feel better," he urged.

"I feel like a big baby." Horrified, I buried my face into the side of the water bottle. The revelation in the President's words kept running through my mind over...and over...and over. I managed to swallow a gulp of water.

"You're not a baby," Leevi reminded. "My father gave you the shock of *your* life." He smoothed back a few loose strands of my hair. "Ted, if I die of old age remember that merely means we have *both* survived and lived a long life," he tried to assure me.

"What if I gave you the gift and then *I* died later—would you die also?" I asked weakly, looking up into Leevi's worried eyes.

"It doesn't work in such a way," The President replied for Leevi. "My son would live until his own death." President Koivu didn't have an apologetic tone.

I laughed, overwhelmed. "Leevi, you're chances of living to a ripe old age are looking pretty good about now." No wonder he was always cocky and confident.

"I'm not afraid of death," Leevi said, trying to sooth my worries. "Ted, in my opinion death is merely an adventure we all should go on...eventually." He still was looking concerned for me. "Are you feeling better?"

I nodded. "A little."

"Please realize what my father is asking of you is a big responsibility, but the A.O.G would protect you—I won't let anything bad happen to either of us."

I knew Leevi was speaking the truth. It *was* to both President Koivu and Leevi's benefit to keep me alive. Why was I panicking? *Should I be happy*? *No, I most definitely shouldn't be happy.* If I pledged my gift to

Leevi it would only provide the H.A.S with *more* reasons to kill or kidnap us. If they killed the first son's *Lifer* it would be a particularly personal blow to the President of the A.O.G.

"President Koviu, I cannot understand why you'd want *me* to do this for your son—your blood? Shouldn't Leevi be pledged to someone stronger and more resilient...someone who can protect *him*?" I asked.

"There will be shiftie protection for both you and Leevi," The President said sternly. "Miss Owens," his voice softened, "finding you is a miracle for the Koivu family. You truly are a gift to *all* shifties."

"Why?" I asked, glancing back and forth between father and son. "Why would I be a miracle for your family?"

"Because," President Koivu cleared his throat, "You're the *only* unpledged person we can locate with your...particular gift." The President clapped his hands together. "Now, enough talk." He took his seat again. "Are you willing to take such an oath?"

"Do I have a choice?"

"Ted, don't feel like you must," Leevi reminded. He returned to his chair and reached for my hand. "I can take care of myself," he said. As I took his hand, I remembered his cuts and realized how dangerous it could be to live a day in his shoes. He was a good enough guy and I was certain his heart was full of good intentions. Plus, I suspected President Koivu would force me to take this oath—whether I agreed to or not. If I could walk away with no strings attached—would I?

The truth: I would not. If Leevi was killed and I had not pledged my gift to him, for the rest of my life, I would remember the role I had played in his death.

The truth was I had already made up my mind.

193

"President Koivu," I said with a decided edge to my voice, "I'll do it—I want to help."

Leevi should have had his goofy tilted smile working unexplainable magic, but instead he looked worried. He shifted nervously in his chair and held my hand tighter.

"Ted," Leevi said, leaning towards me, "You realize your relationship with Ka—"

"What does this have to do with, Kane?"

"Please spare her such insignificant details," President Koivu interrupted. He opened the laptop on his desk and fiddled with his keyboard for a moment. I think he was opening a document or maybe his e-mail. The President stared at the screen reading until his eyes opened wide in surprise. "Miss Owens—Leevi," The President said, with an all business tone, "Please join both hands—we've run out of time."

I reached for Leevi's other hand and noted his palms were clammy. Doing so required me leave my chair to kneel in front of him as I was not sure what else to do.

"Ted, please don't kneel before me," Leevi scolded. "If we have to make this oath," he said, "I want us to be on equal ground. Let me come to you—we can stand." Leevi stood and pulled me to my feet. "You don't *have* to do this," he whispered near my ear. "Ted, you *can* say no."

"I have to..." I said, shaking my head, "Seriously, I think you need my help."

Leevi squeezed my hand. "There are side effects from the bond," he whispered again.

I didn't have time to ask what they were because President Koivu began.

"Leevi Koivu," he said, "If ever needed, are you willing to accept the gift of second life from Miss Owens? Are you willing to be bonded to her?"

"Only if Teddy is certain of what she promises—then yes—I'm willing to accept her gift and the bond," Leevi said. He looked particularly pale as he held my hands in his.

"Miss Owens," President Koivu turned to me with his icy gaze, "Are you aware once you make this oath to Leevi—it will be irreversible?"

"I do. Don't worry, Leevi," I said quickly, "I understand." Still, it felt like a band was tightening across my chest, limiting my capacity to breathe.

"Do you?" Leevi asked, his mesmerizing eyes staring down at me with a searing intensity.

"I want to get this over with," I said with a slight nod. *If Leevi kept stalling I was totally going to freak out again.*

"Miss Owens," the President continued, "Because you understand what you promise—and because Leevi willingly accepts your gift—you're now of a position to make a bondable promise to one another." He clasped his hands together and then held them to his chin. "You may go ahead," he directed, pointing with both his pinkie fingers. "Make the oath—promise Leevi Koivu your *One Life.*"

Leevi's silvery eyes looked unsure and his grasp on my hands was so tight I was losing the feeling in my fingers. A few strands of shaggy hair fell over one of his eyes and his lips pressed together into a thin line.

"Thank you," Leevi held my gaze. "I'll find a way to return the favour," he promised.

Sudden as a gust of wind rushing into the room, I could feel a powerful sense of purpose deep down in my bones and I knew this was the right thing to do—even though I barely knew this guy. Words—guided words—began to form in my mind and across my tongue. Words put there by Leevi's father. They were magical words, words that would make up the oath of a bondable promise.

"Leevi Koivu," I said, "I want you to accept my gift of *One Life*." My voice was courageous and sure. I felt locked into a magical spell, but found I still could look up into Leevi's herculean eyes. "Leevi, I promise this gift only to you and if this oath is ever broken I will willingly face my death. Today, I do vow if you're ever tragically hurt I'll come to you—I'll save you." I said confidently, "Leevi Koivu, I agree to be bonded to you."

The room was literally simmering with intensity. The unbreakable oath had been made on my part. Leevi removed one of his hands from our tight grasp and with a serious expression he gently placed a warm palm to my face. Through his touch I could sense his appreciation for my sacrifice. My insides were churning masses of conflicted feelings. It was the strangest sensation I had ever felt—almost like riding a rollercoaster.

"Miss Owens, only because you're willing," Leevi said with the utmost sincerity and warmth, "I accept your gift and promise." Leevi removed his hand from my face. I shivered. It was odd but I immediately missed his touch. "Theodora Owens," Leevi spoke with finality, "I accept your gift and I agree to be bonded to you."

Ugh, he used my birth name, which was a minor piss off. This really was one of the only circumstances where I would be willing to forgive someone for calling me the T word.

A moment of silence passed and I don't know
what I was expecting... maybe a trumpet to blare in
triumph? We had just made a life-altering oath after all—
and in my opinion it was being poorly celebrated. As
though sensing my disappointment Leevi carefully
released my other hand and took the single step necessary
to close the space between us. Without flinching away, he
leaned forward to take my face gently in both his hands.
My hands were free and no longer under the trance. I
could have pushed him away, but I didn't.

Was it wrong that I loved the feeling of him being
so close to me?

Leevi smelled like freshly fallen rain and nothing
like the expensive cologne scent I had expected from
him. Right then I should have hated myself for wanting to
burry my face into his shoulder; however, before I could
fully process his intent, Leevi leaned down and kissed me
ever so soft and sweet. The kiss was on the lips and it
was—*then all the angels sang*—nice. The kiss was the
kind where all the air in one's lungs draws out. Drawn
out by pure lusty attraction. It was the kind of kiss any
girl in her right mind would lean in to deepen. Kissing
Leevi just felt right—and damn good. My head felt fuzzy
and my blood was pumping madly. This was wrong. I
shouldn't feel so strongly—I barely knew Leevi. Also, I
did have a sort-of boyfriend I really cared for...*and*
President Koivu was sitting right there staring at the
screen on his laptop. The man was completely unaware
our kiss was a cataclysmic—earth shifting—event.

Couldn't the President feel our acute passion?
Wasn't the floor moving?

Leevi broke the kiss, pulling away. Wow. That
kiss had held our bondable promise to one another. It
should have felt only as though Leevi and I had kissed

out of duty, but the problem was that it didn't feel out of duty—not even close. A wild attraction and passion was still lingering around us, deep and powerful. If the President wasn't there I might have jumped right back into Leevi's arms.

Deep down, I knew we had crossed a thin line...and now there was no going back.

Chapter Twelve

Unbreakable

3:30 P.M. EST, Sunday, November 7th

President Koivu pressed the enter key on his laptop with purpose then closed the top. He put both hands flat on his desk, still not even minutely moved by our powerful moment.

"It's done," he said. "Leevi Koivu. Theodora Owens." The president stood up. "The unbreakable promise has been sealed," he said with the tone of a judge casting a verdict. "The bond is officially complete."

Less than a minute after being 'officially bonded' Leevi and I were dismissed from the President's study.

"What just happened in there?" I asked Leevi as I walked out, torn between tears and euphoria. I found Paul waiting for us in the hall.

"Are you alright, Teddy?" Paul asked. He studied me with an odd expression. "You look flushed—what happened?" His keen eye only made me flush a brighter shade of tomato red. Frick, I couldn't even bring myself to meet Leevi's gaze now. Leevi had paused behind me in the hall. I anticipated he was waiting to hear my answer to Paul's question.

"Nothing," I said weakly, "I'm fine." Instead of meeting Paul's concerned gaze, I concentrated on the tile floor.

"Leevi—stop." Paul stepped in front of Leevi. He placed a firm hand to his chest as he tried to walk past. "Did he ask her to make the oath?" Paul asked urgently, studying Leevi's expression. "Blast." He pulled his arm away and ran a hand over his hair. "He did—didn't he?"

"I know you hate it when I skive around a subject," Leevi shrugged, "So yes, the oath was made. What did you think was going to happen?"

"Piss off—and the horse you rode in on," Paul growled. He looked about half a second away from punching Leevi squarely in the face. Sensing the danger, Leevi took a step back.

"Paul!" I stepped between the two. "Chill, seriously." Paul continued to look at Leevi like he was a grub worm. "It was my decision," I assured him. "I wanted to help Leevi."

"The hell it was your decision!" Paul said, "I've made the same bloody oath, so I know right well how it works."

He looked beat, like it was Leevi who had punched him in the face. Looking back and forth between me and Leevi, Paul sighed in defeat. "This pisses me off more than either of you will ever know," he said. "Teddy, I had hoped the President would give you more time...to adjust." Paul shoulder's sagged as he looked past me at Leevi. "Congrats, lad. Your parents fancied this would happen," he said. "They are both surely relieved the issue is sorted out."

Leevi stepped around me and put a hand on Paul's shoulder. "Paul, I want you to know I'm beyond gratitude for what Teddy did for me." Leevi glanced over at me. "She was courageous in there, but I'm sorry if I wronged either of you in any way."

I frowned. "Why would you think you wronged *me*?" I asked.

Paul interrupted, "You really are a lucky bastard." Paul sounded worn down. "You've pissed me off, lad. However, all I can say is the best to you both." He looked over at me. "Teddy, I think well of you. It was the right thing to do—to make the oath. You have a good heart, my daughter."

My jaw dropped. It was the first time anyone had called me *daughter* with such affection.

"There has been a drastic change of plans," President Koivu said as he stepped out of his office behind us. Our touching father-daughter moment had been interrupted. "Follow me—Branimir and Mila must also hear this news," he said with a gruff voice and then brushed past us.

****

A change of plans? The President's words were on repeat in my head.

Five minutes later we were all sitting on the sectional in the living room. I was seated between Mila and Paul—Leevi stood off to the side. For some reason Leevi was in a brooding mood and seemed content on staring aimlessly out a window, possibly wanting to keep his distance. Branimir stood near President Koivu with a look of concern furrowed into his brow. Naturally, President Koivu was front and center. The President wore a weary expression as he cleared his throat, clutching his iPhone like it was a lifeline to the outside world—which it was.

"First off," he said, "as you know there has been an incident in Canada." I sat up straighter. "Delmont has asked me to send additional reinforcements, as the Canmore shifties have faced a few more difficulties than they can manage." My gaze narrowed. "Paul, Mila, and Branimir," The President said, "I want you three to take my jet to Alberta. Once you arrive, Delmont will debrief you on the situation. Make note, I am considering the deployment of a group of Memory Eaters later—if required."

"What exactly has occurred, Mr. President?" Branimir asked. He looked down at his cell to note the time. The President didn't answer Branimir's question because I stood up.

"I want to go with them to Canada," I said, before Paul could manage to pull me back down to sit.

"Going is absolutely not an option. Now—have a seat—Miss Owens," The President said, shaking his head in refusal. "You must stay here with Leevi. Your father will soon return to Europe," he reminded me with a gravelly voice and stern expression. "It's now your sole responsibility to stay safe—for Leevi."

"But—" Paul managed to get a hold of my hand, cutting me off as he pulled me back to sit on the coach.

"Don't be cheeky, Teddy, remember your place— your bond," Paul lectured. "Don't bite your arm off to go where you have not been invited."

"What about K—" Paul cut off my protests with another firm squeeze to my hand. "Ouch!" I glared at him.

"*Isä*...we will go to Canada as well." Leevi's voice drifted over from by the window. "Teddy will come with me," he said.

"Neither of you are going anywhere," President Koivu said absently. He was staring down at his phone. "You're both too important to the organization." What were Paul, Branimir, and Mila—minced meat?

"I'm going *isä*," Leevi said sternly. "I rarely speak strongly against your will."

"Leevi, I don—" The president raised his eyebrows.

Their stubborn gazes met. "*Miellyttää*," Leevi said. There was a sharp edge to his voice to rival the President's.

President Koivu raised his hands in the air in frustration. "Your *äiti* will never forgive me." He clenched his fists. "Go—and be careful."

"*Kiitos, isä,*" Leevi said in thanks. I was not surprised Leevi had managed to get his way in less than two minutes flat. His father probably knew his son would have argued until he was blue in the face.

Paul's iPhone picked yet another inopportune time to begin to vibrate in his pocket. He pulled it out. "I'll ring her back, later," he muttered after glancing down at the caller ID.

****

Turns out Jo, Leevi's mother, sure could pick the worst times to make a phone call. Why was she always phoning Paul anyway? I clearly saw President Koivu holding his cell in hand. Why didn't the woman phone her husband?

After the announcement about the trip to Canada, President Koivu held a private meeting in his study with Branimir and Paul. In the limo on the way back to the flat Paul immediately rang back Jo, then had a hushed conversation with her. My ears perked up every time he called her "luv". If someone was to ask me I was darned sure those two were having an affair. If the President ever found out what they were up to, Paul would surely be up a river without a paddle. It was obvious that Paul was a senior leader within the A.O.G organization. I was surprised he would be stupid and rash as to have an affair that could jeopardize his career—and his relationship with President Koivu. But it was possible I was just jumping to false conclusions. For all I knew, Paul was merely good friends with Jo, or maybe she and the president were divorced.

When we arrived back at the flat it was late in the afternoon. Paul and I each packed one bag, then dressed in our winter gear and rushed down the staircase. We took the elevator to the lobby in silence. The limo was still parked in the street waiting for us.

"To the airstrip, Grigor," Paul instructed the driver.

Arriving at the airstrip we were greeted by a waiting private jet. Out my window I could see Branimir and Mila boarding, both also dressed for frigid winter weather. They paused at the top of the steps and waved as Paul and I exited the limo.

A moment later, Paul and I stepped into the aircraft and were met with a vanilla smell, a custom off-white interior and plasma televisions. The first person I noticed was a uniformed flight attendant serving Leevi a Champagne and orange juice. The attendant was a petite and attractive young woman—I'd guess she had to be three or four years older than Leevi. Her thick brunette hair was tied back into a neat ponytail. As we shuffled in, Leevi glanced away from the flight attendant and waved.

"*Hei*! Paul, Teddy." Leevi called out. His signature sideways grin was plastered on his face.

Paul turned off his cell phone, and then waved back to Leevi.

"We made it, mates," Paul said as he took the empty window seat next to Branimir. Wearing her iPod earphones, Mila was sitting in the aisle seat in front of Branimir and behind Leevi reading Charlotte Bronte.

Should I take the window seat next to Mila, or the aisle seat next to Leevi? I bit my bottom lip in contemplation.

"Ted—come sit by me," Leevi called me over, holding up his Champagne flute. He looked amused over my internal seat selection conflict. "We can celebrate your joyous and early return to Canada," he said boisterously.

"Bloody hell, Leevi—put a sock in it," Paul grumbled. For forty, the Brit really could be a grumpy old man.

"Hey," I shuffled past Mila and took the seat next to Leevi. "A little early in the day to be drinking—don't you think, Leevi?" I glanced at the Champagne flute.

Leevi took a sip. "Nothing like Champagne and orange juice to brighten up a day," he said.

"I didn't know you turned twenty-one since yesterday?" I shot back.

"You've caught me—Officer Owens—I'm not twenty-one until July 1st next year. But here's the good news: the legal age for drinking in Alberta is eighteen—thought I'd get a head start."

I sighed. "Wonderful, I've promised my gift to an alcoholic."

"Actually," Leevi stared at the champagne bubbles in his flute, "You have nothing to worry about. To be honest, it's only a rare occasion I drink. However, today I'm celebrating."

"Really...celebrating what?" I asked, then added quickly, "And don't make me regret asking."

"Isn't it obvious," Leevi smiled into the flute, "Our new bond."

I unzipped my jacket. "Should I be celebrating?" I asked, clipping on and adjusting my seatbelt.

"No, but this is nice." Leevi held out his Champagne to gesture between us. "We have a chance to talk." He pointed at the flute and then glanced around for the flight attendant. "Where'd that attendant go? Do you want anything—soda? Juice?"

I shook my head. "I'll just have water, if I feel thirsty."

"Suit yourself." Leevi leaned back in his seat, glancing over at me out of the corner of his eye.

"Leevi?" I cleared my throat.

"Yes?" he replied.

"I was wondering about something—you can totally tell me this is none of my business."

"Okay..." Leevi raised a single eyebrow in that alluring way I never could, "What's on your mind, Ted?"

"I was wondering..." I turned around to make sure Branimir and Paul were busy, and indeed both men were in the midst of a deep conversation. Mila was still distracted with her book and iPod. I leaned closer to Leevi. "Who made the bondable promise to your *isä*?" As our shoulders touched, a wave of strong attraction surged through us. Shocked, I sat back in my seat. *What the heck was that?* The noise of the jet's engine had drowned out Leevi's answer. We began to taxi down the runway. As our speed increased I found myself fearful and clinging to Leevi's arm. He didn't seem to mind.

We lifted into the air, climbing higher and higher.

"Nervous flyer?" Leevi asked. He stroked my hand, offering me his shoulder to lean on.

"No one warned me flying is scarier in a smaller jet." As if on cue, we hit a patch of turbulence and I lurched harder into Leevi's arms. He put a reassuring hand to my head, holding me to his chest until the turbulence dissipated. For bonus points, the guy somehow had managed not to spill a single drop of what was left of his Champagne. Once the jet had levelled off I allowed myself to take a deep breath and sat back in my seat.

"Sorry," I said. "Talk about invading your personal space."

"Don't apologize. You were scared," Leevi said, not at all put out.

"I didn't hear the answer to my earlier question." I remembered. "Who made the bondable promise to your father?" I asked, again.

Leevi leaned close to my ear. So close, I could feel his chest move up and down with each breath. "Delmont Owens," he said.

"My uncle?" I covered my mouth, then jerked my hand away. "How would that work? He doesn't even live in New York—what if something happened to the President?"

"Keep your voice down." Leevi motioned down to the floor with his hand. "Delmont Owens is often in New York or travelling with my *isä*—they manage just fine." At least I finally had a good reason for why my uncle was barely around the manor.

"Wait—who is Paul promised to?" I asked with a barely audible whisper.

"I thought it was more than obvious," Leevi said. He took a swig of the little bit left of his Champagne. "Paul is bonded to my *äiti*—my mother—Johanna Virtanen-Koivu."

I gave Leevi a look, which clearly said *really, your mom*? He interpreted my facial expressions and nodded grimly.

"Isn't that...weird?" I asked.

Leevi shrugged. "Both of my parents have been bonded since I was a child. I've had a lot of time to get used to the idea."

My curiosity got the best of me. "What kind of relationship does Paul have with your *äiti*?" I added quickly, "—not that it's any of my business."

"Their relationship is...I *think* as you're assuming." Leevi seemed okay with talking about Paul and his mother. "Ted, before you freak out, let me explain," he said. "For years after being bonded my *vanhemmat*—my parents—claimed they would never let their bonded partners get in the way of their marriage." *Must not have been a binding promise.* "They *both* wanted to remain loyal to each other, but neither could change the fact that their self-preservation instincts had them running to their bonded partner whenever they were faced with a problem."

"I don't get it," I said.

"Let me explain," Leevi said. "You see, a bonded partner is the only one who can provide a comforting level of emotional support in times of trouble—much as an unbonded partner may try. The bond, for reasons I've never been told, offers both parties a feeling of safety and contentment." With a nod, Leevi handed the Champagne flute to the pretty flight attendant as she passed by. She smiled back sweetly.

I frowned. "How do your parents manage their jealousy?"

"They don't," Leevi admitted. "They have since decided to live apart."

"Crazy—and that's really sad. Are your parents getting a divorce?" I asked.

"No, not an option for shifties unless my father agreed to it," Leevi said, insulted. "He *never* would."

Old school marriage rules. "I assumed—sorry, Leevi." A promise of monogamy must not have been included in his parents' vows. Poor Paul...he was probably in love with the wife of the President of the A.O.G. How scandalous! He'd never be able to openly be with her. "Leevi, is Paul like another *isä* for you?"

"I only have one *isä*," Leevi said, being short with me. His tone insinuated that I knew nothing. "Paul is Paul," he said. "We are close and I care for him like family. He will never be my *isä*."

"It was incredibly rude of me to ask such a stupid question." I put a hand to my chest, feeling horrible.

"Paul is *your isä* and he loves *you*," Leevi said softly. He reached for my hand and intertwined his fingers with mine. I found this new need to cling to him weird.

"Paul hasn't acted like an isä...all these years." Sinking further into my seat, I had to fight the need to snuggle into Leevi's chest.

"He would never have left you without good reason," Leevi said, gently letting go of my hand.

Why did it feel like I was sitting next to a warm and welcoming fire? Here I was feeling like I had just come in from the cold. I put a hand to my mouth as I remembered his touch.

"Leevi?" I asked, "If Paul had a relationship with Jo for years—what if you're my half-brother?" Seriously disturbed, I slowly lowered my hand.

Leevi made a choking noise. "Don't think such nonsense!" he said, horrified. "Ted—I'm 100 percent certain Paul is *not* my *isä*." He looked conflicted.

"Why don't you enlighten me?" I asked.

Leevi and I both glanced behind us. "Branimir has gone to sit with Mila," Leevi noted. "Why don't you go ask your father to enlighten you?" he suggested. "Paul's the only person entitled to tell you about his past."

Paul was sitting alone and doing nothing more than staring out the window. The sunlight was filtering through the window and reflecting off his loose golden hair.

"You're right," I said, unbuckling my seatbelt. "I'm ready for some answers." I stood up and walked up the aisle toward Paul.

"Hiya," Paul looked up at my approach. "Have a seat, Teddy," he said and gestured to the seat next to him.

"Thanks." I sat down, clipped the seatbelt on and felt nervous. "Paul...what happened when I was born?" I decided to jump right to the point. "Angelique claimed you didn't want to be a part of my life? She went so far as to even suggest you might be dead."

Paul took a deep breath, "Way to start with the hard questions, Teddy. Angelique—that *tar*—she never did quite *know* me," he sighed. "When we first met I was a nark." Paul fiddled with a folded up airplane magazine in his hands. "At the time Angelique went by the name of Lynette Luke."

Angelique's name used to be Lynette Luke...the name of her alter ego?

"Lynette was an impressionable girl—a mug— with no family and no money," Paul explained. "She wanted to belong...anywhere. The H.A.S offered her a life that was attractive for someone in her position. I always fancied she was the kind of girl who was easily led to make piss poor decisions. I was right, because she accepted the H.A.S's radical thinking without a right question."

"I cannot imagine Ang—I mean Lynette—being impressionable and making poor decisions," I sneered.

"It's mighty terrible how she has turned out, Teddy. A real twit," Paul shook his head. "There was a time when Lynette was in better control of herself. I do suppose she always had a dark side—a wonky side." He raised a hand to touch the side of his face. "The girl's head was in shambles."

"Uh yeah, I have marks to prove it," I said under my breath.

"I'm sorry if she hurt you," Paul said. "Luv, I'm sorry for missing so many years of your life—I feel like a real arse." He lowered his hand. "I never imagined Lynette would be so crass. I thought the two of us had a platonic friendship. Please understand, I never fancied her in that way."

"Did she seduce you?" I asked, conjuring uncomfortable images in my mind.

"She tried," he sighed. "I didn't realize the depths of her obsession with me. When it finally became apparent her obsession was out of control, it was around the time I had to abandon the H.A.S. Lynette was gutted and she wanted to hurt me in any way possible." Paul closed his eyes. "The damage Lynette caused," he said, "It was sick and irreversible."

I always knew I had been an accidental pregnancy, I thought.

"Paul, what did she do exactly?"

"For one," he said, "I barely had a chance to be a part of your life." Paul stared out of the window. "I would have been your father—in the traditional sense—had Lynette not taken you away," his voice wavered. "After she took you, I was in a bloody shambles for ages. I wanted to die. Honestly, I think Lynette had wanted to make me snap and suffer—forever."

"We have each other now," I said reassuringly and put my hand over Paul's, a bit unsure about how exactly to comfort him.

"For this I'm lucky," he said, with a thin smile. "What you need to understand is...before I was bonded to Jo, I was in love with her childhood friend, Liisa."

"Holy, you were quite the heartbreaker back in the day!" I noted with two raised eyebrows.

"After we graduated from secondary school," Paul explained, "Delmont and I wanted out of London. We decided to travel the world and were real young buggers on the piss. We liked to knee it up—party. Travelling was our one goal before we made a formal commitment to the A.O.G. We were both afraid we'd only have a few short years to faff around and made sure to enjoy every bloody minute."

"Spare me the details," I interrupted. "Anyways, where did y'all go?"

"Like I was saying, we backpacked through Europe. We lived in Canada for a while and had a smashing good time learning to ski and raft. We travelled through the U.S, making the drive from Los Angeles to New York City. After New York, we spent three months mucking about in Australia. Before we returned to Europe, we did a four-week stint in Tanzania and climbed Mount Kilimanjaro—it was bloody brill," he said, gazing off into the past.

"Is there any place you two haven't been?" I asked. Next thing he was going to tell me they'd climbed Mount Everest.

"Nah, we never went to Asia," Paul said, disappointed. "There was a trip to China in the works for a while, but after Africa we went to visit family friends in Finland—the Koskinens. They were kind enough to invite us into their home," he said. "After all of two weeks in Helinski I fell in love with the Koskinens' daughter, Liisa."

"Wait—how come you never ended up with this Liisa?" I asked, all ears.

"First off, realize the Koskinens are distant cousins of both the Koivu's and Virtanen's—I think fifth or sixth cousins." Paul tilted his head as though to relieve a pain in his neck. "Liisa came from a lineage of shifties who took the continuation of their bloodlines *seriously*," he said, emphasizing the last word.

"Like European royals did in the past—because they wanted to preserve their royal lineage?" I added helpfully.

"I fancy you've also heard shifties have a difficult time conceiving?"

"Yes...I've heard." I considered what Paul was saying, but then a scary thought came to mind. "Wait— are Leevi's parents related?" I was definitely a bit bothered by the thought.

"Very distantly, but remember most shifties of the same species only have so many options. They usually end up partnering with distant relations for lineage preservation and reproductive reasons—in this case the lions," Paul said.

"Okay, so whatever, you loved Liisa, how wonderful, but what do the Koskinens have to do with me?"

"I didn't only love Liisa—I married her."

"I get it," I said with a sly grin. "Let me guess what happened to Liisa. Did she divorce you after you impregnated Angelique—or wait—maybe she stuck with you and then filed for divorce after you pledged your gift to her best friend, Johanna Virtanen-Koivu?"

The story of my conception was worse than I feared. The truth was my father was a chronic playboy and I was Paul's mistress' bastard child.

"Teddy—bloody well stop," Paul said, growing annoyed. "Now you're jumping to conclusions and I'm not done explaining. You see, less than a hundred years ago President Koivu would have been considered a King—yes—the Koivu's are considered of royal shiftie lineage. My *One Life* gift was bespoken to Johanna, therefore when I made the bondable promise to her it was essentially done only to offer a great service for a shiftie Queen—a great honor."

"Wait a minute—a Queen?" I asked, shocked. "Is Leevi a prince?"

"Not anymore," Paul said. "The shifties demolished their monarchy system in the 1920s to accommodate the wishes of the gifted for a democracy. For example, others with special gifts are the Memory Eaters, Gift Seekers, Oath Binders, Truth Seekers, those with One Life and a few other groups. Even with the demolished monarchy, the Koivu's, and therefore the shifties, have monopolized the highest levels of the A.O.G leadership. The leadership is voted on by the members of a special council. Nearly all those councillors have royal lineage in their blood and they will forever be loyal to the old monarchy. Once Leevi's father retires or passes away your Leevi will take over the role—though I must say, I think the current President Koivu intends to live forever."

The Koivu's were monopolizing a powerful leadership position? Not at all shocking.

"After Delmont was bonded to Jiri Koivu," Paul continued, "Jiri thought it would be suitable to have Johanna bonded to Delmont's identical twin with the same gift—which was such a rarity we were like trophies for the Koivus. He was the President—I didn't have a choice in the matter. I asked him to reconsider and bond me to Liisa, but Jiri refused. Liisa insisted if I couldn't be bonded to her then I *should* bond to her *best friend*. Liisa always was selfless when it came to her friendship with Johanna." *Talk about a bunch of convoluted relationships.* "We knew sod all about the issues we would face once bonded to one of royal lineage."

Tell me about it. "How do I fit into this story?" I asked. "What happened to your marriage?"

"I have a photo in my bedroom of me with two young women. Did you see it?" Paul asked.

"Sorry for snooping. I saw it—when I was looking for my bedroom."

"Don't say sorry," Paul said. "I'm glad you saw the photo. It's a picture of me with Liisa and Johanna." Those girls *weren't* Paul and Delmont's sisters...farewell to my dreams of being an unusually fertile family.

"Bollocks..." Paul let go of my hands and clasped his together, "I don't know how to bloody well tell you this."

"Just say it, Paul," I urged, "I'm tougher than you think."

"Teddy, Liisa died when you were a baby." Paul's words were coming out so fast they rolled over each other. "Lynette shot and killed her to get back at me. Luv, I never slept with that twit Lynette—*Liisa* was your real mother."

L.A. CADIEUX

Chapter Thirteen

True Feelings

8:30 P.M. EST/ 6:30 P.M. MST, Sunday, November 7th

Liisa was your real mother.

I gasped. "What?" Even with the engines working overtime, the jet was very quiet. It was as though someone had reached over and turned down my internal volume modulator. "That can't be." My mouth had fallen open. I was shaking my head back and forth, struggling to organize my thoughts. Of course the stupidest thing came to mind first. "I'm Finnish!"

Paul reached for my hand and held it firmly. "Your mother was Finnish. Luv, you know I'm of English descent." I must have looked too stunned to reply, so Paul continued, "Once I had successfully taken out the leader of the H.A.S American chapter, I was immediately relieved of my nark position by the A.O.G and returned to Europe. I came right back to Finland—to you and Liisa."

"This isn't fair," I raised my voice. Two lone salty drops escaped my tear ducts. I feared the two lone drops were only the beginning and that soon a stream of tears would run down both sides of my face. I hated to cry. Crying was for the weak. My eyes were blurry, my bottom lip was trembling and I felt like screaming or breaking something—anything. I never understood why people in the movies liked to attack pillows when they got angry. Right then, if I had the chance I wouldn't have minded to make the plane snow with goose down feathers. "Everything—everything—I've been told my whole life was a lie!" I choked out.

Paul's eyes glazed over as he remembered back. "Somehow, Teddy, the bloody H.A.S discovered where we lived. When the bastards came to Finland I think they intended to assassinate me...in retaliation. All I know was that Lynette came with them. It was a bloody Wednesday, around one o'clock, and I was away on A.O.G business in Paris and would return that evening— at seven o'clock—I'll never forget it. That afternoon, they managed to slip past Liisa's lone shiftie guard. There were usually two guards on duty but that afternoon one was on an unapproved lunch break. The bastards got lucky—even the security system had malfunctioned earlier in the day. The A.O.G technical team was coming to repair it around five o'clock."

I wanted to cover my ears because the truth hurt about as bad as a knife slicing into my chest. With each word the invisible blade burrowed closer to my heart, plunging in oblivious to bone or flesh.

"The bastards shot and killed Liisa." If a dead man could speak he would sound like Paul. "There was a silencer on the gun and the devils had enough time to snatch you from the crib."

"How could Angelique, or Lynette—whoever she is—lie to me?" My voice was thick with building anger. "She killed my mother—she took me away from my father."

"You were only eighteen months old," Paul explained. "Afterwards Lynette had created fake passports, social insurance numbers, and birth certificates. Upon her return to the U.S. she quit the H.A.S and emptied out her bank account. She changed her name to Angelique Owens—and yours to Teddy

Owens. I never thought to search for an *Owens*." Paul shook his head. "She named you after *my* grandmother, whom I had mentioned to her on one occasion, Grandma Theodora Owens."

"Theodora isn't my real name?" My real parents would never be so cruel.

"Your birth name was Lahja Liisa Owens—Lahja means *gift* in Finnish."

"Lahja?" I ran the name over in my mind. It was a nice name.

Paul patted my hand, wearing a pained smile. "You were our Lahja—we loved you," he said. "Liisa thought up the name the wee moment you entered the world, our tiny six-pound, nine-ounce gift."

"Paul, why didn't you come for me?" I asked.

"We exhausted our bleeding resources searching for you. We weren't even right sure if you were alive," Paul said. "Only Johanna could know the extent of my pain at that time...because of the bond. Other than Delmont, she was the only person I had to lean on. Without Jo I would have bloody well died having lost both my wife and child. It was unbearable. It took me ages before I could come to a point where I managed the painful loss...before I could imagine living. If I hadn't been bonded to Jo...I don't know what I would have done."

"I was alive." I wiped away my tears and sniffled. "I was alive," I repeated. "Did y'all stop searching for me?"

"We never quit," Paul said. "Lynette had bought the house in Corpus Christi for cash and she only kept an unlisted phone number." This was true, my whole life we only had an unlisted number—Angelique claimed it was to limit 1-800 callers. "For years the A.O.G searched to no avail and then by a bloody miracle in early September a social services agent, Mrs. Rivera, called Delmont. She said a woman the police had in custody was ranting about her brother-in-law Delmont Owens. She'd called seven Delmont Owens' before finally tracking your uncle down at his work number. Mrs. Rivera explained she was searching for Angelique Owens's family, her daughter needed somewhere to stay or she would become a ward of the state."

I felt my insides go numb and leaned into my shaking hands. "Oh my God," I said. "This is all making sense. Angelique is a fraud and I have forgiven her time after time...after time," I said quietly. "I...I thought she loved me. I thought she was my mother."

"You forgave Angelique because you are a good person." Paul pulled me into his arms and smoothed down my hair. Paul smelled like all spice.

"My whole life I've worried I would end up crazy like her."

"You won't go mad," Paul assured with a soothing voice. "You're not Lynette or Angelique."

Paul held me like I was a little girl. "When they told Delmont the name of Angelique's multiple personality—Lynette—Delmont realized he had in fact found you—or in a way—you had found him," Paul said. "He was ecstatic but was held up in Atlanta with President Koivu. Ms. Beth Lillian—his most trusted employee—swiftly made arrangements to relocate you to Alberta. We thought you should be safe there until I could obtain permission to leave Europe. Even President Koivu kindly called in a few favours with the Canadian and U.S. governments to fast forward the paperwork process."

"The President probably only helped because of my gift," I sniffed.

Paul shook his head. "I don't think so. The President couldn't know for certain if you had inherited *One Life*. He helped because you're Delmont's niece and you have royal blood in your veins. Delmont told me the staff at the manor quickly realized you had no knowledge of a gift, or me, or of your colourful past."

"I really didn't know." I glanced up at Paul.

"When Delmont called me Jo and I were trying to get back to Helsinki. There was a string of bad luck. Only hours before I had informed Jo I was being tracked by a group of those bastards. If I acted harshly and hopped onto the first aeroplane back to the U.S., Jo could have been killed. Worse, I would've been too bloody far away to help her...and therefore would die with her. I was trapped by my duty...and distance. Delmont promised to care for you until I received clearance."

"I hate her." I wiped away any remnants of tears. I was tired of secrets and tired of lies, and tired of tears. "I hate her so much," I said with more anger than I realized was pent up inside of me. "I hate Angelique for what she did to our family," I growled.

"As you've done before, you must learn to forgive the twit," Paul said. "It's clear she's mad. It hasn't knocked me out of my trousers to find out Lynette believes she'd conceived you."

I shifted away from Paul. "Thanks for telling me the truth," I nodded slightly, thinking. "Now I need some time to process all this information—you understand—this is a lot for me to take in." To make matters worse I had a sudden urge to rush down the narrow aisle and throw myself into Leevi's arms. I peeked up over the seat toward Leevi and saw him turn around quickly. The Finn had been listening to our conversation. Every muscle in my body was pleading with me to go to him. It felt like all my nerves were tingling and there was a growing pit in my stomach expanding into the now familiar feeling of tightness across my chest. A moment later I was all but breathless, overtaken with feelings of loneliness and sympathy.

Holy crap! I realized with a start—I was feeling Leevi.

I was fairly certain these were *his* feelings. *He was torn about coming over to console me.* Damn it, this must be another side effect of the bond. *Someone could've warned me.* Maybe I should go over and talk to him...if only to get rid of this aching feeling inside me. There was no way Kane would understand if I followed through on these new urges...or maybe he would and that's why he'd been so hesitant to become involved with me. Still I couldn't run to Leevi with all my problems because I was Kane's sort-of girlfriend and needed to sort through those feelings. In good consciousness I couldn't throw myself at someone else—even if he was my bonded partner. *If I get up I can say sayonara to my sort-of boyfriend.*

Wonderful...on top of dealing with the fact my whole life had been a sham, now I had an unalterable bond to contend with.

****

11:40 P.M. EST / 9:40 PM MST, Sunday, November 7th

I hated the bond with Leevi and we had not even been bonded a full twenty-four hours.

After Paul was done tormenting me with our tragic life story, I decided to attempt a full-fledged battle against this ridiculous need to be close to Leevi. Battle Strategy #1: relocate to the seat farthest away from Leevi. Even with the shortness of breath and growing pit in my stomach, I desperately needed a few minutes alone. Battle Strategy #2: No more tears. I was never a big crier and my crying quota was up for the rest of the year. Battle Strategy #3: Instead of an emotional breakdown I would build up a mental stone wall and concentrate on trying to climb it. Battle Strategy #4: Be thankful for the truth and try to look at the bright side. I could have spent the rest of my life thinking Angelique was my real mother. I could have worried until my dying day that her mental illness was hereditary. Heck, without her mental breakdown I would never have found Paul...I would have never met Kane...and I would have never met Leevi.

"Please store any loose items and prepare for descent and landing," a female voice instructed through the speakers.

Though it was night I could still see we were descending into the beautiful shadows of the Rockies. The mountains were covered with a fresh layer of sparkling snow, which at night was varying shades of grays and cobalt blues. Below a mountain lake was covered with a layer of ice and black splotches of evergreen forest stretched on for miles and miles. I knew we were headed for the manor's airstrip. I would soon see Kane. I would have to tell him about Leevi.

In a few hours it would be midnight in Alberta—officially Monday morning. I had left the manor in the early hours of Saturday. *Why did it feel as though a few weeks had passed?* Emma-Lynn didn't even have two days to rally her troops and plot their plan of attack—

with one intention—to steal Kane back. Emma-Lynn was a girl who wouldn't give up until she was shouting, "Victory!" If she ever met Leevi she'd probably be sinking her claws into him too—not that it should matter.

When the jet landed smoothly on the airstrip, it was as though I had spent five hours trapped on a *Six Flags* emotional rollercoaster. The rollercoaster had several steep inclines and even more gut-churning twists. The largest twist had a blinking banner strung across its length, which said *Leevi Koivu*. Speaking of Leevi, before we began our descent my bonded partner had purposefully walked by my seat upon return from the washroom. He knew I wanted to be alone so without a word placed my black ski-jacket over the aisle seat next to me. I had left my jacket with him before I went to speak with Paul. It was a nice gesture. Leevi continued to surprise me.

I put the jacket on and pulled out my cranberry scarf, mittens, and toque out of the zip-up pocket. When the jet door was pushed open I was the first to exit. As I stepped onto the metal staircase I saw the night sky was clear and sparkling with stars. There had been a massive snowfall since I left and the temperature had dipped severely. Fred, the taller and darker estate guard, pushed the stairway up to the jet and stood below it rubbing his gloved hands together.

"Fred? Hey," I greeted him as I jolted down the stairway—nearly slipping on an icy step. *Ugh, Leevi, please stop worrying about me,* I thought as a feeling of fear and concern washed over me. The frigid air registered and took a big bite into my skin. "Brr, what's the temperature out here, - 60?" I asked Fred. I had to slow to carefully step down the last three steps.

"Glad to see you again, Miss Teddy." Fred laughed at the scrunched up expression on my face. "Actually, Miss," he said, "The temperature is -25 degrees Celsius or -13 degrees Fahrenheit."

"Fred, it is flipping cold," I grumbled. "We've made a mistake and landed in Antarctica."

"Maybe New York is starting to seem like a more attractive option," Fred said with a grin.

"I think you might be right," I admitted. To no avail, I attempted to burrow into the collar of my jacket. My teeth were chattering together and I was fighting another urge to find Leevi. That stupid urge was beckoning me to burrow into his arms—to use them as a source of warmth. Crap. This probably meant he was feeling drawn to provide his body warmth—as Paul would say—bloody awkward! I probably *should* have waited for the others but I saw Leevi was descending the stairs. I turned my back to him and blushed, then noticed the manor lights were on beckoning to me as though a search party waving their lanterns. Taking off I started to jog toward the main pathway when I saw Paul's clone approach.

"Uncle Delmont!" I shouted, sprinting toward him. He welcomed me with a wave.

"Teddy, glad you all arrived safely," he greeted me. He looked drained.

"What's wrong?" I asked, stopping.

"I'll explain inside," he said with a hoarse voice. I glanced past my uncle and saw the bundled up figure of Ms. Lillian rushing up the pathway. Her faux-fur lined hood was tied tight around her face. Leevi, Paul, Branimir, and Mila approached from behind me. I could hear them all shuffling back and forth to fight the cold.

"Hello there." Ms. Lillian waved a gloved hand in welcome. "Come now," she said, "We must all head for the manor at once—you'll all catch cold."

"Yes, head inside," said Uncle Delmont. "Renaldo, good job," He shouted and waved toward Fred.

Fred was Renaldo?

"Ted?" Leevi fell into step beside me.

"Hey," I said with chattering teeth. "It's colder than when I left." Walking together, Leevi and I followed after the party headed for the manor.

"I've never visited *Three Sisters Manor* in the winter," Leevi laughed. "This weather is no different than what you'd get in Finland this time of year, but this weather does make New York seem like a tropical vacation." Leevi reached over to link his arm with mine. The aching in my stomach drained away as though a plug had been pulled. Even the band across my chest loosened. "Ted," Leevi scolded, "You're freezing—you should've brought another jacket."

"Sorry, boss." I rolled my eyes. "I thought one winter jacket would be enough. I didn't know it was goin' to be -100 outside." Leevi moved closer. I noticed if we leaned on each other the proximity helped to make the less enjoyable parts of life more bearable—weird.

"That's better." Leevi took a relieved breath.

"Oh, Leevi," I said. "I'm sorry." He had been battling the same tight band across his chest.

"Nothing to be sorry about."

"This whole bonded arrangement thing." I winced. "It sure is more complicated than I could have ever thought. Be honest with me, Leevi, were all my roller-coaster feelings on the jet making *you* feel sick?"

We kept walking along. "Doesn't matter," Leevi said.

"They were—weren't they?"

At the same time we shifted closer to one another, both equally glad for the sense of security we felt. If this kept up Leevi might as well carry me into the manor.

"I had expected as much." Leevi sighed. "Ted, don't worry about how the bond makes me feel—I can take it."

"Leevi, will there always be this heavy weight across my chest?" I asked, "Will there always be a gnawing pit in my stomach when we're separated—even by such a short distance?" We both slowed slightly. Now the others were a good fifteen yards ahead.

"I...I'm not sure." Leevi admitted. "You should ask Paul, because frankly I'm interested to know myself," he said. "Ted, I feel the need to protect you." I could feel his internal conflict. "I want to take away any pain you may incur...when you cry it's as though..." Leevi's voice trailed off. "Just...try not to cry if you can help it."

I can keep care of myself.

"That intense, hey? How do Paul and Uncle Delmont handle the distance from your mother and father?" I asked, feeling terrible. "You know, without feeling as though they are being tortured from the inside out?"

"Not sure," Leevi sighed. "Maybe the longer we are bonded the easier it will be."

"Let's hope so," I said. Overhead a bald eagle's cry shrilled through the night. Alarmed, Leevi lifted me off the ground and up into his arms. "Leevi!" I held on. "Whoa, it's okay. I think the eagle is a shiftie."

He put me slowly down. "I think you're right." I noticed the silver in his eyes had started to glow a bluish white color. Oh no. "Leevi—fight it," I ordered. I could feel his body rippling and shaking and faint cracks were appearing in his skin. "We're almost in the manor," I reminded him.

"I've never had trouble controlling the trans…trans…transformation…" Leevi trembled. He looked confused.

I pulled him to a stop and reached up to put my mitten-covered hands on both sides of his face.

"Look at me," I ordered. "No, don't close your eyes." Leevi tried to close his glowing silver eyes again to make sure I couldn't see them. "I don't care about your eyes—whatever—look at me," I whispered loudly. I could feel his panic setting in. I found myself becoming entranced by the glow and had to give my head a good shake. "Good," I took a deep breath and exhaled. "Just like me, take a deep breath." He shook his head. "I know the air is cold, but the oxygen will help you to calm down." With hesitation he took a couple deep breaths and winced as the cold air rushed into his lungs. It only took a moment before Leevi stopped shaking and his skin cleared up. His breathing slowed again to an even rhythm. "There you go," I encouraged. "You're doing great. That light in your eyes, it's dimming now." Leevi was clinging to me. I felt lightheaded from his exhaustive effort to stop the transformation. It was so bizarre that I could feel him. I could feel he was afraid to rip out of his clothes. He was afraid to transform into a lion in front of me. I tried to imagine the sight. Surely he must be a gorgeous lion.

"Ted?" he asked. I felt a surge of lusty desire rush through me.

"Yes?" I swallowed my embarrassment.

"I can tell." Leevi took advantage of our close proximity to kiss my neck. The warmth of his breathing made my back arch. "I can tell," he said with a husky voice. "You want to see me shift. You're interested and excited by the idea...if you want...I can show you."

Honestly, I wanted to see him shift. I had only seen Kane and Emma-Lynn shift. The transformation had been incredible but scary to watch up close. "No. We don't have time—don't show me," I ordered. "Leevi also, no more kissing—remember I need to sort things out with Kane." I peeled myself out of our embrace. Defiant, Leevi reached for my hand. "And—" I snatched my hand back. "I'm going to have to watch how I feel around you from now on."

"You *wanted* me to kiss you," Leevi said arrogantly.

I stubbornly stared at the scar above his lip. "No—*you* wanted to kiss me."

"Ted, you can't fight this!" Leevi shouted. Frustrated he ran a hand over his head. "If you are in love, cold, scared, happy...or having desires—I will damned well feel them. You will damned well feel mine too—so get used to it."

"Doesn't mean we can't try to control it," I argued back.

He clenched his teeth together and wanted to shake me silly. "Ted, this bond, it isn't something you can modulate like the volume on a television. Are you so naïve? How can you even *consider* having a boyfriend under the circumstances—do you like to torture me?" he asked with a pained expression.

We were near the manor entrance now and the others had already gone inside.

"No!" I cried out. "Of course not, it's just...I have to talk to Kane about this bond. It's just, I don't know if I want to end things with him because of this bond," I admitted.

"Like I said—you *want* to torture me," Leevi scowled. "Plus, Ted, are you *in love with* Kane? Do you *care* for him the way you used to—before we met?"

"Sorry to interrupt—Mr. Koivu—Miss Teddy."

Leevi and I glanced toward the manor in tandem. Mr. Green, dressed in his winter gear, was holding the front door of the manor open for us. "Please," Mr. Green urgently gestured for us to come in. "It is cold and the other parties are waiting."

Leevi grabbed my hand. "Let's go," he said. With his touch Leevi's feelings pounded through me like the roll of a tidal wave made up of several sensations at once. The most predominant feeling was disappointment and frustration. "You're confused—I can tell," he said.

"Am I?" I asked surprised. "What—now you can read my mind too?"

"No," Leevi shook his head trying to knock out the intoxicating feeling. "I know you don't want to talk about this right now." He pulled me toward the door. "Come on, Ted—you're freezing."

Leevi released my hand before we walked through the door. He didn't want to, I could tell. He was doing it to be respectful of Kane. I hated how disappointed I felt, it was odd. As we walked inside we both stomped the snow off our boots on the welcome mat.

"Hurry in," Mr. Green instructed. He looked as exhausted as my uncle. "Miss Teddy," Mr. Green smiled weakly, "We are glad to have you back so soon."

"It's good to be back, Mr. Green." I cast a concerned expression his way.

Mr. Green closed the door and locked it. Inside, the space in front of the grand staircase was bustling with activity. I tried to gauge how Leevi was feeling but couldn't get a clear reading.

"Oh," I whispered to myself in realization. Unless Leevi was having a strong feeling about something or we were touching, I was pretty sure his feelings came through kind of like radio static.

Upon our entrance Uncle Delmont raised his voice and directed, "Quiet please." He paused waiting for the chatter to hush. "I'm glad you all have come here tonight. The H.A.S have dared to threaten our homes and those we care about... "

Looking around, I saw Mrs. Abasi and her daughter Mrs. Jordan near the staircase. Next to them stood Barney the guard, with Koko at his feet in cat form near the French door entrance to the parlour. Off to the side I was surprised to see Emma-Lynn, Whitney, John, and Connor. I sighed. They were all glaring at me. It was as though I had never gone.

Leevi raised an eyebrow in question. "What's going on?" he asked.

"Nothing...only half the town is visiting the estate tonight." I burrowed my face in my mittens.

I lowered my hand and met Emma-Lynn's gaze for a moment. Of course she rolled her eyes at me.

"You'll have to explain later," Leevi said with his usual tilted grin. I thought of what Leevi had suggested outside, about how my relationship with Kane would torture him. The image of Emma-Lynn seeing me kiss Kane, as we made snow angels, popped into my mind. I blushed. Where *was* Kane anyway? I took a step toward Ms. Lillian and Leevi followed.

"Ms. Lillian, where's Kane?" I asked.

"It's best if your uncle explains, my girl," Ms. Lillian said. She looked around me toward Uncle

Delmont who was still talking loudly. His voice was full of an authority that made me stand up straighter.

Uncle Delmont raised his hand. "A number of civilian shifties," he said, "Have been kidnapped. Tonight is a search and retrieve operation. Remember, we want minimal casualties from our side. The goal is *not* revenge—it is retrieval."

"Kane!" I gasped. Paul and Leevi both cast me apathetic looks. Warm feelings of condolences emitted from Leevi. I *knew* something was wrong when Kane didn't call me back.

Ms. Lillian leaned toward me. "A series of unfortunate events have dropped beloved Kane into the hands of the enemy," she whispered.

"Bloody bastards," Paul said, pissed off.

"No." I choked back a sense of dread. Leevi reached for my hand, offering me his calm and security. "Don't," I warned, pulling my hand away.

My uncle's voice raised another level. "Those kidnapped have been tranquilized and encaged in an abandoned cabin near a lake—about three miles away. The H.A.S have suggested they want to complete a hostage exchange. However, I highly doubt they will follow through on their promises," my uncle said. "We will comply with their requests only with the intent to attack the cabin and complete a rescue."

"Brother," Paul spoke up with an equal tone of authority, "I know these sods too well. Who are they requesting in exchange for the hostages?" Uncle Delmont's gaze shifted to me.

Wonderful, the look on my uncle's face said it all—they wanted me.

Paul's stance became rigid and defensive. "Piss off, Delmont. There's no way," he growled.

"She must," Uncle Delmont said. "This is our best option."

"Delmont, I'm not going to haggle," Paul said. "You know bloody well Teddy has been bonded to Leevi." A surprised murmur erupted from the group of civilians and manor residents. "Brother, forget this daft idea," Paul stood his ground.

"This is big news." Emma-Lynn's murmurs were the loudest. "Teddy's been bonded—to Leevi Koivu." Emma-Lynn cackled like the Wicked Witch of the West. "Not really surprised, but I cannot wait until Kane finds this one out."

"And you're such a heroine," I said under my breath.

Emma-Lynn turned to Whitney. "I tried to warn Kane this would happen."

"We all knew with what she was gifted," Whitney said sadly. "My mother told me she comes from the royal bloodline," Whitney voice was filled with a gossipy tone. "As an Owens' daughter my mother said it was a given they'd have her promised to Leevi."

"Really?" Emma-Lynn's grin was devilish.

Connor shook his head and glared at me. "Kane will flip a kidney," he said.

"Kane knew this was a possibility," Whitney said, hugging John's side. John stroked her long blond hair. "Mr. Piers tried to warn Kane about what happens to the gifted—like Teddy—Kane told John all about it."

"It's his fault for falling for her," John said, staring at me bitterly.

Paul put a supportive arm around me. "Forget them," Paul said. He glared at my ex-school mates.

"I didn't mean to wrong him," I said to Paul, glumly.

"Luv, they don't understand." Paul squeezed my shoulder. "You didn't wrong him—Kane knew. You know if there's one thing I've learned through the years, it's that sometimes we can't choose who we fall for."

I glanced over at Leevi. His dagger-like glare was focused on Emma-Lynn and company. The young group of civilians were oblivious that they were walking a very thin and dangerous line. Leevi was angry over their ridicule of me, and our bond. Without question, I suspected he would take somebody's head off if they took their ridicule of me further.

"I realize Teddy is bonded," Uncle Delmont said, clearing his throat. I noticed he was doing a fine job ignoring the murderous stares emitting from Leevi.

"My mom told me her name isn't even Teddy." Emma-Lynn laughed to Whitney. "Her *real* name is Lahja. All our parents know her story."

Oh god, Leevi was about two seconds away from shifting. Emma-Lynn needed to shut-up—now.

"Emma-Lynn..." Connor warned, noticing my horrified expression. "Real classy, why don't you make fun of her for being kidnapped now?"

I felt my face flush in embarrassment. Everyone really did know my life story—but me.

"Whatever, just saying." Emma-Lynn shrugged. I knew she didn't regret hurting my feelings.

Uncle sent a warning glare in Emma-Lynn's direction. "Enough civilians! This isn't a high school popularity contest. Grow up—we're a team. I doubt the H.A.S would know about Teddy's bondable agreement."

"Delmont, I don't want her involved in a hostage exchange with these bastards—they're dangerous," Paul said. "She's my daughter and I should have some say in the matter."

"Teddy," Uncle Delmont said my name, but spoke only to Paul, "must be a part of the exchange. It has come to my attention one of the agents has a particular interest in Teddy—beyond her gift." Uncle Delmont paused and was staring at his brother waiting for him to clue in.

Bits and pieces of the puzzle began to fall together in my mind.

"She's come for me, hasn't she?" I asked. "It's Angelique—isn't it?"

"Bloody hell." Paul hugged his chest. "I wish that tart would go away."

My panic was growing. "It's her! Angelique's the only one who would know I was in Canada—social services must have told her." I stared at my uncle, afraid. "The rest she could have pieced together. I can guarantee you—she wants me back." As much as facing Angelique scared me, I knew Kane was in danger. I had to do anything I could to save him...even if it meant risking my own life.

Paul turned to Leevi. "Mate, make sure this is what she really wants," he requested. "Jo is probably going mad right now," Paul said wearily to himself.

"For the first time in my life," Leevi leaned towards Paul, "Paul, I know exactly what you mean." Then Leevi reached for my hand and squeezed it gently. "What do you want to do, Ted?" he asked, studying my face. Leevi slowly moved closer and placed an arm around my waist. I knew this was his attempt to gauge my true feelings. Also, I knew the close proximity would help us both breathe freely again. The weight from the bond was at times unbearably heavy on both our chests. As Leevi's body pressed closer to mine, I could feel a rush of emotions and realized he was terrified for me—he was terrified I would die. He placed a hand on my cheek and looked into my eyes. For a crazy moment, I thought he was going to kiss me. "If anyone ever hurts you," he said quietly, "I promise to avenge you."

Yep, he sure did want to kiss me. Oh wow...he wanted to do more than kiss.

Then, I felt a wave of decision barrel through me. "Delmont?" Leevi said softly. He lowered his hand from my face. "My only wish is that Ted doesn't go alone." He took a step away from me without breaking eye contact. "It's too dangerous," Leevi said sternly, "And she's not ready to deal with the H.A.S."

"She won't be alone, Leevi." Uncle Delmont's tone suggested he understood Leevi's concern. "Paul and I will also be present for the exchange."

"Delmont? Why doesn't Paul deal with Angelique—or Lynette—whoever she is?" Branimir asked. "We don't have to risk Teddy."

"If we comply with their orders," Uncle Delmont said to Branimir, "It may provide us with more time to surround the cabin and save all the hostages."

"Brother," Paul said, "You know right well I would have no problem going in as a lone pawn."

"Think about this situation objectively," Uncle Delmont asked Paul. "Sending both of you in is my best option to minimize casualties. I want to avoid a catastrophic battle and all this talk is stalled action. I already have President Koivu's permission to move forward with this strategy."

Leevi looked unconvinced. "You do?" he asked.

"Yes," Uncle Delmont said, "And Leevi, yes, your father was more than hesitant to agree. The President *is* fearful," Uncle Delmont said, further leveraging his decision. "He realizes there is a significant risk to the life of his son—and his bonded partner. If he didn't believe in us there's no way he would send in Teddy."

Tired of pretence, Leevi took me in his arms and rested his head on top of mine. At nearly 5'10'' I'd rarely felt short but Leevi had several inches on me. Connor and John were scowling at Leevi's open affection for me. I should have separated myself from Leevi, if only because Kane's friends did not understand how our bond worked, but I couldn't...his arms were the only place I felt safe. Right then, I needed to feel safe.

"Realize, brother," Paul said tensely. "I can't bloody well stand to lose my daughter to these bastards again."

I lifted my hands in surrender. "There's no need to discuss this matter anymore," I said. "I want to help the capture shifties—I'll go. Seriously, this isn't a big deal for me." I felt Leevi's level of worry pique. Letting me go was not going to be easy for him in any shape or form.

Uncle Delmont cleared his throat. "In a moment all those willing to fight will need to shift outside." He pointed to the door. "You will travel in packs. Our first goal will be to surround the first kilometre around the cabin. Once Teddy and Paul are delivered the enemy's lookout will need to be taken out—I want this done in one sweep." My uncle pointed to Branimir and then Mrs. Jordan. "I want the fastest moving shifties to attack the agents on the outside perimeter." He pointed to Ms. Lillian. "The slower and bulker shifties will take up the rear." He lowered his arm. "Remember—we only have a few minutes. If an agent escapes and sets off the alarm, we storm the cabin and save the hostages, then everyone will need to retreat for the estate."

"What weapons are the agents carrying?" Leevi asked.

Uncle Delmont turned to Barney. "What did you see, Garret?" he asked.

"Francis reported there are three snipers. The rest—maybe five or six agents—are carrying knives and handguns," Garret, a.k.a Barney, explained.

"Have those bastard snipers set up on the outside perimeter?" Paul asked.

Garrett nodded. "Yes, sir, up in trees."

"I'll send Francis back in to scout before we attack. He can fly overhead to locate the snipers' exact location," Uncle Delmont explained. "Francis, report the snipers' locations to Ms. Lillian and Maria Abasi. These two ladies will provide the pack with further directions."

"My pleasure," Mr. Piers replied.

"Where will you be, Mr. Owens?" Mrs. Jordan asked my uncle.

"I will be with Paul and Teddy." He turned to me and Paul. "Prepare to depart."

Paul and Leevi glanced at each other, worried.

"I'm ready," I said quickly.

"You, there—Connor—I want the bears to meet near the estate gates!" Uncle Delmont shouted his orders.

"Connor's a bear?" I stared at him, weirded out.

"There are a few bears here," Leevi replied under his breath. "I can smell them."

"Eww." I scrunched up my nose.

Leevi nodded. "To be honest, I've never been a fan of bear smell."

"Ms. Lillian will update Renaldo—he will be your pack leader." My uncle raised his voice, commanding our full attention. "The cats and wolf will be led by Branimir," Uncle Delmont pointed at Branimir. "Don't let his smile fool you—this is a shiftie skilled in all areas of battle." Uncle Delmont smiled. "Follow his directions *without* question."

Uncle Delmont took Branimir aside.

"Branimir," I heard him say, "I want the jaguars to take out the snipers. The wolves, lions, and panthers, should attack with a second wave. I want the bears to follow in with a third wave—the dogs should attack in a fourth wave."

"Yes, sir." Branimir shook his head with vigour.

"In Bulgarian body language, that means he understands or agrees," Leevi explained to me.

"Oh, I was confused for a moment," I admitted.

"Once the drop is complete," My uncle continued, "I will attempt to join the battle." He shouted, "Does everyone understand?" He looked around.

The words, "Yes, sir—understood," erupted from the pack in unison—well, from everyone expect for me, Paul and Leevi. We were still a bit unsure about this plan.

"Then let's go—outside," Uncle Delmont ordered.

I took a moment to look around as everyone began emptying the room. Anyone without the last name of Owens was probably a shiftie. I stared at the back of Ms. Lillian's head—good lord—what on earth does she transform into?

"Everyone is so brave..." I continued to stare at Ms. Lillian, a gentle woman by nature, but also apparently courageous. *I have to do this for Kane.*

"You're braver than you think—or you would be hightailing it out of here," Leevi said as he put a hand on my back. I sighed with relief.

"I don't think so."

"Ted, we can dispute that afterwards." Leevi snuggled into my neck to calm me. He wasn't nervous because the guy had the most enviable strength and a reckless streak at least a hundred miles wide. By mixing in barrels full of royal arrogance, Leevi easily fit into my stereotype of a lion.

We were the last to step outside.

"Tonight, Ted, remember *Ei halu halaamalla lähde.*" Leevi leaned back and touched my cheek gently with the palm of his hand. His words were thick with his Suomi accent. "Desire won't fade with embraces."

"Leevi, I..."

"I know you have your thing with cougar boy, but think about that—okay."

"Leevi, I want you to stay safe," I said, trying to grin playfully. "Behave," I touched the arm of his jacket. "Don't make me come to your rescue."

"Same to you *kaunis ystäväni.*" He lowered his hand.

"What does that mean?"

Leevi smiled. "My beautiful friend."

"*Kiitos,*" I said, truly complimented. "Tell me, Leevi, are most guys from Finland as direct with their feelings as you?"

"Finnish men are known to be shy and indirect—unless they have a few spirits in them," Leevi explained.

"Really?" I laughed. "What on earth happened to you?"

Leevi put his gloved hand to my face, again, causing a shiver to slowly drift down my spine. It was a gesture I was really coming to like—a lot. "I was homeschooled," he replied with a smile. "Also, I did spend all those winters in southern Europe. I think I've been tainted by the Spaniards' romantic streak. Most men from Suomi would consider me too sarcastic and forward." Standing so close to Leevi, I savoured the wave of longing which transferred through us.

"Don't change." Our faces were so close now I could feel his breath warming my cheek.

The first loud pop startled me. I shrieked. Leevi laughed and taking advantage of the situation he swept me off my feet. "It's alright," he said, holding me tight. "They are only shifting." I felt a warm rush of comfort and security. It was honestly unhealthy, maybe even dangerous, how good it felt to be near him.

"Shifting—I nearly forgot," I said relieved. Then, as if on cue the night erupted with several more pops and the stomach-churning cracking sounds. Leevi gently set me down. We stood together as the front drive turned into something from a horror movie. It was not beautiful, but definitely mesmerizing. Human hair became fur. Human faces cracked and warped into monstrosities with razor sharp teeth. Eyes shone intensely, glowing blue or golden.

"Teddy, we're leaving in less than five." Paul walked towards me and Leevi. I hadn't even noticed him leave I was so wrapped up in Leevi—stupid bond.

"Okay," I nodded weakly.

Leevi squeezed my hand. "Hey, Ted, we do need to talk again after this is all over?"

"I'd like that."

Leevi let go of my hand, but only out of necessity. He hated to walk away, but bravely did. He stopped to unzip his jacket and hang it on a statue: a stone angel pointing up into the twinkling night sky. Next he took off his dress shirt and I blushed for the hundredth time, as it was impossible not to notice the deep lines of muscles across his back and stomach. His muscles rippled without effort. I hadn't realized it before, mainly because I had not seen him without his shirt on. Leevi started to unclasp the belt on his dress pants.

"Teddy, I know you will be brave tonight." Paul's voice made me jump back and tear my gaze away, startled.

I turned my back to Leevi and his gorgeous exterior that was about to crack apart, only a cocoon for the hidden beast within. "Nope, no cowering tonight," I said, tomato red. "We all need to face this problem head on."

"Jolly good," Paul said with a wink. "And don't worry, we'll keep you safe."

"I'll be fine. No one else seems worried." I jumped as Leevi's body popped and cracked into place behind me.

"Just because they don't show their worry, it doesn't mean they aren't," Paul said.

"Paul, how come I can't feel Leevi change?" I wondered, wanting badly to turn around and steal a glance.

Paul sighed. "You will soon enough, luv, and it's not for the faint of heart. Enjoy not sharing that part of the bond...yet."

When I looked back over my shoulder most of the warping had ceased. Leevi was also no longer standing near the stone angel. All the shifties were standing in two neat rows and to be exact there were two black wolves, a light colored grizzly bear, a black bear, two jaguars, a white-haired panther, a pit bull, a golden retriever, a red haired tiger, a blond tiger, and then slightly off to the side...a gorgeous blond lion with a glossy mane.

"Amazing." It was the only word I could muster.

The lion had a thick mane of unruly white sand hair and it stood proud and regal. Its glowing silver eyes considered my reaction, which must have encompassed the dictionary definitions of wonder and amazement.

"Are you afraid?" Paul asked.

"No, how can I fear him—them?" I said in awe. Leevi was inside that beast of a lion. I took a step forward and felt my heart rate increase. Incredible...the height of his shoulder on all fours was taller than my shoulders standing upright. Leevi, in lion and human form, was a fearless prince among his paupers. "Leevi, you're beautiful," I whispered, putting a hand out toward the lion and wondering at his powerful presence.

Paul was laughing uneasily at my awestruck expression. "In Suomi, you would say *sinä olet kaunis* or *upean*," he explained. "Jo taught me."

"*Upean*," I repeated, with stilted pronunciation. I could tell the lion understood and was pleased.

"Five hundred pounds of Koivu," my uncle said as he approached from the direction of the garage. He walked past me, back to business. "Paul, Francis is flying toward the cabin." He raised his hands. "Bears!" Uncle Delmont shouted and pointed at the grizzly. "Depart to meet Renaldo at the estate entrance." He then pointed at the larger wolf. "Cats and wolves—follow Branimir." Uncle Delmont turned to me and Paul. "Brother, we'll drive with Teddy to the cabin."

"This is it?" I asked, nervous.

"This is where you go big or go home, luv," Paul said, still agitated with the whole situation. "If I have my way, these mugs are going home."

Uncle Delmont pulled his keys out of his jacket pocket. "Jump in," he directed, gesturing toward the X5. I heard the car unlock as Uncle Delmont hit a button on his keychain.

Paul linked his arm under mine. "It's time to go big," he said.

I swallowed a sick feeling in my stomach. "Big, right."

Paul started to lead me away from the departing shifties. I caught sight of two jaguars as they bounded into the night and shivered.

"Ouch," I winced and held my chest.

"This is the bloody worst part. I'm sorry, but you must take a deep breath and keep walking," Paul said with a firm grip on my elbow." Paul and I had barely walked ten yards away from Leevi and I was already bent over in pain as the pit in my stomach grew.

"I can do this." *I have to do this,* I kept saying bravely over, and over, again in my mind. *I have to do this for Kane and for the other innocent civilian shifties.* Behind me the lion growled with disapproval. When I glanced back, he had trotted off to follow a pack led by a large black wolf, Branimir. They were heading the opposite direction from us. I was nearly bent over with pain and clutching my side now—how could Leevi take the pain with such ease?

"I see your bond is growing stronger." Paul wasn't doing a great job in trying to console me. "Bloody hell."

Chapter Fourteen

Paranoid

1:40 A.M. EST Monday, November 8th */ 11:40 PM MST, Sunday, November 7*[th]

My uncle drove under the speed limit down the icy mountain road, everyone in the vehicle quiet with anticipation. Tonight, Paul would face the woman who killed his wife. I would face my 'mother', and the woman who killed my real mother.

"What should I say to Angelique?" I asked.

Paul turned his head slightly to glance into the backseat. "Nothing, luv… let me do most of the talking."

"As soon as we enter the cabin," Uncle Delmont said, "Look for the agent with keys to break the hostages out." His advice was more helpful. "Also always—always—search for a way out, Teddy. If things get bad, look for anything that can be used as a weapon, but do stay by Paul."

"What about Leevi? I'm bonded to him and I don't know how to use my gift… if he dies—"

Paul put a hand up to stop me. "Teddy," he said, "Believe me, Delmont and I understand all too well why you're right concerned. We have to trust the bugger to act responsibly—for everyone's sake."

"*Tonight* is only the beginning for you and Leevi," my uncle added glumly. "You both will soon begin to fully understand the heavy responsibility, and complexity, associated with being bonded to anyone in the royal bloodline through an unbreakable promise. You can help him best by trying to stay calm."

"You pissed away a big part of yourself," Paul said sullenly, "when you promised Leevi your gift."

"Tell me about it," I said, trying to feel calm and collected.

Uncle Delmont pointed ahead. "We are approaching the turn off to the cabin," he instructed. "Say no more."

My stomach flip-flopped in apprehension. This was it. Tonight would be my most heroic moment or I could die—or worse—Leevi *and* I could both die. All I knew was Kane needed to be saved and we had to succeed. My uncle turned down a snow-covered driveway lined with towering pine and spruce trees. Earlier another vehicle, or two, had driven down the same road. Inside I could hear the crunching of winter tires as the rubber dug and gripped at ice. After taking a sharp bend in the road we caught sight of a trapper-style log cabin. A soft yellow light was seeping through the windows, creating an illusion of harmlessness. The cabin's roof was covered with sparkling snow and knife-like icicles. Out front were two black super cab pick-up trucks.

"Agent sighted—gun drawn," Paul whispered to his brother. "He is standing behind the wood pile at nine o'clock."

"Agent at...one and three o'clock...and behind the outbuilding," my uncle said, staring straight ahead at the cabin. "Two more are on the inside right and left windows—both with guns drawn."

"Do y'all have night vision or something?" I whispered, leaning forward. "I can't see anyone."

Paul nodded toward the cabin. "The tart is here, doing a piss-poor job of looking out the window." Great...an Angelique sighting...this could get interesting real fast. My uncle parked behind one of the trucks and turned off the ignition. Everything was eerily quiet until a surge of squealing winter wind jostled the SUV.

"Let's go," he said gruffly. "Teddy, don't make sudden movements—" Uncle Delmont opened his door, "—and keep your hands visible." I looked down at my mitten-covered hands, then pulled them off and stuffed them into my jacket pocket.

Paul came around the truck to open the door for me. "You all right?" he asked.

"I'm okay," I said, stepping out to meet the frigid wind, which swirled around my legs.

My uncle, Paul, and I stood in a small cluster and stared at the cabin like it was haunted. In a frosty pane of glass a head covered in a full ski mask popped into view. The masked head tilted to the side as the person studied us, then motioned for us to come inside with a gun-wielding hand.

"Cowards," Paul growled. "They won't come outside to meet us."

"I expected as much." Uncle Delmont motioned for me and Paul to follow him toward the cabin's front door, but not before he inconspicuously dropped a handgun into the snow near one of the H.A.S trucks. He whispered to me, "I don't like to bring weapons, but just in case."

When we reached the door of the cabin Uncle Delmont raised his fist to knock. The door swung open.

"Come in," a deep female voice greeted my uncle.

"Oh hell." My heart plummeted to my stomach. It was a voice I knew. I immediately felt conflicted.

Uncle Delmont wore a sour expression as we shuffled into the cabin. "We finally meet in the flesh,

Angelique," he said. "Or Lynette—whichever you prefer."

"My name is *Angelique Owens,* has been for years," Angelique snapped back. She actually looked a whole lot better than the last time I had seen her. Her dark hair was clean and tied back in a ponytail. There was a lively spirit in her brown eyes. The stay at the hospital must have been rehabilitating for her. "Teddy—my daughter," she said with enthusiasm and opened her arms to me. Obviously, Angelique had expected me to run up and give her a hug like a homesick puppy.

Yeah, not going to happen.

"Teddy, come to your mother," she urged, instead pulling me into an unwanted hug. "I've come all this way to save you from these wretched people." I glanced over Angelique's shoulder and saw the corner of a metal cage. The cage was in a back room—I think a lone bedroom. Within I could hear animals pacing back and forth in their cages, one growling low and violent. "They are liars—don't believe anything they've told you," she whispered near my ear. "Nothing any Owens can say is truth."

My chest constricted. I wasn't sure if I wanted to slap Angelique across the face or turn and run away. *This woman had hurt me.*

Paul nudged me from behind. *Oh right...I needed to put my personal feelings aside.*

"Teddy? Have they cut out your tongue?" Angelique grabbed my shoulders.

I swallowed and weakly gave Angelique a hug. "I'm glad to see you—I hope you are feeling better." I felt slightly nauseated. Her arms wrapped around me...this was a familiar hug...a hug which used to offer me comfort when I fell and scraped my knees or had a nightmare. As a little girl I used to seek out hugs from

Angelique—back when she was kind. The times I remembered fondly were long before she became sick with substance abuse, eaten from the inside out.

Was I turning my back on my own mother? What if the Owenses were lying? Really, Angelique had every reason to be paranoid.

"You cut your hair," Angelique noted as she reached out to touch a few strands. "You look beautiful—like a grown woman."

"I've been well cared for," I said, plastering a smile on my face.

"I'm glad your father found you," Angelique admitted. "I thought he might."

"It's been good." I looked over at the Owens brothers. To my left one of the masked agents moved closer to the doorway. I took note that another agent was standing off to the right near the kitchen table—also with his gun drawn. Both agents wore all black and had hunting knives strapped near their gun holsters.

Oh, no.

Angelique was wearing the same black on black, only minus a ski mask, and her gun was stored safely in a holster.

God save us all. Angelique was carrying a gun.

She released me. "You're safe now," she said, then turned to Paul. "Paul, you're handsome as ever." Angelique put one hand on her hip. "It's about time you returned."

Paul met her gaze and smiled brightly. "Indeed," he said, "Luv, I took too bloody long, but now I have come for you. Darling, I want our family to be together."

Angelique's bottom lip quivered. "I had lost all hope," she drew out her words.

Paul pushed a few stray strands of golden hair off his forehead. "I had a difficult time to find you." He drew a hand out to show he meant no harm. "Your tracks were covered."

"I took good care of our daughter," Angelique purred, "Our Teddy."

"I can see you love her." Paul reached out with a single hand. "Lynette, we can leave here together—just let the hostages go with Delmont," he urged. "Then we can be together *forever*."

Props to Paul. In my books this was an Oscar-calibre performance, or at least worth a best dramatic actor Golden Globe.

Angelique shook her head. "Call me, Angelique, Paul." She closed her eyes tight. "The shifties are evil—genetic anomalies—all of them should be killed."

"You said the shifties would go free if I delivered Teddy," Uncle Delmont interrupted. He ran a hand across his forehead in an identical way to Paul. "As you see we kept our promise."

"And #3 don't trust them," the masked man to the left warned. He had his finger on the trigger and pointed the barrel of his handgun at my uncle's chest. "You know this is a trap—as you said, they lie."

"Number 1 is right," Angelique agreed. She bit her bottom lip. "The H.A.S must break their promise to you, Delmont." She shook her head. "Understand, as a mother I would have promised you anything to get Teddy back, but I have to break that promise." Her words made me cringe.

"I know you would do anything for me, *mother,* but these innocent shifties should be freed—they are my friends," I demanded.

Angelique choked back tears as she glanced toward Paul. He was frozen, staring into the barrel of #2's gun. "Paul." she smiled widely. "Teddy called me *Mother*—our daughter—she never calls me Mother."

"Believe me," Paul's eyes never wavered from #2's gun, "I understand."

"This one needs to leave—now," said #1 gesturing towards Uncle Delmont. "Open the door." The agent pushed my uncle's chest with the barrel of his gun. "Consider the fact you're leaving with a beating heart a *gift*."

"I can't say this has been a particularly pleasant visit," Uncle Delmont said with a foot propped in the front door. He pulled it fully open. "I do look forward to our next meeting though," he said with sarcasm.

#1 placed his gun squarely at my uncle's temple. "Get out of here, princess." My body went rigid. "You ever watch *Pulp Fiction*? You know the scene with Marvin in the car?" #1 asked my uncle. "How about you get out of here before we recreate such a scene? We wouldn't want any blood on those expensive clothes," he jeered. My uncle stepped back. "Oh—you're scared!" he laughed. "Too bad your brother isn't so lucky tonight. He has a long standing debt to pay with the H.A.S—but don't worry, princess—your day is coming too."

"Thank you for the warning." Uncle Delmont bravely turned his back on the barrel of the gun, then courageously walked out the door, leaving it wide open.

"Asshole!" #1 shouted and kicked the door shut. It closed with a loud slam.

As #2 stepped closer to Paul I heard the sound of keys clinking together. My gaze zoomed in on a key bracelet around his wrist. There were four keys attached to the bracelet. Taking my uncle's earlier advice, I searched around the cabin for an inconspicuous weapon to use if necessary. My gaze landed on a weatherworn garden rake leaning against the wall nearest the kitchen table. Outside, Uncle Delmont drove away.

"Mother, can I see the hostages?" I asked, casually as I could manage.

"Why would you want to do that?" asked the gruff voiced agent, #1.

Angelique touched my face. *A gesture I only appreciated when coming from Kane...and Leevi.*

"I want to tell them goodbye." I spoke only to Angelique.

She smiled. "My friends," she said, "I told you my girl is smart—she will support the H.A.S."

"Your daughter might be a smart girl, but I don't trust her one lick." #1 trained his gun on Paul. He was immobilized, with the barrels of two guns pointed in his direction. "We were made to be fools—now this Nancy owes us his life," #1 said.

I screamed inside my head. *Leevi—hurry up! It's getting ugly in here.* Why couldn't I feel him? *I have to free Kane.*

Paul jutted his chin out. The man deserved props for such fearlessness.

"I thought you loved me?" Paul said levelly to Angelique. "You wanted our family to be together?"

"I did, Paaull," Angelique whined like a little girl. "I had to learn my lesson after y'all killed our leader— you abandoned me. What if you are lying again? What if you're trying to take *my* daughter from me?" Paul's neck muscles tightened.

It was probably taking all of Paul's strength not to launch a verbal tirade. "I thought she was *our* daughter," he said roughly.

I opened my mouth to defend Paul, but closed it with a frustrated expression. I should stay silent.

"You really do think I'm stupid—don't you?" Angelique angrily asked. "You abandoned me for *that* woman—that woman who took my baby."

Whoa, Angelique really was losing her marbles.

"You know I had to kill her," she said, with a psychotic giggle. "I had to protect Teddy." Paul's green eyes flashed with a ferocious anger and he began to shake with furry. Wiggling out of Angelique's grasp, I slowly edged closer to the rake.

#1 put the barrel of his gun to Paul's temple. "You want to kill her—don't you?" #1 asked with a grin. "She insulted your dead wife."

Paul shook his head and closed his eyes. "No. I don't."

#1 was going to murder my dad—execution style—in front of me.

Leevi! I felt a surge of ruthless rage roll through me. Leevi was not far away now and he was pissed off and going to tear apart a few H.A.S.

L.A. CADIEUX

Chapter Fifteen

Deadbolt

12:30 AM MST, Monday, November 8th

I was staring in horror as the barrel of a gun was shoved into Paul's temple. I shuddered as another wave of Leevi's all-consuming wrath flooded through my system. The wave was violent and vibrated through every nerve in my body.

He's hunting...and hungry. I hoped he had heard—or felt—my cries for help. If only I could free Kane.

Kane had the killer instincts of a cougar and could move at least six times faster than I—or some stupid H.A.S agent.

"#4, you can start the snowmobiles," #2 spoke into a small voice transmitter clipped near his collar. The direction his gun was pointed never wavered. "Ready for a little late night joy ride," he sneered at Paul. "A good night for some ice fishing—don't you think?"

"Daddy!" I screamed and rushed forward. I never made it to Paul—pushed roughly to the floor by #1. On the way down, I hit my head against the side of the table and fell onto the wooden floor with a dull thud. Pain split across the side of my head, at the same time a vicious vengeance vibrated through my body. The vicious energy's intensity knocked the breath out of my lungs more violently than the hit to my head. As Leevi's deadly wrath tore through my insides the pit in my stomach grew to the size of a watermelon. I blacked out for a moment.

When I came to again blood was trickling down the side of my face. It puddled onto the floor and into my mouth.

"Teddy!" I heard Paul and Angelique shout in unison.

"#1—you moron!" Angelique screeched. "That's my daughter you're man-handling."

"How about you tell your daughter to mind her own business?" #1 growled back. Someone knelt beside me. I felt a warm hand feel my neck for a pulse.

"She's alive," #2 reported. He stood up. "The others are waiting for us by the lake. We should take care of this Nancy before anything else happens."

"Hear that, Pauley? You're going swimming." #1 laughed evilly. "Your snowmobile ride into heaven is ready."

"Before I go swimming—you'll be taking a bloody ride straight to hell, bastards," Paul said with a murderous edge. The act was up.

"We'll see." #1 had a smiling edge to his voice. "#3, you come with me—#2, you stay."

"Aw, boss," #2 complained, "I don't want to babysit."

"I'm staying with my daughter," Angelique shouted with insult. "She's injured!"

#1 sneered. "You're coming with me, #3 and that's a direct order." He looked around. "Who's the most senior agent here? Oh right—me!" I felt Angelique's hand rest on my blood-matted hair as she knelt next to me.

"My daughter needs to be bandaged up," she said urgently. "She's bleeding."

"She's fine," #1 said annoyed. "Kids can bounce back from anything. Come on, let's go." The door to the cabin opened. The frigid air rushed in and boots shuffled and then crunched over snow. The door closed with a loud bang.

This was not a part of the plan. Now what?

I had to do something soon, or Johanna Virtanen-Koivu was going to lose the man she was bonded to—and possibly her son. I certainly didn't want to lose my father for a second time.

"Good riddance," #2 muttered towards the door. "Bet the fishes are hungry under all that ice."

I listened to #2's heavy footsteps walk away. He had left me alone to bleed onto the floor. Groggy, I struggled to open my eyes and saw #2 set his gun on the kitchen countertop. While muttering to himself, he opened the small fridge and began to dig around. If I shifted slightly to the left...I might be able to wrap my fingers around the rake.

Here's to hoping buddy hasn't had his tetanus shot.

Every small movement made me feel nauseated because of a splitting headache—considering my current circumstance a minor setback. I reached out and stretched my arm to a new length until my fingers brushed the splintering wooden handle—it scratched against the wall. I froze and played dead. To my great relief #2 continued to rummage through the fridge, none the wiser of my conscious state. Carefully, I dragged myself forward the extra inch and grabbed hold of a chair leg with my free arm. Supporting myself, I plucked the rake from the wall and used the chair to slowly pull myself up. Wincing, I touched my head and glanced down at my blood-drenched fingers. I had seen this episode once on one of those emergency room television shows: a woman with a head injury is rushed into the ER as the narrating doctor explains how head wounds bleed the worst.

If I could stop the bleeding—and if there was no brain swelling—my injury was probably minor.

#2 popped his head out of the fridge and made my heart skip a beat. He placed a package of bologna and a jar of Heinz Mustard on the countertop.

"Damn," he said, "Where are those cheese slices?" He stuck his head back into the fridge.

Tightening my hold on the rake, I didn't dare breathe as I crept toward the agent. I paused mid-step as #2's head emerged again. Without glancing behind him #2 closed the fridge door, holding onto a package of generic brand cheese slices.

"Shiftie lover," he said absently. "I'd offer you a sandwich but—" His eyes opened wide as he glanced over a shoulder and saw me. With adrenaline pumping through my veins and with my feet planted to the floor, I swung the rake with all my might. The swing was powered by Leevi's wrath, which was still swimming through my muscles and veins. With a loud crack the rake made impact. The agent's head flew back dramatically. It took all of two seconds before he crumpled to the ground in a limp heap. Blood puddled through a ski mask eyehole.

I snatched his gun off the counter and then pulled the keys off his wrist, stuffing them into my jacket pocket. With my free hand I snatched a kitchen towel off one of the cupboards and held it against my head wound.

"Good riddance—freak," I spat out as I staggered over #2's legs on my way to the back room. Smelling the agent's blood, the shifties were nearly mad with hunger. In their animal forms, pacing and growling, encaged— they were practically begging to be freed. The cage took up three-quarters of what was once a bedroom and was separated into four cells. Inside the closest cell were two angry white and brown pit bulls. In the other four growling tigers with orange and white stripes and a pair of black bears. But the cell that held a part of my heart was where a pacing brownish-tan cougar was found. When the cougar saw me it emitted a cry and pushed up against the door.

"Kane, are you alright?" I dropped the towel and rushed to his cage. Swiftly I took the keys out of my pocket and fumbled through them. The first two didn't work—just my luck. To make matters worse when I got to the third I dropped them onto the floor.

"I'm sorry, Kane!" I gasped with frustration. I snatched the keys back up with my sweaty and bloodied hands and fumbled again with the third key. Impatient, the other animals paced up and down their cages.

At least their tranquilizer shots seemed to have worn off.

As I stuck the third key into the lock, I jiggled it. "Listen, Kane," his growl was threatening, "Look, chill out, they took my dad to the lake—they are going to kill him," I swiftly explained. "#4, #3 and #1 went with him."

Triumphant, I unlocked the padlock. The cage door swung open with a heavy bang but before Kane could lunge past me a heavy arm reached out and wrapped tight around my throat. The tight hold over my neck stifled a blood-curdling scream as I struggled with asphyxiation and scratched wildly at the strong arm. #2 easily plucked the gun out of my hand and pushed the cold barrel up against my temple. He snatched the cage keys out of the lock and stuffed them into his pocket. *Not. Good.* A dangerous growl rumbled through Kane's throat as he stared down my assailant.

"Kitty," my assailant's voice was shaky as he now realized I'd released Kane, "—don't do anything hasty—or the girl will die." #2 started to pull me out of the room by the neck. The gun barrel dug deeper into my temple and I made a choking noise. Kane growled again and inched forward. "What did I say—stay back, kitty," #2 shouted. "Stay back or else the shiftie lover dies!" His finger tightened around the trigger.

"Kane," I gurgled, "Stop." Kane stopped. His golden eyes opened wide in horror.

"Listen to your girlfriend." The agent kissed my earlobe. I whimpered through my gurgles. Kane's wild eyes narrowed. I might not be able to feel Kane's emotions but it did not take a genius to guess what he was thinking: if he had the chance #2 was going to end up torn into several ragged pieces.

"Kane, please," I pleaded. The agent's hold tightened across my throat again cutting me off mid gurgle. "Hear that," he said. "She's begging for you to listen." Kane hesitated which only gave #2 enough time to dive out of the room while maintaining his hold on me. #2 slammed the door in Kane's roaring face. With a violent crash—half a second too late—Kane smashed into it. #2 reached up with his free hand and locked the door's deadbolt. I heard another smash as Kane's sharp jaws and claws attacked the wooden barrier violently.

What moron puts a deadbolt on an interior door? Murderous roars ricocheted off my ear drums as Kane's claws pummelled at the door. The other shifties were also freaking out, within—all thinking their one chance to be saved had expired. *Would they all turn back to their human forms soon?* The door shuddered with the force of another of Kane's vicious impacts. The heavy weight on my chest wasn't helping me to take a badly needed breath. I had to do something quick. I wasn't a doctor but I knew suffocation would cause me to black out. Kane threw all his weight into the door again, and a loud crack vibrated through the cabin as the door splintered. As #2 dragged me towards the front door his hold loosened for a moment as the cage keys fell out of his pocket. He kicked them away from my grappling hands, then kneed me in the chest. They skidded to a stop halfway hidden beneath the refrigerator.

"You'll regret," I gurgled.

#2 jammed the barrel of the gun into my ear and elbowed me in the jaw. "Shut up," he whispered evilly. "Don't forget who has the gun! I don't give a rat's ass about your wack-job-of-a-mother." He licked my ear. "I'll have you—then I'll put a bullet in you." He spit on my face and dragged my limp body toward the door. The door swung open and smacked me in the leg, which hurt a hell of a lot more than his words. "You deserve everything you get," he said.

Why did I deserve this? This bastard was more of an animal than Leevi or Kane could ever be. As I struggled to drag my limp body over the threshold #2 kneed me in the stomach.

"Stand up—move!" he ordered.

He pushed me and I staggered out and fell into a snow bank biting the inside of my cheek. Numb all over, I couldn't feel the cold.

"Get up!" #2 shouted. He grabbed my hair, pulling me out of the snow only to throw me in front of one of the trucks as though I weighed little more than a child. I slammed into the vehicle and crumbled to the ground in pain. "I said get up!" he shouted again, wiping blood off his eye.

Was he blind? I couldn't get up—even if I tried.

"We're taking a truck out of here," he said. I could see blood was trailing out of my mouth, soaking the white snow red. As he leaned over me, the agent shoved the gun into my cheek. "Don't make me haul you into the truck," he warned.

"I'm not going with...you," I said, with a gravelly voice. My tongue felt swollen. Snow and blood filled my mouth.

"If you're not coming with me," #2's words were slow and deliberate, "then you're going to meet your father." He kissed the side of my face hard. "Your time is up." My fist closed over something hard poking into my back.

Leevi! Everything in me screamed in agony and terror. Where were the shifties? They should have been here long ago—had they abandoned me?

#2 picked me up off the ground and threw me against the truck. He held me up by the neck against the truck's front grill and kissed me again—hard—this time on the lips. When he pulled away I saw there was a glossy trail of both our blood drenching his lips down to his chin.

"Sit up!" he ordered. When my neck lolled to the side #2 slapped me across the face. "You deaf? I said sit up!" Somewhere, somehow, I found the last vestiges of my strength and courage. Maybe these last vestiges were not even my own...it could be the bond lending me a fraction of Leevi's greatest assets. Whatever it was the heaven-sent, final burst of strength helped me to stay upright. I intended to die staring my enemy straight in the eye. My expression was one of only unyielding hatred and defiance—my last stand. I could feel the dark hand of death closing in on me with each passing second as my breath rattled in my chest. My only solace was the knowledge that Leevi and Kane would arrive soon and it was highly unlikely my assailant would live to see the light of another day.

From what I could sense if Leevi arrived first, this bastard's death would be deservingly brutal. #2 took three steps back. He pointed his gun at my chest.

"Goodbye, shiftie lover," he said sickly sweet. His finger tensed.

I grasped onto the only opportunity I had left and opened my mouth to release a blood-curdling scream and a shattering roar and cat's cry erupted through the night. As I screamed I pulled out the handgun I'd hidden behind my back just as I felt air and fur whoosh past my face, and pulled the trigger—in tandem two gun shots rang out—my shot had been knocked off target. A furry body fell into a lump in my lap as the agent's gunshot hit the animal in the chest. I slumped back on the ground and dropped the gun. Mere seconds later I heard the agent scream in agony, followed by the sound of crunching bones. I opened my eyes and saw a cougar on top of the agent and I felt no pity. I closed my eyes. #2 was looking his brutal death in the face. Kane would spare no mercy. There was another round of bone crunching noises, then the sound of an animal ravaging at its prey. The ravaging was followed by a dizzying silence as the cougar froze and listened to something. I could feel his steady gaze on me.

Then I heard shouting. A man screamed in agony and there was another gunshot. I felt a massive rush of fear followed by a numbing peace. My eyes flew open. *Leevi.*

I'm not dead? I struggled to push the furry body off of me but quickly realized there was nothing left in my fuel tank. All I could manage was to lean over wheezing and lie sideways in the snow. I whimpered as a sharp pain shot up my side and across my chest—I probably had a couple of broken or bruised ribs. Where the agent had stood I could see a cougar was finishing off the job— tearing my assailant to shreds. At least it appeared he was not intentionally consuming that garbage.

"Kane..." I gurgled, "Um, oww." I coughed and weakly put a hand to my wounded head. My other hand was tangled in the limp mass of blond fur pinning me down...my hero. Feeling extremely tired but knowing I should fight sleep, I struggled to open and close my eyes enough to see Branimir and Mila leap out of the forest, then head into the cabin—still in wolf form. Behind them a bald eagle came swooping out of the sky and landed gracefully on the front step. I watched in an almost dreamlike state as Mr. Piers shifted in record time and rushed into the cabin to check on the hostages. He didn't seem the least bit concerned about being fully naked. I tried to sit up again when I again heard faraway human screams and worried they were coming from the cabin. The screams were from the direction of the frozen lake. Then I heard two more gunshots ring out and my weakly beating heart was zapped back into action, as though shocked with a defibrillator. Near my head a telltale pop had me reach up to cover my face as loose fur scattered over me.

About ten seconds later the furry body pinning me down was moved away gently and loose tendrils of sandy fur were wiped from my face. "Ted—oh God—what did he do to you?" Leevi asked. His worried voice was like the sun basking across my skin on a gorgeous summer day. He was alive. When he touched my head gently I felt a rushing sense of security, which came from being near him. It felt so good, even as I struggled with so much pain. All his other feelings were also profound, but right now the security was what I needed.

"I...tried to shoot...him?" I gurgled, through a blood filled mouth. "Brave." Leevi ran an arm over his mouth to wipe away dripping blood. Apparently he'd had a run in with one of the agents. Then he touched my lower back gently and ran his other hand down my arms and legs. I think he was checking for broken bones. I struggled to look around for Kane.

"Ted, yes—you did great. Very brave. Stay still. I don't want to hurt you worse than you already are." He continued to evaluate my injuries. "Delmont!" Leevi yelled. "Both these ladies need immediate transport back to the medical center. I need something to stop the bleeding—and a blanket!"

"Leevi...it's not so...bad," I tried to ensure him. I tried to take a good breath but I kept coughing and wheezing. "Kane...saved me."

"Ted, it's bad." Leevi gently lifted me into his arms. It took me by surprise to realize he was buck-naked. He hugged me close as I tilted my head toward the ground, spitting out the blood in my mouth. When I looked up into his eyes I saw a pained expression. The worst part was there were two tears running down his face.

"You lie, Ted. I can feel your pain—it's horrible." He stroked my bloodsoaked hair, "*Minun Kaunis*, my beautiful, you've lost a lot of blood." Weakly, I reached up to capture those two tears with my fingers.

"Don't cry...please," I pleaded. The tears rolling down Leevi's face were worse than any of my bodily injures. The pain from those two drops was like someone had kicked me in the stomach, well, someone had kneed me in the stomach, but right then all that mattered was making him feel better. "Leevi," my voice cracked, "stop."

"I'm so sorry." Leevi reined in his emotions in as he kissed my forehead. "I'm making this all worse." I wrapped my arms around his neck and we both took a moment to catch our breath. The two streams from Leevi's tears froze to his cheeks and he calmed down, the sense of security I needed to feel returning.

"No, you're…making…it better."

We held onto each other until a vehicle drove wildly up. It braked loudly to a stop. Leevi continued to hold me like a baby and kissed me gently on the forehead again.

"Where's Kane?" I asked, trying to search for him.

"Could you ever love me, Ted? Like you love him?" I found myself staring up into Leevi's silver, still slightly glowing, eyes. I spat out a mouth full of blood.

"I..." Surprised, I coughed a couple times because my throat was sore, at least my breathing was getting clearer. Leevi stroked my blood stained cheek with the side of his hand. "Leevi..." I didn't really know what to say next. "I'm tired," I said weakly, spitting more blood out.

"Try to stay awake—you probably have a concussion."

"I'll try." I felt Leevi's hold tighten around me. He looked up.

"Can we talk about this later, *pyydän*—please," Leevi said hoarsely to someone nearby.

"Dude, I hate to ruin your moment but I need someone to take a look at my arm—and we have a situation here." It was Kane and he sounded upset. *Did he hear what Leevi asked me?*

Before Leevi could reply Uncle Delmont slammed the door shut on his X5. My uncle's boots crunched through the snow frantically as he rushed to open the passenger doors. I knew he was preparing to transport me...and my hero. With a jolt, I thought of the wounded shiftie. Growing frantic I made a poor attempt to pull at Leevi while trying to search for the furry mass—where I had seen Leevi lay down the limp shiftie. Relieved, I sensed Kane was already there, treating my hero. I coughed to clear my throat.

"A shiftie took a bullet for me—who was it?" I asked into Leevi's shoulder weakly.

"Cat, how is she?" Leevi redirected my question to whoever was treating the furry mass.

"The bullet hit her heart," Kane answered back, clearly not amused with Leevi. "She's gone," he said with a tired and weary whisper.

"No—no," I wailed. I buried my head into Leevi's bare chest until I couldn't bear my own pain any longer. There was only one shiftie with that color fur: the golden retriever. I knew who it was. "Ms. Lillian!" I shrieked, my hysterics building, causing me more pain.

"The woman was selfless to the end—she met a heroic death," Uncle Delmont said, coming up from behind Leevi carrying a blanket, two pairs of pants, and shirts. He tossed a pair of pants and a shirt to Leevi, and the others to Kane. "Beth loved Teddy like a daughter, she told me a number of times," he added sadly.

"No." I buried my injured face into Leevi's chest. He used his t-shirt to stop the bleeding from my head, pressing it gently to the wound.

"Stay still, Ted." Leevi put a hand to my chest and I cried out in pain.

"Leevi, we must take Teddy now—she may need surgery—at the very least several stitches." It felt like someone had skewered that old knife into my back again.

"Ms. Lillian was too good a person," I cried out. "This shouldn't have happened to her—she shouldn't have done it. The bullet was meant for me." I could feel Leevi's concern for me build but I sensed a masked sorrow as well, as though he was trying to hide his emotions from me. "She had accepted me...for me." I began to shake all over. "Ms. Lillian was kind and cared about everyone. She was concerned about my welfare...and now she's gone. It's my fault because I have a gift—and now I can't even save her!"

"Teddy, don't blame yourself," Uncle Delmont pleaded. "Beth would hate if you did."

I wailed, "This is my fault." I began wheezing again.

"She was a wonderful woman and now we need to celebrate the life she had." My uncle swallowed in a poor attempt to hide his own emotions and made me suspect his feelings for Ms. Lillian had run deeper than he cared to share.

"Mr. Owens, I need to go with Teddy to the bunker," Kane said quietly. I could tell by the edge in his words he was daring Leevi to challenge him.

"Ted needs *me* right now, KP." Leevi clenched his teeth together. I knew he was ready to scrap if necessary to keep me safe.

"Last I heard, Dude, *Teddy* was pretty much *my* girlfriend—how about you go put on some clothes," Kane suggested as he pulled on his pants.

Oh no ... they will end up fighting this out. I doubt there's any way Leevi would leave me right now.

"I'll tell you what she doesn't need!" Uncle Delmont snapped at both boys.

"—Two pissed off cats fighting over her," Another person with a thick British accent finished my uncle's sentence.

"Paul!" I cried out. I put a hand to my sore mouth in relief. "You're alright." I winced.

"I never even made it out onto the lake—Leevi and I were too much of a match for those bastards." Paul sounded shaken up and was covered in a thick fleece blanket, his hair wet. His freezing cold hand touched my forehead. "Leevi," he ordered. "Put her in the vehicle already, you prat, she needs to see the doctor."

Leevi stood, holding me in his arms. He headed for the passenger seat of the truck and gently laid me over the seat. In tandem, we winced in pain. My shock was starting to wear off and my neurons were processing the extent of my injuries. Leevi placed my hand on the t-shirt held to my head. "Keep pressure on this cut," he directed. Reaching over, he put a soft palm to my neck. My neck was hurting worse than the cut on my head. "*Kaunis*," he said sadly, "Your neck will be badly bruised." Leevi moved his hand and ran his thumb up and down my jaw.

"Doesn't matter," I sighed. "I'm alive." My words only made me remember Ms. Lillian. I felt broken inside and out.

"Leevi, you're doing a great job with Teddy, but I would like you to drive with me in one of these H.A.S trucks," Uncle Delmont's voice interceded. "I know it's hard for you. However, I need a few minutes to speak with you. We also need to make a couple long distance phone calls, and you do need clothes. KP, you're wounded and need to go with Paul and Teddy to the clinic," Uncle Delmont instructed. Leevi ran his hand over my tangled hair.

"Ted needs me," Leevi argued. "Surely you understand the distance is difficult for us right now—it will be painful for her. Hasn't she been through enough?"

"I fancy Delmont's right," Paul said quietly. "Leevi...I will be with her—don't worry." Weakly, I reached up to touch Leevi's face.

His silver eyes turned to me in concern. "*Kaunis*, what's wrong?" he asked.

"*Kiitos*, Leevi—for everything," I said weakly. "But Kane and I need to go together." Leevi opened his mouth to protest. I shook my head. "I'll be fine—call your mother and tell her everyone is okay." I felt a wave of defeat and heartbreak ripple through Leevi's hand. He pulled his hand away and backed out, like he'd been slapped.

"I won't be far," he said hoarsely. Once Leevi was out, Kane climbed into the back and laid a blanket over me. "She has a concussion," I heard Leevi explain to Paul.

"Well, that's bloody obvious—it looks like she's seeing birds flying in circles 'round her head," Paul said. "Mate, put on your trousers and we'll see you at the bunker." Paul slammed the passenger door shut. The sound of the slamming made my headache worse. He slipped into the driver's seat...and more gently closed that door and started the vehicle. *Ugh.* I didn't have to see Leevi's face to know he felt my pain.

"Is there anything I can do to make you feel better?" Kane asked taking my hand and intertwined his fingers in mine. I saw him wince and for the first time noticed the blood running down his other arm.

"Kane!" I shouted in a raspy voice, struggling to sit up in a panic. Paul backed into reverse and pulled forward.

"Teddy, lie down. It's nothing a few stitches can't fix," Kane insisted. He released my hand and pushed the t-shirt Delmont had handed him onto the arm wound.

"What happened?" I leaned back, feeling a course of concern from Leevi smash into me. He had easily sensed my panic. Uncle Delmont would probably have to physically restrain him from chasing us down the road.

"Talk to me," I said with a rasp. "Kane?"

"Yes?" His voice sounded hesitant, like he knew what was coming next.

"Do you know already about what happened in New York?" I asked.

Kane leaned his forehead against the back of the passenger seat. "You mean...you already made a bond with cocky Koivu?"

I shuddered. "Yes."

Kane turned his head to look down at me. I saw jealousy flash across his face and felt remorse.

"Are you mad?" I asked, just wanting him to hold me.

Even though it hurt I shifted my head to stare into Kane's eyes. If he wasn't holding onto his upper arm wound I would have reached over to squeeze his hand...but it wouldn't help the weight across my chest.

"I'd be lying if I said no." He took a deep breath and stared down at me with sad eyes. "You know this makes things even more complicated for us," he said gently.

"Kane, be honest," I pleaded. I felt tears welling in my eyes and struggled to fight them, the last thing Leevi needed right now was a swift kick in the stomach.

"What?" He frowned.

"Did you know I would be bonded with Leevi in New York—when I left?"

"My grandfather told me...there was a strong likelihood it would happen," Kane admitted guiltily.

"Still, you wanted to date me?"

"Teddy," Kane said in exasperation. "I tried to fight it for months—fighting it was impossible. You're ridiculously charming and the craziest part is that you don't even try."

"Believe me—I tried, Kane," I laughed weakly, wincing.

"I didn't notice you try," Kane said sadly. "It doesn't matter because in our case the course of love never did run smooth."

"You're a Shakespeare thief—you know that, right." I smiled through cracked lips.

"The guy was a poetic genius." Kane smiled back. "You caught me."

What would Kane think...if I told him Leevi was seething with jealousy about now? Gosh, it really was awkward how *sometimes* Leevi and I could easily sense each other. At least our bond should grow weaker with the distance.

"Teddy, I was so worried for you." Kane studied my face, clenching his fist. "The agent I killed asked for everything he got when he dared lay a finger on you." My face fell as I remembered the image of the cougar standing over the agent's mangled body. Leevi was a lurking voyeur to my more intense emotions, so I had to fight back emotions, yet again. Kane leaned down to kiss the unharmed side of my split lip softly. In the past it had been easy to get lost in Kane's kisses...but right now it felt like Leevi was standing there watching. *This whole situation was impossible.* Kane and I pulled away at the same time. Leevi's jealousy had jolted through me again. Paul was probably trying not to watch us in the rear view mirror.

"Teddy," Kane said huskily, "You're going to leave me again—aren't you?"

I was about to promise never to leave again. I wanted to tell Kane I loved him more than he could imagine. Heck, I even opened my mouth to say the words...Only, as much as I tried the words didn't come out...because they wouldn't be fair to him.

"Did I say something wrong?" Kane asked. "Are you in pain?" He noticed my troubled expression.

"No—well yes, about the pain—but there are a few things we need to talk about." I forced myself to smile painfully.

"Teddy, can you see yourself falling in love with *me?*"

Yes! Wasn't this the question of my life?

"Paul?" I called out weakly, not ready to say more.

"Yes, luv?" My father was concentrating especially hard on the road. "The gunshots down at the lake—what happened?"

"Those shots were poorly aimed," Paul explained, his eyes never wavering.

"Are all the agents...dead?" I asked thinking of Angelique...feeling sad.

"One injured bastard managed to take off on foot toward the forest. He turned back to take a poorly aimed shot at me and Leevi took him out. The sod, lad could have got himself killed leaping at an armed agent."

"What about Angelique?" I asked, spitting out a little less blood.

"She managed to escape by running down the water's edge. I chased her, but I couldn't track her after a certain point—she's gone." Paul didn't bother to mask his frustration.

I was not sure if I should be upset or relieved. Right then, I didn't want to think about my complicated feelings for my ex-mother.

****

Paul parked in the garage off the manor. Once in the garage Kane showed us a secret entrance into the tunnels—which he claimed led to the bunker below the helicopter pad. The entrance resembled a door to a tall tool cabinet.

"Paul?" I asked, holding onto Paul trying not to fall on my face from nausea.

"Yes, luv?" Paul answered.

"Why didn't Uncle Delmont use the helicopter...with the guns?"

"The shifties will only resort to using weapons in their human form, if they must. They are usually more effective in their animal forms. Those bastards would have heard the helicopter approaching—and would have shot us down," Paul explained.

"Oh," I said. We fell back into silence and I was totally going to puke if I didn't sit down soon. I leaned on Paul as we stumbled into the infirmary. It was the same room I had discovered the night I climbed the tree. Kane winced as he went to sit down in the lone chair and was starting to look pale. Once I was sitting on the infirmary room table Paul helped me out of my winter clothes.

"Luv, I'll return shortly with the doctor," Paul said holding my jacket and boots. "You're going to be right fine." He left.

Everything hurt.

"Teddy, you're pretty tough for a girl." I knew Kane was trying to make light of the situation. With a grim expression, in the better light he studied the bruising on my torso and face.

"I don't feel tough," I croaked lying down on the infirmary table. Kane tossed the bloodied t-shirt he'd been holding on his arm into the stainless steel sink. He found a clean towel and ran it beneath warm water. When he turned off the tap he wrung out the damp cloth and turned to gently begin wiping the blood off my face and shoulders. It did not take long before the white cotton was soaked red. Kane frowned as he shifted his target to concentrate on the cut on my scalp and I closed my eyes, trying to fight the pain as he removed the t-shirt and dabbed at the wound.

"You'll have to shower in order to get most of this blood out of your hair," he informed as he handed me a clean towel.

"I figured." I wheezed.

"Keep putting pressure on your head wound. You have an ugly gash—definitely needs stitches," he said tossing the bloody towel in the sink.

"No surprise there." I gritted my teeth together as I held the towel to my cut. "It has bled a ton."

"Do you have a headache?"

"It has dulled a lot," I said wearily. "I'm just tired, my chest hurts, and my breathing is still difficult."

"Maybe it's a partially collapsed lung? Also, you need to be hooked up to an IV to replenish fluids," Kane said. "How's your mouth?"

"It's not bad, compared to my head." I put my other hand up to my mouth. "One tooth might have knocked loose—I might need a dentist to look at it. The inside of my cheek has a huge bite out of it." The last injury was my own fault when he threw me up against the truck.

"Do you need anything else before the doctor arrives?" Kane asked. I opened my eyes and stared at my hand. *Yes, I want everything to be like it was before this intrusive bond.*

"No, but thanks." I studied my nails. There was dried blood, fur and dirt stuck in places Kane couldn't reach. I lowered my hand to grip the edge of the stretcher bed. "Kane?"

"Need anything?" he asked, wincing as he took a seat again. He looked weak and I noticed the deep gash in his arm was bleeding again.

I shook my head. "What happened to your arm?" My gaze narrowed in on the wound. "You should keep care—don't worry about me. It looks bad."

"Arm's fine." He placed a hand on the stainless steel counter to steady himself. "Dude, it's a funny story actually."

"Funny." I frowned. "Really?"

"I'll get to tell my friends about the time you shot me." Kane tried to laugh but it came out as more of a groan.

"I what!" I jostled and it felt like all the cuts and scrapes on my body screamed at me for mercy. "I'm sorry, my head injury is causing me to hallucinate. Did you just say I shot you?"

"Stay still, Teddy. You're going to hurt yourself." Kane smiled weakly. "But yeah, you shot me. The bullet grazed my arm—I'll survive." My mouth was throbbing and my chest felt like it was going to explode. However, I still managed to gape in horror.

I coughed and clutched at my wheezing chest. "I'm...I'm sorry. My arm was knocked when the golden retriever..." I trailed off and put the back of my hand to my neck. Kane and I sat listening to the water rushing through the pipes outside the infirmary for a long time. The reality of the magnitude of the woman we lost set in and burrowed deeper into our minds and hearts. I'm sure Kane also considered how close my bullet came to fatally harming him.

Quite the paradox: the girl with the ability to save a life nearly took a life...and she is partially responsible for the death of the best woman she has ever known.

"The estate won't be the same without *her,*" I said, staring at the ceiling.

Knowing whom I meant, he said grimly, "No, it definitely won't be the same...she was the glue that held this place together." Kane stood and looked down at me. He leaned in to look into my eyes supporting his body with a shaking arm on the table next to me. I immediately felt lightheaded...followed by Leevi's annoyance. "She was pretty much my mom over the last two years."

"I didn't know her long...but I feel the same way." I struggled to take a deep breath. "This is my fault."

"It's not. This is the risk we all take while fighting the H.A.S." Kane murmured near my ear. I took a deep breath of his forest scent. "She risked her life to save you—because she believed in you."

"She shouldn't have."

"She did." He paused. "I do."

I glanced at him in surprise as I continued to put pressure on the throbbing cut on my head. "You do?"

"What is going on with Leevi Koivu?" he pulled back. "I've heard colourful stories about the Owens brothers...and Leevi's parents."

What did he want, intimate details? It's complicated...

"How do you know Leevi?" I asked with a sigh.

"Every shiftie knows about the Koivus." Kane shrugged and then grabbed at his arm. "I know him because the guy came out here to visit, the first summer I lived at the manor. We hung out—it's not like we're best friends." *Makes sense.* "Do you know much about Leevi's past...with girls?" Kane asked trying to sound off-hand.

"No—what do you mean?" I sat up wincing. Kane pulled me with one arm to his chest. I breathed in his forest smell, and for once I was just relieved he could not smell me.

"Leevi has been around the block a time or two," Kane said. "You catch my drift? It's a known fact the guy doesn't have a lot of respect for the boundaries of other people's relationships."

"I don't care what he's done in the past with girls—that's up to him." I pushed my hand against Kane's chest, pushing him back enough to look into his eyes.

"Just making sure you have the full story." Kane shrugged again. "I don't want the dude slobbering all over you—it would be a mistake."

I wasn't exactly shocked to find out Leevi had a sordid past—I had suspected as much. I closed my eyes. *If only Kane knew the truth.*

"Leevi doesn't even have a girlfriend," I noted. A thought crossed my mind: Was I going to sense Leevi's feelings when he *slept* with a girl? How could another girl ever match our intense connection? With the bond...if Leevi were with someone else...would it really feel like *torture*? I hoped I wouldn't have to find out anytime soon.

I had to be honest with myself. What I had with Kane was passionate and true, but the kind of heat Leevi and I could conjure because of the bond—even when simply talking. It scared me. What would our connection be like in bed? Bad—bad—I totally shouldn't go there. Here I was thinking about Leevi's sex life and feeling a sense of ownership over him. *Stupid bond.* He was a single guy and should be able to bed whoever he wanted—whenever he wanted. Only...I wouldn't be able to live in the same country as him if he bedded random girls every night.

"That dude should go get a girlfriend—and leave you alone," Kane said angrily. He had knocked me out of my thoughts by sounding awfully territorial.

"What are you worried about?" I asked annoyed with his tone.

"I'm worried because the dude's a player, Teddy." He paused to stress the point. "He's the kind of guy who'll tell you all the right things to mess with your emotions. I know you're bonded and I sure have a lot of questions about that—just don't let him get to you. I'd never treat you like he could."

Funny...Al said the same thing about you, Kane. I lay back down. "Kane, you really have no clue." *Tonight made me realize how much I love you.*

L.A. CADIEUX

Chapter Sixteen

A Gift or a Curse?

2:02 AM MST, Monday, November 8th

Kane was staring at me oddly. "What should I have a clue about?" he asked. "Did something else happen between you two?"

"Yes—we made the unbreakable promise." I prodded at my neck with a finger.

"What exactly did you have to promise?" Kane's asked, his voice sounded icy.

"You know. I promised him my *One Life*."

"What else?" Kane urged me to continue.

"As you know, he's a royal, my life is bound to his now." I stared down at my blood soaked fingers. "If Leevi dies...I die."

"You're bonded to the heir of the shiftie world. I figured it wouldn't be a trial and error sort of assignment." He ran a hand over my hair, and I leaned my head back enjoying his touch.

I reached up to for his hand. "What Leevi and I did is forever—and ever," I said softly.

He cupped my face with one hand. "Teddy, is it true he can sense your feelings?"

I blinked. "Yes...it's true." It had to be wrong how badly I wanted him to kiss me, even with my injuries.

As though he had read my thoughts, Kane leaned forward, guiding the tilt of my head until our lips met. As we kissed my thoughts went all fuzzy as his lips moved slowly over mine. I reached up to grip at the back of his neck, but the pain emitting from my cut lip flared. I pulled back with a pained wince.

"Kane," I gasped for air. "We shouldn't have done that."

Kane stepped away. "Guess it was a message," he said huskily.

"You don't need to send any messages," I said as the fuzz in my head started to clear. *The kiss was mutual.* Under the current circumstance I certainly couldn't approve of vengeful kissing.

"Look, Teddy, the dude needs to realize what we have together."

"Kane, we don't need to prove anything to Leevi. He can feel what we have togeth—"

"Message received," Leevi's pissed off voice came from the doorway. He was wearing a fiery expression.

I turned bright red as Leevi's silvery eyes shifted from Kane's to mine. There was a tragic shadow in them.

"I *felt* your message," Leevi said. A wave of anger and hurt washed over me. Whoa, I *really* must have been distracted by Kane's kiss—I should have easily sensed Leevi's approach.

"Kane, you smelled Leevi coming!" I shrilled. I should have thought of this possibility a long time ago. "You knew he was there." I pointed my finger at both of them with a warning glare. "Not cool—and Leevi, you're no better." I glared tossing my bloody towel at Leevi. "Feels like you both are trying to lay claim to me—I'm not an animal!"

****

Paul and Koko paused in the doorway arriving just in time to see me shouting at Kane and Leevi. Koko was wearing a white doctor's coat and was holding a cooler—which probably held medicine. They stared back and forth between the three of us. Leevi was still angry. Kane was looking at me with a guilty expression.

"It was a selfish move on my part—I'm sorry, Teddy," Kane admitted.

"Don't *ever* do that again, Kane Piers," I growled. "Y'all, as of right now—" I said, steaming with frustration. Leevi's terrible mood plummeted even further. "—I need time to think about what *I* want. I need stitches—please get out." I pointed to the doorway. Amused, Koko and Paul grinned at the boys.

"Listen to the girl, Leevi," Paul said. He shook his head. "She wants you buggers gone, so hit the road."

"*He* can't imagine what Ted really wants." Leevi pointed towards Kane.

"*He* has no clue what I feel for *Teddy*," Kane countered.

Leevi's gaze narrowed. "Ted can tell him what I'm feeling." Leevi was feeling rage, jealously, adoration—more intense—maybe love. I put a hand to my head and tried to decipher if the love feeling inside *me* was my own for Kane or for Leevi. It was probably Leevi's feelings for me. Ugh. It was likely I was directing all these emotions at both of them.

"Teddy," Kane flicked his hand toward Leevi as he sat down in the chair again, "is this dude what you want—this playboy?" He scowled. "The guy doesn't even know your name."

Wasn't this every girl's dream—to have two hot guys fighting over her? Guess what, it's overrated.

283

"Her name is Lahja," Leevi scowled back. "And it means gift—*my* gift." He added, his tone dripping with menace, "And all it takes is one word from her, me, or my *isä*, and you won't remember anything about the last few months—the memory eaters are on their way to take care of the local shifties…and to calm things down around here."

Kane paled. "Koivu, that's fighting dirty," he sputtered.

"Stop with the threats." I threw my hands up in the air. "Kane—I'm not dating him, and I'm *so* not playing this game right now." I thrust my chin out and stared them both down. "Out, Leevi!" I ordered, feeling exhausted.

"Ted, what about the hurt?" Leevi asked. A wave of worry washed over me and the pit in my stomach contracted then expanded. "You need me," he said with an edge of panic.

"No, Leevi, I *need* stitches. I *need* a shower. I *need* to eat and I *need* sleep," I said, growing more agitated.

Koko headed for the medical cabinets and began to organize her supplies to treat me. Paul held the door open. "Leevi—don't be daft," he said. "Mates, we need this room." He nodded at Kane. "I'll do your stitches in the infirmary down the hall."

Kane stood and as the boys stepped out, both casting threatening glares at each other.

****

12:15 P.M. MST, Monday, November 8th

Ten stitches in my scalp.

Three stitches in my upper lip.
Two stitches in my eyebrow.
A bitten tongue and inner cheek. Four more stitches.
A loose tooth.
One black eye to ice.
Several bruised ribs.
A partially collapsed lung—luckily it was fairly minor.
A missing patch of hair.
A razor sharp sore throat.
Several more bodily bruises.
A sort-of breakup with the most popular boy at school.
A bondable promise, a hell of a lot more complicated than I expected.
The death of the best woman I had ever known.

All were the result of *One Life*, a mentally ill liar named Angelique, and my first run-in with the H.A.S. Somehow I had barely managed to survive the worst night of my life.

It was noon before I was all patched up and my stomach filled with liquids. I'd already started to bruise, swell up, and looked like I'd run through a car wash— sans car. Mrs. Abasi had brought a liquid breakfast tray over to the infirmary before I began my walk back to the manor with Paul. The sun was shining and the sky was clear. The temperature had warmed considerably. The estate was a winter wonderland and even the birds were chirping joyfully. Paul seemed comfortable to just walk along with me, respecting my need for silence. I'd learned earlier from Mrs. Abasi there would be a memorial and ash spreading ceremony on the estate tomorrow for Ms. Lillian. All with abilities are cremated in private crematoriums because they don't want humans to find inconsistencies or genetic mutations in their DNA or bone structure.

"Paul?" I broke the silence.

"Yes, luv?" he said.

"I have this pit in my stomach." I frowned. "I don't know how to explain this...but there's a heavy weight constantly on my chest—and it won't go away...unless I'm with Leevi."

"Luv, that's normal," Paul said. He shortened his long steps.

"How do you deal with being away from Jo? If this feeling is *normal*."

"It's never easy," Paul admitted. I studied him and saw the purple circles under his eyes. He was tired—and we both badly needed a shower.

"Do you get used to it at all?" I wondered.

"In a way you never do," Paul said sadly. "You see, Teddy, a lot of the weight has to do with worrying about your bondable partner. As time goes on, you'll learn to trust Leevi to stay out of bad situations when you're apart," he said. "The trust makes it...easier, but the worry is always there."

"This is Leevi we're talking about." I snorted. "I'm going to be worried for the rest of my life."

"Leevi's all piss and vinegar," Paul said with a smile. "You two will work it out, but if he keeps giving you a hard time—let me know. I'll have a few words with the prat."

"Thanks." I grinned, then reached up to touch my swollen stitched up lip. "So...last night was a super bad situation. It must have been hard for you...and Jo." Paul looked up into the expansive blue sky and his long tangled hair swirled in the winter breeze.

"It was tough," Paul said basking in the sun. "But soon...I'll return to Jo."

"Where am I supposed to live—while you're gone?"

"In New York—at my flat. You need to learn more about *One Life*, and I think Sapientia Academy is the right place for you to learn how to manage your gift...and the responsibility that comes with it."

I glanced over at Paul in surprise. "Luv, I'll visit fairly often and you'll be right busy with class and training," he explained. "Also, the Koivus will keep mighty good care of you. I don't think you will be lonely, but do let me know if you are. If you would prefer you could go live at *The Plaza*."

"As tempting as that offer sounds," I said quickly, "The flat is fine."

"In a few weeks," Paul said, "I'll fly back to New York and this time I hope Jo will return with me. I want us to all spend Christmas together." He looked pleased at the thought. "If you'd like," Paul said, "for New Year's, I'd be glad to fly out some of your Canmore friends for a visit."

Would Kane consider coming for a visit? It was probably too much to hope for.

"My friend, Al, will love that." I loved the thought of bashing around New York with her. Speaking of Al, I still had to call her.

The manor towered ahead of us. Outside, a sad Mr. Green was standing in the main entrance with a snow shovel in hand. He waved glumly when he saw our approach. Paul and I waved back. I stared down at my red mittens taking a moment to remember Ms. Lillian. A thought about an earlier conversation she and I had shared.

"It's inevitable, isn't it, Paul?" I whispered. "Who I end up with?"

Paul linked his arm with mine and patted my elbow. "I can't say if it's *inevitable*."

"No, but I'd bet it would make life a lot easier."

"Luv," Paul said softly, "you're going to drive yourself mad. Don't over analyze."

"I guess I am."

Paul sighed. "Blast, it is difficult being in love—is it not?"

"Seriously, that's a massive understatement."

He stared up at the manor. "Unfortunately, Teddy, I don't have all the answers. I haven't bloody well sorted out my own love life yet."

I groaned. "Don't say that! Leave me at least with a little hope of getting it sorted out."

Paul laughed. "I hope you have more luck than I."

"Paul, you don't have to answer this...but do you love Jo?"

"Jo is the wife of a shiftie royal—the President of the Alliance of the Gifted," Paul said swiftly. "As a loyal A.O.G. service member it doesn't bloody well matter what I feel." His gaze shifted to stare at his feet as we walked. "Without a miracle we will never be together in the official sense," he said.

"It doesn't seem fair," I said.

"Well, life isn't always fair."

"What about President Koivu and Uncle Delmont's relationship?"

Paul coughed into his hand. "Everyone knows it's a tricky situation for them," he said. "But out of respect for Jo, the matter is not discussed."

"Okay...but you know something?"

"What?"

I thought back again on my earlier conversation with Ms. Lillian. "I think Ms. Lillian was in love with Uncle Delmont," I revealed. "She once mentioned to me she'd fallen in love with a younger British man—a man she'd met over the summer a long time ago," I explained. "I think her love for him was the reason that she never married."

Paul patted my shoulder. "You might be right," he said. "I'm sure Delmont loved her back, but in confidence, I did once talk with Delmont about his relationship with Ms. Lillian."

"What did he say?" I asked interested.

"Delmont admitted to me he fancied her—said he always had," Paul said. "You see, Delmont had to make a hard choice...and he chose not to be with her because of his gift's responsibility. If he married Ms. Lillian he would have done her a great injustice..." Paul sighed.

"Really?" I said. "I think she would have understood the bond—after all she'd stuck around all these years despite it all."

"I believe Delmont was right to keep their relationship only on a friendship level...his relationship with the President is complicated—and there is real love there."

"Will you ever marry again, Paul?"

"I no longer desire marriage," Paul said shortly.

"What about Uncle Delmont?" I asked, wincing because my swollen lip was throbbing. "Would he ever marry?"

"Nah, I'd be mighty surprised if Delmont ever chose to tie the knot."

****

10:32 A.M. MST, Tuesday, November 9th

I fumbled around in my bed. With eyes still heavy with sleep I gazed at the clock on my cell.

"10:30 a.m.!" My head fell back on my pillow. An arm covered my eyes. I had slept twenty-two hours. "God!" I groaned. My bruising and stitches were throbbing. "If you're listening I seriously need some Superman-strength Tylenol. It feels like someone has smacked me across the head with a two-by-four." I rolled over on my pillow. "Ouch!" I winced as the stitches on my head and lips pulled.

I opened one eye as something warm and wet licked my nose. "Hey, Koko." I reached out to pet her silky black head. "Aw, did you stay here to make sure I was alright?" There was a meow in response. "Thanks, I apreesh—you're a good doctor."

I sniffed. Aromas of banana and strawberry wafted up through my nose. My mouth watered in response. I sat up and gingerly touched my head and rib cage. "Did you bring me breakfast in bed?" The black cat's head shook back and forth. On the night table was a breakfast tray with a fruit smoothie and a bottle of water placed on top. Fighting pain, I hung my feet off the bed and reached down to place the tray on my lap. "Seriously," I said to Koko. "I haven't been this hungry in a long time—Ms. Lillian was always making me eat..."

My mood plummeted as I remembered the events from the day before. Fighting tears I sipped carefully on the straw. As a single tear managed to escape, I swiftly wiped it away. I sighed. "I need sunshine." Holding the tray I stood and limped over to the window seat.

There was a light knocking on my half-opened door. Koko's little head flipped around to stare. She bounded off the bed, then scurried out of the room.

"Come in, Leevi," I said still staring out the window, past the ice and snow, towards the blooming interior of the greenhouse. Mr. Piers was inside watering the hydrangea. I found myself looking for Kane, but he wasn't there. It was another day here...as if nothing out of the ordinary had occurred the night before.

I looked up as Leevi strode through the doorway barefoot. He was holding a mug of coffee.

"*Hyvää huomenta*—good morning," he said. It was odd to see him dressed casually in blue jeans. Leevi was wearing an understated white golf shirt with a long sleeved blue shirt underneath. *Here I was in my pink cotton pyjamas.* Of course, Leevi would know I had woken up—stupid tear. Leevi hesitated by the bed for a moment and grimaced at my condition. A wash of peaceful energy enveloped the room with the addition of his presence. There had been a gentle humming energy floating into the room since I had woken. It was the bond, I realized—the humming was the sense of security because of Leevi's presence in the manor.

I moved the breakfast tray off my lap. "Good morning, Leevi," I said warmly. *Now please stop looking at me like I was hit by a semi truck.* Holding my smoothie in one hand, I ran the other carefully through my hair. Good thing I had showered, but because of the cuts I didn't use shampoo or conditioner. Not that the state of my hair should matter to Leevi—he was stuck with me for the rest of my life—morning hair and all.

"Are you feeling better, *kaunis*?" Leevi asked. He sat down next to me. Too groggy to fight the bond I shifted closer and leaned into Leevi. He put one arm around me, careful not to spill both our drinks, or to hurt me.

"I'll survive," I said. I took a sip of my straw and then lowered my cup. "Did you speak with your family?"

"*Kyllä*, they were relieved to find out we are all fine."

"They both must have been terribly worried?" I stared down into my straw.

Copying me, Leevi stared down into his mug. "You know, Ted," he said. "I've spent far too many years feeling sorry for myself...there was a time when I was convinced my parents cared more about their bonded partners than they did for me."

"Leevi, that's not true!" I scolded. "I saw how much your father cares—he just has a different way of showing his feelings."

"You wake up on the wrong side of the bed?" he asked with a grin.

"I can't believe you would even ask me that," I muttered.

"What I'm *trying* to say," Leevi continued, "Is now I understand how well they actually dealt with...a terribly complicated situation."

I turned my face upward to stare into his silvery eyes. I hated to admit it, but I seriously wanted to cling to him. When we were this close it was becoming more and more difficult to distinguish my feelings from Leevi's.

"Over the last day," Leevi continued, "I've had a lot of time to think." He paused. "Ted, even with this bond you shouldn't have to give up a single thing your heart desires. As much as I hate to say it...this does include Kane." Leevi's face contorted like he'd eaten a sour candy. "You have already done much for me by promising your gift—you deserve the world."

"I promised you my gift because I wanted to," I reminded. "Yes, my relationship with Kane is...more complicated now."

"Lahja, you're my gift." Leevi stared out the window. "I don't want our bond to be a curse for the rest of our lives. I don't want you to make decisions against the will of your heart. I need to support what matters to you...no matter the difficulties that may lie ahead for us. I'll always protect your best interest," he added. I felt like it was a loaded statement. It was easy to sense something heavily weighing on his mind.

I placed the smoothie on the window seat next to me. I inhaled his scent of freshly fallen rain and found myself reaching for his hand like a supportive friend. Somehow a simple gesture turned into much more when I intertwined my fingers through his. Leevi looked so...unsure. It was a cute expression on him. He stared down at our joined hands. The familiar feeling I associated with happiness flooded the room. *Our relationship will never be easily defined.*

"*Kiitos*, Leevi," I said softly. "For everything."

"Have I ever told you how hot it is when you speak Suomi?" Leevi smiled, brushing a strand of hair away from my eyes.

"Leevi...are you trying to hit on me?" I asked with a mock serious tone.

"Sorry." Leevi's hand froze on my forehead. "I guess this is the part where you break the bad news to me."

"Bad news?" A silence settled over the room. I took my hand back.

"I'm going home to New York tomorrow," Leevi revealed, and a wash of sadness wafted between us. I could also sense he had made an important decision, a decision which didn't please him. "If you want to stay here with Kane, I understand."

"Leevi—we're bonded," I said in shock, though a portion of my heart was ecstatic at the thought of staying in Canmore with Kane.

I studied him as he avoided meeting my eye, having probably sensed my uncertainty. "No, Leevi." I shook my head. "I should go back to New York." We shouldn't be separated.

Without Ms. Lillian, Three Sisters Mountain Manor was no longer my home.

"Last night Paul told me, with time, it will be easier to be apart," Leevi admitted. "He said it's only really hard at first." I saw his troubled expression. My lips parted in question.

"After last night, Kane will probably never talk to me again," I reminded him.

"I think you're wrong, my Lahja. Actually, I know you're wrong." Leevi met my gaze and his eyes simmered. "He loves you. You should *want* to live in New York," he said. "You shouldn't have to be dragged away from your home like a hostage."

"Wait, I have one request," I said carefully.

"Anything, *kaunis*." Leevi touched the hair near my stitches softly. Paul had warned me yesterday there would be some potentially nasty scarring when my wounds were healed, but for now I was just glad to be alive...and Leevi had his own scars I had yet to learn about.

It could have easily turned out different if it was not for Ms. Lillian taking that bullet. "All I want is for you to take me to a show on Broadway—as friends."

"Is that all you want?" Leevi smiled. "It's done. I'll personally take you to a show on Broadway—and we *won't* call it a date."

"Thanks, Leevi." I reached up to give him a hug.

"You smell sweeter than the flowers in Hawaii," he murmured.

"You can smell me?" I pulled back in surprise.

"Hmm-hmm, it's because of the bond."

"Leevi?" I leaned within half an inch of his lips.

"Hmm?" he murmured. Delighted, Leevi's lips parted and a wash of desire flooded the room, then slowly an inkling of sadness diffused the passion.

"What time is the ash spreading?" I asked pulling back, remembering today there would be a difficult good-bye. "And where?"

Leevi shook his head, disappointed. "If you're up to it—at one o'clock near the birch tree by the helicopter pad." He stood and headed for the door. "I'll see you there...but Ted?"

"Yes?" I asked.

"There is something we need to talk about." He paused in the doorway and glanced back. "It's to do with your lack of smell."

"Let's talk about it on the plane back to New York," I said. Our gazes met for a moment and we exchanged a smile. We could feel the other's appreciation for our private shared moment. I knew he could sense much as I fought it, I needed him...and he needed me.

****

12:55 P.M. MST, Tuesday, November 9th

As the manor staff and houseguests began to gather near the birch tree—the same tree I'd risked my life and limb on—I took a shaking breath of crisp mountain air. The leaves had tumbled to the ground for the winter and the tree sparkled like a diamond from frost and sunlight. I closed my eyes and listened to chickadee songbirds happily celebrating the life of a truly good soul. Even though my body was in pain, I couldn't imagine a more pristine and peaceful day.

When Paul and I had arrived we found Mr. Green standing by the tree dabbing at his eyes with a handkerchief. My arms were tight across my chest and I burrowed my neck further into my scarf as Paul approached and offered the old butler a comforting arm. Over the last couple of hours all I kept thinking about was what Ms. Lillian had said to me, about how she didn't *need* a man in her life to be happy...she was far from alone.

"You okay? Teddy, you sure got beat up." A voice behind me jarred me from my reverie.

"Kane." I jumped, and my heart leapt into my throat. "I'm fine—just sore." I rubbed my mitten-covered hands together and we exchanged tentative smiles. "I was thinking. You surprised me."

"We've all been thinking a lot about her." Kane shook his head. He was wearing blue jeans, a black jacket, and his arm was slung in a sling. *Note to self: guns = bullets = injuries.* His toque was pulled down over his ears and his cheeks were pink from the chilly air. The curls in his hair stuck out in the back the way I loved. Kane looked handsome, and like he belonged in the forest with nature—it was what I liked best about him. "Teddy, I owe you an apology for how I acted toward you...and Leevi."

"Don't worry." My gaze darted to the tree line where my Uncle Delmont had appeared. "It was a horrible night for everyone—all is forgiven. How is your arm?"

"I'll survive." He shrugged his good shoulder. "No big deal."

My uncle approached us holding a golden urn. He stopped beneath the tree to exchange a solemn hug with Mr. Green and Paul. As Ms. Abasi, Mr. Piers, and Mrs. Jordan arrived they fell into step beside Mr. Green. They all exchanged solemn nods and then joined hands and formed a crescent around my uncle. Paul tilted his head to invite me and Kane to join in.

"Shall we?" Kane offered me his uninjured arm. I paused only because I felt Leevi approach. A glance back revealed he had indeed arrived with hands stuffed in his pockets. His shoulders were pushed up to his ears to protect from the bite of the wind. When our gazes met his eyes flashed in the sunlight, and I saw his concern was for me.

"Let's do this." I put my arm through Kane's, waving Leevi over to join us with the other.

"Ted. Paul," Leevi acknowledged as he fell into step between us. We all joined hands, and immediately my emotions felt more in control.

As my uncle Delmont broke into a recited a prayer, he battled tears. To watch a typically composed man nearly crack was heartbreaking. I clung to the two young men on either side of me, using them as a grounding force to keep from crumbling to pieces.

"...To the wind and earth we send your ashes. Go, and may your spirit find peace in a place of solace."

My uncle recited a prayer then spilled the ashes slowly into the direction of the wind. The ashes caught in the breeze and scattered around the tree trunk as the songbirds sang. I could envision the pristine old tree's rebirth in the spring when it would once again become surrounded by lush grass and wild flowers. It was a perfect and beautiful resting place for Ms. Lillian as her favourite past time was walking the trails to marvel at all of nature's miracles.

When the last of the ashes had scattered, I slowly exhaled the breath I'd been holding in. Exchanging a sad smile with Leevi and Kane, I let go of their hands and clasped mine together. Paul patted uncle Delmont's back and then turned to nod at me with an expression of apathetic condolence. He placed a hand on my shoulder. "Teddy?" He studied me, reading me as only a father could. "Luv, you look like you've made an important decision."

I patted his hand. "I have."

I love Kane—I really do—but I can't keep him in the background as a 'potential' boyfriend while I figure out my bond with Leevi. Ms. Lillian would have reminded me not to put all of my happiness in the hands of young men. She'd have instead encouraged me to focus on developing a closer relationship with the man who needed me most...and he was looking at me the way I'd always hoped he would.

"New York, New York, here I come," I said wistfully and waved farewell to Kane. His face fell in shock as my decision dawned on him.

"Teddy—wait!" He reached out to me.

My heart was breaking, but I turned away and joined arms with Paul. "I have to be with Paul." I took a shaky breath. "Kane, you know I love you, but I have to learn about my ability. We still have our love, but this—" I pointed between me and Leevi, "—is not fair to you."

"We'd figure it out...together." Kane lowered his arm.

"This is my decision."

"Bugger has gone and fallen hard now, hasn't he?" Paul shook his head and waved goodbye to Kane and Leevi. We turned to depart for the manor. "Could've warned the prat what kind of trouble comes with it."

"Paul." I squeezed his arm. "The comments aren't making this easier for us." Paul shot me an apologetic glance. All the while I could feel Leevi watching us with a blank expression. His apathy regarding Kane's feelings became more apparent with each moment. I knew his pleasure about my decision was mostly about his fear of suffering from the physical torture of separation—I could feel it—but surely there were harems of girls waiting for him back in New York to torture *me* with.

"*Kaunis!*" I turned my head slightly to glance back at the Finlander. "Manhattan will capture your heart—you'll see."

Indeed, I was far from alone.

The End

www.lacadieux.com

Evernight Teen

www.evernightteen.com

	DATE DUE		
Oct. 2/15			

Made in the USA
San Bernardino, CA
26 June 2014